*AT LUDLOW'S MILL . . .*

There was something there, glittering in the
moonlight. A vague shape changing as it wove
towards her and around her, a phantom with no
more substance than a flashlight beam swinging
in a fog. Only the eyes, two slitted pinpoints of
hell light, watching her with their unblinking
stare, and *beneath them*. . . .

The girl fell to her knees, whimpering. . . .

**A novel of supernatural suspense**

**LUDLOW'S MILL**

ATTENTION: SCHOOLS AND CORPORATIONS

PINNACLE Books are available at quantity discounts with bulk purchases for educational, business or special promotional use. For further details, please write to: SPECIAL SALES MANAGER, Pinnacle Books, Inc., 271 Madison Ave., Suite 904, New York, NY 10016.

## WRITE FOR OUR FREE CATALOG

If there is a Pinnacle Book you want—and you cannot find it locally—it is available from us simply by sending the title and price plus 75¢ to cover mailing and handling costs to:

Pinnacle Books, Inc.
Reader Service Department
271 Madison Ave.
New York, N.Y. 10016

Please allow 6 weeks for delivery.

_____Check here if you want to receive our catalog regularly.

R. R. WALTERS

# LUDLOW'S MILL

A TOM DOHERTY ASSOCIATES BOOK

PINNACLE BOOKS                    NEW YORK

LUDLOW'S MILL

Copyright © 1981 by R. R. Walters

A Tor Book

First printing, July, 1981

ISBN: 0-523-48006-7

Cover illustration by: Don Brautigon

Printed in the United States of America

Distributed by Pinnacle Books, 1430 Broadway, New York, N.Y. 10018

## AUTHOR'S NOTE

In classical mythology there existed a creature, one of a class of man-devouring monsters, commonly represented with the head and breast of a woman and the body of a serpent.
It was called a lamia.

# Ludlow's Mill

# PROLOGUE

In spite of the humid heat of the Florida summer night, the eternal chill was deep within her. And with it came the ancient hunger of the moon change, twisting in her like a gnawing cramp. She coiled lower behind the turk's cap bush, feeling her body scrape against the foliage, knocking a handful of the red bell-shaped blossoms to the ground, and looked intently before her. A hundred yards or so to the east, the narrow road emerged from a stand of pine into the moonlight and came straight across the pasture land like a grey scar traversing the tender earth. Along it, in a few moments, her meal would come.

She pulled back deeper into the shadows, so smooth and unencumbered without the cocoon of a mortal body enshrouding her. For a brief instant, fury raged in her that she must return to one; that only a mortal body could continue her eternal life and allow her to experience the urgent emotions the mortals lived by. But the anger shrank in upon itself and faded away. The burden of the flesh was not too heavy in relation to the joys gained. Her mouth moved; her tongue darted out, tasting the sultry air for vibrations.

After the meal was finished, when a partial warmth

again flowed through her veins, she'd return to the host body she'd left in its waiting coma and to life among the humans of this quiet village. She liked it here, its shadow-dappled forests and birds sailing on spread wings in the hot sky. And there were ancient whispers in the air. Here she often felt that she had returned to the primeval times when the human creatures were fewer and the air and grasses were sweet to smell.

She felt the vibrations now. Close. Coming closer. A membrane slid over her eyes, and the road and all around it became tinted with a reddish-amber hue. Her long body moved, tiny tremors of anticipation rippling along its sleek muscles, finally knotting and bunching for movement.

The hunger flared potently within her; a redness replaced the amber hue, and the girl became a crimson creature walking through a russet landscape.

She was sturdy, dressed in a blouse and jeans, heavy in the hips and thighs as were so many of the modern female mortals. She was perhaps sixteen, the age when sexual wants should be forming within the female.

An excitement as consuming as the hunger was in the lamia now. Her throat grew taut, and she could feel the pulsing of her heart in it, a heavy thudding beat in tempo with the girl's soft footfalls on the sandy soil. Her tongue flicked out.

She waited.

Far away, automobiles rushed through the darkness chasing their fans of light. The drone of engines and the swish of tires on night-hot asphalt were a muffled undertone to the chirping and whine of insects. The sound was an irritant. She listened for a moment, yearning for the ancient voiceless nights when the world was reluctant to move after the sun went down.

The girl sauntered towards her. Nine more steps. Six. Two.

The lamia eased through the foliage and moved onto the perm. Moonlight eddied around her.

For a few seconds, uncomprehending, the girl stared at her. Then the young face crumbled as the mind behind it knew terror far beyond its capacity to contain. Her brown eyes bulged and rolled desperately, refusing to focus on the thing in the road gliding towards her out of the darkness.

"Oh, God!" The girl stepped backwards. "Who—What are you?"

The lamia moved closer, silently. She could not speak without a possessed body acting as her interpreter. Never, through all the ages, had the desire to do so been upon her. It was a gibberish of vibrations on the air, a chattering which brought as much trouble to the humans as it did good.

Her tongue flicked out. The girl whimpered and fell back another step.

For the first time she hissed, and raised her head, staring at the girl with eyes flamed by unholy hunger. The girl moaned deep in her throat and stood where she was, terror draining her responsive reflexes.

The lamia raised herself higher, her head swinging from side to side. Her throat muscles worked in anticipation.

The helpless girl moaned again as her frantic mind tried to fight off its paralysis, to understand what her eyes were seeing.

But there was no physical definition. The girl knew only that there was something there, glittering in the

moonlight. A vague shape changing as it wove towards
her and around her, a phantom with no more substance
than a flashlight beam swinging in a fog. Only the eyes,
two slitted pinpoints of hell light, watching her with
their unblinking stare, and beneath them two long
curving and monstrous fangs, with a forked tongue
darting in and out between them. Wildly, she tried to
put a definition on the thing. Serpent? Maybe, but this
thing was too tall at times. A dragon? No, no. There
was no such thing. There was no description this side of
reason.

When the lamia raised herself until her glowing eyes
were even with the girl's, the prey surrendered docilely.
She fell to her knees whimpering, mewling little
incoherent shards of sound.

With a final dreadful hiss, the lamia sprang, entwining herself around the robust one of the girl. The girl fell
to her back. Spasms heaved her torso, but her sturdy
hips thrust only once as the lamia coiled around her
head, pulling it back and stretching her throat into a
taut arch bulging upwards towards the hungry mouth.

Watching the frantic pulse surge through the taut
throat, the lamia hissed. The sight of the throbbing
warmth and strength beneath the tender skin was a
sweet agony within her, sending chills along her nerve
lines. She tightened herself around the warm body,
pushing the girl's head back until her strained throat
appeared ready to burst and fountain the blood within it
upwards.

At that instant, a choking sound forced its way from
the girl's vocal chords, and she heaved upwards in a last
desperate thrust of strong muscles, her hands groping
blindly for something to clutch.

The lamia hissed and pressed around the writhing body, squeezing air from the struggling lungs, twisting the neck until she heard a tiny grating sound. The girl squealed and went limp.

The lamia lowered her mouth to the bulging throat, her breath sounding in her flared nostrils, and sank her fangs into the great vital artery, into the thick warm blood.

Later, she pushed the body into the roadside ditch. She was content. Extinction had been averted for another changing of the moon.

She moved swiftly across the fields. The waiting body was ahead, toward the source of the cool breeze that blew when the land became hard and brown and cold. When she arrived there and reentered the body, she'd rest . . . and the next day, also, if she could. Always a sensual calm claimed her after one of the meals . . . and after that would come the primal want, sending her forth within the possessed body to seek a young male human. It would be a ravenous desire this time. The blood tonight had been thick and fulsome.

The lamia entered the opaque darkness of a stand of pines.

# CHAPTER 1

Standing at the end of her driveway, Karen Sommers looked up and down the narrow macadam road; north towards the orange groves hidden behind a gentle rise in the land, and then south, in the direction of the village of Grove Center. The morning air was crisp, still fragile and damp with ghost mists from the night just passed. She drew a slow deep breath, inhaling the lingering perfume of the night-blooming jasmine on the weightless air. Within an hour, she knew, this same gossamer air would be heavy and humid under the sun-burned sky of Florida in June. The jasmine aroma replaced with the smell of dust and dry leaves.

She picked up the morning newspaper lying in the driveway; its plastic bag had torn when the delivery boy tossed it from his car. The dew had seeped in and stained a portion of the front page, obliterating the weather report. That didn't really matter, she thought; the weather seldom changed during the summer months . . . continued fair with the chance of afternoon showers. Yet, she frowned, it didn't seem too much to wish that the *Orlando Sentinel* would replace the delivery box knocked over some months previously by an unknown night driver.

"Damn it!" She surprised herself with her own anger. The ripped plastic and the damp paper within it seemed an example of everything that was wrong with the world. Everyone was filled with arrogance, indifference and thoughtlessness. What has happened, she wondered, to America? Greed! Me first! To hell with the other person! That, she answered herself, that is what has happened.

She started back towards her old house, its size dominating the oak trees with their dirty grey beards of Spanish moss hanging limp in the quiet air. The house, with its veranda and curlicued steamboat Gothic carvings, was a relic of the unconfused era before the structures of society began to decay. It looked as sturdy and eternal as the world had looked thirty years ago when she was a young girl. A langorous, innocent time.

With some vexation, she saw weeds pushing up through the gravel and shell mixture along the center of the driveway. Sometime in the near future she'd have Jeff pull them—and then wondered whether he'd do it on the first asking or whether she'd be forced to command him or even resort to bribery. Right now, the way she felt, there'd be no bribe. He'd do it because his mother asked him to do it. Fifteen-year-olds! She sighed. Had any time in history been worse to bring up a child, especially when you were trying to do it yourself? From what she could see, none of the kids nowadays wanted to accept demands on them, no matter how minor. Show indignation; talk back; sneer at the adults; or run away. Those seemed to be their answers.

But not when it came to something they were interested in for themselves, oh, no, not then. Then it was all eagerness, with all the time needed to devote to whatever the interest was. Like the Jay-Cee baseball clinic Jeff was attending three days a week. Nothing could keep him away from that, rain, hail or high water. Whoa! Knock that thinking off, woman! she scolded herself. You've gone too far. That clinic was building Jeff's future. It might help him make the varsity next year. And two years on that, with his ability, could lead to a scholarship. Not a big one—baseball scholarships weren't big. But every little bit would help.

Jesus, she thought, you're in a fine and jolly mood this morning. You'd better shape up, gal, before Jennifer thinks her older sister is a gold-plated grouch and cuts short her visit.

Red berries sprinkled the grass beneath a pepper tree; she decided to pick up a few to plant in one of the pots she kept in the garage. She started towards them when, behind her, a car stopped at the end of the driveway.

"Karen!"

She turned. Lois Rutherford was leaning out of the passenger window of her dusty green Toyota, her pudgy face reminding Karen of a full moon topped with white froth. In spite of the early morning coolness, Lois' leathery skin shone with perspiration. She delighted in conveying bad news.

After a moment's hesitation, Karent went back down the driveway and stood by the car.

"Morning, Karen. Have you heard about the poor Simpson girl, Shirley?"

"No."

"She was killed last night. Murdered!"

"Oh, God!" Karen suddenly felt awkward and very helplessly mortal. "How?"

Lois Rutherford drew a deep breath. "The poor

child's throat was gouged open and the blood sucked from her dead body."

Karen stood very still. All the magic went away from the morning. "Where did it happen, Lois?"

"About a mile from her house on County Road Three. She was on her way home from baby sitting for Doris and Sam Franks."

"How terrible." Karen felt hollow with fear. County Road Three was less than five miles away.

"There's a fiend among us, a devil." Something ugly was apparent behind Lois Rutherford's eyes, an almost physical warp, changing her into an inexplicably hostile creature. "This means no woman in Grove Center is safe, do you realize that? We're all potential victims. That girl may be only the first. We women ought to do something to protect ourselves."

This was how it started, Karen thought, how the veneer of civilization was stripped away. "There are the police and the sheriff's department, Lois."

"Incompetents! All of them!"

Karen nodded, opened her mouth to disagree, then realized there was nothing to say. Hysteria was like a bubbling well behind the other woman's eyes, and hysteria could not be reasoned with. Karen felt apprehension coiling in her, too; however, she knew she could control it because, so far, her deeper realms of consciousness were untouched by its tentacles. She would not permit herself to be injected. As much as she disliked admitting it, even to herself, the death of the Simpson girl was still an impersonal event. The dying had happened to another, to someone they hardly knew, it had not invaded her family. Jason had once told her that that was how it was in battle—if the guy down the line from you got it, well it wasn't you.

"The police have means, Lois, and I'm sure they're doing their best."

It was weak and escapist. The fat woman thought so too, apparently, because she snorted and pulled her head back in the window. "I hope you're right, Karen; but you're being like so many others these days. Turn your head away and the problem will disappear." She rammed the transmission into gear and accelerated the little car in a spray of sand and gravel towards Grove Center.

Karen looked after her, suddenly feeling guilty. Lois was right. She, herself, was an answer to the questions she'd just asked herself. She *was* indifferent! And indifference was one of the great plagues decimating humanity today.

As she walked slowly to the house, her mind turned deep into itself and saw only little dark shadows around her, in the oak trees, the morning doves cooed their welcome, but the morning had lost its joys. It had become empty, as though nothingness lay beyond the jasmine and gardenia bushes surrounding the lawn.

When she entered through the side door, both Jennifer and Jeff were in the kitchen. The dome tea kettle was on the range, the first puffs of steam erupting from its short spout. About now, she thought, it would begin to give short little whistles, had not the round button thing which did the whistling fallen out last March. Neither she nor Jeff had been able to find it. Some of the fun of using it was gone, she had to admit.

Jeff was collecting a bowl and the cereal box, Jennifer was going through the cupboards on either side of the range. "Do you have anything planned for breakfast, sis?''

She laid the newspaper on the drain board. ''No, I'm not much for facing food the first thing in the morning. I usually settle for coffee and toast or an English muffin. Sometimes we have Pop Tarts.''

''That sounds good to me,'' Jennifer nodded.

''What?''

''The Pop Tart, if you have any. I haven't had one for I can't remember how long.''

''We have them. They're in the cupboard over the stove. You can have any flavor you want, as long as it's cinnamon.''

Jennifer found the box of pastries, took two out, and dropped them into the toaster. While she was doing that, Jeff went to the dining nook and filled his bowl with corn flakes. He went to the refrigerator and grabbed hold of a gallon jug of milk.

''You need help with that?'' Karen asked.

''Aw, mom. I can at least pour milk.''

''Okay.''

He undid the cap, lifted the jug, tilted it—and the milk gushed out in a cascade, hitting the pile of flakes and spraying them over the table. ''Damn!''

''All right, that's enough of that language. Clean up your mess with the dishcloth, and while you're doing it remember that's why I use plastic tablecloths.''

''Yes, ma'am.''

Jennifer was leaning with her hips against the drain-board watching him, a small smile hovering on her lips.

Looking at her, Karen forced herself to see Jennifer as a fully mature woman and not as her kid sister. The woman standing there watching Jeff hardly seemed the end result of the thin little girl always tagging along to the park, wanting to know why she couldn't accompany her older sister on dates, and not too happy about receiving a hand-me-down bicycle.

Like herself, Jennifer was tall, nearly five feet nine without heels. She had a ripe body scaled magnificently to proportion. Leaning against the drainboard, with her arms folded under her breasts, she gave the impression of a person who meets life directly, with no nonsense. Her vivid blue eyes were clear and dewy with health, under neatly arched brows and her face was somewhat square, with cheekbones just high enough to have slight model's hollows beneath. The nose was perhaps a trifle too short, but it was narrow at the nostrils, giving the impression of perfect length. Her mouth was wide, full, and richly molded; Karen realized uncomfortably that it was the most sensuous feature of her face. Jennifer's thick waves of golden blonde hair were pulled back with a blue ribbon into a loose pony tail on her neck. Jennifer had had it colored, but if so Karen was pretty sure it was an expensive professional job, not one from a bottle over the bathroom sink. Except for the rich jewelry hue, it looked natural.

She was overdressed again today, Karen saw, like so many visiting northerners in Florida. Her pale blue blouse was opened to show the upper slopes of heavy breasts, and her matching shorts were discreetly tight, snugly binding the strong curves of potent hips and flat abdomen. Around her slender waist a narrow yellow sash was knotted. Her legs were the long tight-muscled legs one associates with a dancer . . . the thighs solid and the calves sturdy. Overdressed wasn't quite the word, Karen thought. It was just that she looked like a visitor, not a native.

Karen smiled at her sister, then stopped, confused. Jennifer was staring at Jeff. Karen saw in those vivid blue eyes, a hint of amber shadows. Her sister's gaze moved over him leisurely, studying him. Maybe it was her imagination, but to Karen, for an instant of time, Jennifer's eyes seemed to lengthen, becoming glowing slits under their long lashes. Jennifer appeared fascinated with the innocent strength of Jeff's young body.

Jennifer's tongue came out, its red tip running back and forth wetly on the ripeness of her lower lip. She inhaled, her chest rising, thrusting her breasts forward against the cotton blouse.

As suddenly as Karen had become aware of it, the strangeness left Jennifer's face. Her eyes, blue once more, stared briefly at Karen in remote assessment, then turned away for the length of several breaths. When Jennifer looked at Karen again, her eyes were dewy and clear.

A clang came from the toaster. Jennifer went to it. "Just like mine," she said.

"What's that?"

"One comes up, and the other stays stuck."

She must have done some exploring of the kitchen, because she opened the correct drawer and took out a paring knife. Muttering under her breath, she dug the stuck tart out of the slot and dropped it on a plate. "A smidgen of black around the edges, but very edible."

Karen got out the cups, spooned instant coffee into them and added the boiling water. "Do you want orange juice?"

"Oh, I don't know. I suppose I should, since I'm in the state which produces it, but I really don't care that much for it.''

"Neither do I. I keep it for young Lochinvar here.''

"I don't like it that much, either,'' Jeff said around a mouthful of cereal.

Karen poured a glass and set it on the table before him. "Drink it. You're not old enough yet to make your objections count.''

"Mom,'' he grumbled, but he drank it.

She sat looking at him, exasperatedly.

"What's wrong now?'' he asked.

"Why can't you do whatever it is I ask you to do without a fuss?''

"I do.''

"Then we've different definitions of 'fuss' ''.

"Maybe.''

She allowed it to drop. It could become a complication, and she wanted none this morning . . . not on Jen's first day here.

No one said much during the makeshift meal. In spite of what she thought she'd seen in Jennifer's eyes, Karen began to feel comfortable. She'd been wrong; she must have been. At this table were the only two people in the world who shared her blood. They were a family; they shared blood-related understandings and awarenesses. She felt close to them.

A sense of closeness had been a long time absent from her life, ever since Jason's death, so horrifyingly unexpected and swift, four years ago. On a pristine April morning Jason and two friends had driven out with a canoe on the car-top carrier; at six-thirty that evening she was in a funeral parlor in Grove Center identifying his body. A freak accident—the canoe turned over by a submerged log, a foot caught in a

fishnet entangled around a too heavy tackle box. A
husband and father, aged thirty-two, was no more. For
a year and a half too many reflecting memories had
been reality, and the present the unreality. But that time
was over now, thanks to Jeff, her work, and lately, a
man named Patrick O'Shawn. It was now a doleful
memory locked away in a far corner of her mind.

Jennifer lit a menthol cigarette with a yellow Bic
lighter and pushed her coffee cup away, leaned back in
her chair. She arched langorously, pluming smoke
towards the ceiling. "This is complete and utter
relaxation, Kar. Is every morning like this with you?"

Karen saw Jeff looking at his aunt's thrusting body.
She forced herself to smile. "I should be so lucky!
During the nine months of school, the mornings around
here are dismal chaos. Would you believe the school bus
comes by here at *six forty-five?* Neither Jeff nor I can
speak that early. It's all grunts and head wags—very
primitive."

Jennifer looked at the burning tip of her cigarette,
then, under her thick lashes, her eyes slid once more to
Jeff. "It still sounds wonderful to me."

"It's cold, too, Aunt Jennifer." Jeff's voice was
tight. "We turn the furnace off at night to save fuel,
and we have to wear sweaters, sometimes coats, to keep
warm in the mornings—right here in the kitchen."

"Oh, that sounds rough, Jeff."

"It is."

Jennifer smiled again. Karen watched her for a
moment through the veil of cigarette smoke. If a smile
could be out of tune, she thought, Jennifer's was just
that. It seemed false, an adjustment of mind and facial
muscles to form a mask behind which to hide some

other emotion.

Averting her eyes and smiling, she said, "I've nothing really planned for the day. I thought I'd drive you around to show you the area."

"That sounds fine to me." Jennifer gazed at a yellow curtain rippling slightly from a breeze. "I want to see everything. You do have it idyllic here. This might just be the place to escape the rat race, to start a new life. You and Jason did."

"It's not all bucolic, Jen." She pulled a Benson & Hedges from its box and lit it. Jennifer had left the lighter on the table. "We have murders here."

Startled by the words, both stared at her.

"Who, mom?" Jeff was looking at her with wide eyes.

"Shirley Simpson."

"Shirley?" His eyes crinkled, then popped open wide. "I know her, mom! I know her!"

"I know, Jeff." She looked at Jennifer. "Jeff and Shirley's brother play together sometimes and attend the same baseball clinic."

Jeff sat staring straight ahead, his mouth working. "She. . . . She was a nice girl."

"I'm sorry, Jeff."

He only nodded. Secrets seemed to be moving through his mind.

"You're excused, if you want to leave," she told him.

"Yeah. Thanks." He pushed himself away from the table and went through the kitchen to the side door. The screen slammed behind him as he went out to the veranda.

Jennifer mashed her cigarette in the ceramic ashtray slowly, watching the white cylinder splay and burst. "A girl murdered, Karen?''

Karen saw some crumbs from Jennifer's tart on the table beside her plate. She dampened a fingertip with her tongue and picked them up. "Yes. A teenager, which makes it so much more gruesome. Her throat was bitten out, and the blood was entirely drained from her body.''

Jennifer glanced at her, then looked once more at the open window. A pulse throbbed in her throat. Finally, in a low voice, she said, "That will be hard for the people here to take, won't it?''

Karen nodded. "Yes.''

Jennifer picked up her cup and turned it around several times in her hands looking down into its emptiness, a pensive expression on her face. "Was she sexually molested?''

"Lois didn't say.'' Karen looked for more crumbs, carefully. She sighed. "It could cause a mild hysteria among some of the women. When Lois Rutherford told me about it this morning, she immediately started talking about the women of Grove Center uniting for protection. Female vigilantes, I guess.''

"That's absurd. You've got a police force, don't you?''

"The town does, yes. But we live in the county. Well, there's the sheriff and, I suppose, the state. They must have investigators.'' She crushed her cigarette out in the tray. "Shirley's death has made me think, though. I don't allow outside disasters to come close to me. I keep them remote, telling myself they are happening to other families and people who I don't know—or hardly know. They are only names on the radio, or blurred photos in the newspaper. But with the Simpson girl's death I can't do that. I'm affected.''

Jennifer nodded. "I understand, sis, but try to keep it like it was—pushed away. Living in a big city, I guess, has made me immune to acts of horror. I know it's different in a small town, where the people are closer to each other and the chances are that you would know whoever is—murdered—but keep it pushed away as best you can." She leaned forward, putting her hands on the table as if wanting to reach over and take one of Karen's. "I'll help you."

"I know." She stood up and took her cup and saucer to the sink. "I think I'd better see how Jeff's doing."

They found him sitting on the porch steps, elbows on his knees and his chin resting in his hands. Without looking up at them, he asked, "Will the police find out who did it?"

"Of course, darling." Karen sat down beside him. "It will probably take some time, but whoever did it will be found and punished. Believe me, son."

Eyes blinked, a muscle tightened in his jaw. "I believe you."

"Thanks. Now," she tousled his hair, "try not to think about Shirley too much, and let's figure out what we can do today to show Aunt Jennifer a good time."

Jennifer said, "I'll tell you what. I haven't completely unpacked yet. How about coming up to my room, Jeff, and helping me? And telling me some of the things to do around Grove Center, so I can tell your mom what I want to see and where I want to go?" She cocked an eyebrow and smiled. "But maybe you'd be embarrassed watching a woman unpack her things."

Jeff blushed and grinned. "No. I—I've seen women's things."

When they had gone, Karen leaned against a porch
post. In the gently curling air the Spanish moss on the
oaks began to sway, while far up near the treetops
hushed leaves spoke shyly to one another. She could feel
the heat moving in with the breeze. A booby trap, she
thought: it was so easy to be conned by the early
morning coolness into believing this would be a day
unlike the others, into planning outdoor activities.

Interlaced with the approaching heat there was an
undercurrent, an uncanny sensation of mild electricity
tingling against her skin. She was aware of a dark and
bitter haunting forming under the surface of her well-
being.

Something this morning had started it. Whatever it
was, it sought grotesque and nonexistent trouble, trying
to create a shadow over Jennifer, making her seem a
person moving obliquely to the grain of life.

With a sigh, she took a last look at the shadowed
patterns of the oaks and pepper trees trembling on the
lawn, pushed herself away from the post, and went into
the kitchen. The satisfaction with the day she had
experienced this morning before picking up the newspaper had disappeared.

The cups with their saucers and the cereal bowl waited
on the drainboard. Turning on the hot water, she waited
until it steamed and then held each under it, giving them
a quick swish with the dish cloth. She shook the excess
water from them and placed them in the draining tray to
dry.

Whatever Jennifer and Jeff worked out to do today,
Karen now knew there was one place she wanted to go.
During the course of the drive she'd take them out to the
old mill ruins on the Ludlow land. It was her sanctuary,

as it had been Jason's. Their psychologist's office. When all the mind's problems were confused and tensions were intermingling, they drove the three miles to the solitude of the tumbled stone walls. Sitting together in the ambient peace, saying to each other all the things that needed saying, they healed themselves and each other.

Jennifer was greedy in her desire to see the area, and they drove back and forth through the small town more times than Karen cared to count. Twice they went past the citrus processing plant with the cotton-white smoke pluming from its tall stacks like a scarf, its acrid smell turning the air sour. Then once around the new Highland Mall shopping center with its buildings looking gaudy and sterile; and three times around the high school and its adjoining athletic field. There a group of boys was half-heartedly kicking a soccer ball around. When that was done, and Karen thought they might return home, Jennifer asked to see the country surrounding Grove Center, so they drove along the half-dozen roads leading into town. She asked few questions, but Karen received the impression her sister was studying the country as one does when establishing landmarks. Jennifer sat motionless. Watching. Perhaps, Karen thought, it was because she lived in the continuous upheaval of a city and found the slow rhythm of a small country village a strange niche in time.

By three o'clock, Jeff, who was sitting between them in the cab of the Dodge pickup truck, was restless. The Friday evening traffic was building, slowing the driving, making him even more nervous. "Is this how we're going to spend every day while Aunt Jennifer is here?

Because, geez, there are ten thousand other things to do."

Karen gave him a rather sharp "no." But Jennifer laid her hand on his thigh, between the bottom of his shorts and his knee, and reassured him. "This is the only time I'll want the Cook's Tour."

"Cook's Tour? What's cooking got to do with it?"

Jennifer laughed and explained.

Somehow they never got out to Ludlow's place.

That evening they sat down to a warm-weather supper of cold cuts, cheese, tossed salad, and iced tea. Around nine o'clock, Jennifer, who seemed surprised at herself as she spoke, said she was still tired from her flight the previous afternoon and, if they wouldn't think her a party-pooper, thought she'd retire. For some reason, Karen was as surprised as Jennifer looked; she suspected that her sister wasn't weary but was making an excuse to leave them. But she made no objection, telling Jennifer to sleep as long as she liked the following morning.

Later, after Jeff had gone to bed, Karen poured herself a glass of milk and stood drinking it at the side door, aware of the rising scent of jasmine. Her mind wanted to form questions and seek answers, to turn over events and place them in neat perspective; but she wouldn't allow it to. She wanted to be aware only of the movement of her arm, only of drinking the milk.

Before going up to her bedroom, she locked the doors, thinking what an idiotic precaution it was, because she was leaving the windows open for coolness. Habit. What creatures of habit we are, she thought, following a daily routine like a sacred ritual and not deviating from it by so much as the turning of a key. Even when we wished for excitement.

Day after tomorrow Patrick would be coming over from Vero Beach, and not a moment too soon. Damn, she did miss him; she, who for so many years had been a one-man woman. Jason would never be gone; memory was not a perishable substance. But events did not remain motionless, and other currents moved in to reconstruct a life, even though the life might come apart easier the next time. Such was the case with Patrick. He was the kindness of a reshaped life.

Perhaps more than anything else, it had been her meeting of him which had been the final victory in her struggle to regain a taste for day-to-day social encounters. Just over a year ago, her booth had stood next to his at the Indialantic Seaside Art Show. His flamboyant sunsets and sunrises over wet marshlands or white-tipped waves depressingly turned her pastel and meticulously drawn still lifes into namby-pamby wash-outs. By the second afternoon of the show, he was sold out.

"Be bold!" Patrick O'Shawn had shouted at her, as she sat glumly contemplating her work. "Be bold, damnit, Mrs. Sommers. Paint from your guts, not your mind. Your mind will shape it, but your guts will give it substance."

He was right, and she told him so, adding that she was eager to return home to put her "guts" into her work. What she had not told him was that she was doing very well as an illustrator of children's books, that what she exhibited was really a venting off of creative frustrations caused by the demands of publishers.

Twice he had phoned from his home in Vero Beach.

Once she had written him a newsy letter describing the new "guts" 'in her work. One day three months later, a Chevy station wagon had pulled into the driveway, and Patrick O'Shawn had begun his regular and increasingly frequent visits.

But this remote feeling of a shadow following her sister would not leave her thoughts. It seemed to have lodged in a crevice in her mind. Why? In the name of God, why? Patrick's arrival, she hoped, would open a relief valve. His exuberant zest, she told herself, would bring her back to reality, and do away with this irrational feeling that darkness was gathering on the perimeters of her life.

As she went upstairs to her bedroom, she felt her desire to see him become an impatient wanting in her awakened body.

The lamia hissed and made her way through the underbrush, stopping in a webbed pool of shadow under a pine tree. There was no sound from the house. No light. They slept. Her tongue flicked out.

The moon was alone in the sky. Somewhere there were stars, but they were hidden behind a high floating haze. Deep within the dark foliage a cricked sawed, its chirping shrill in the stillness of the night, while far away, in the direction from which the cold winds came, a dog barked. It was a warning, and her muscles tightened at the sound.

After several moments, she moved onward through the moon shadows. Ahead, in the direction where the sun sank, the river curled across the land. It was rough and unfamiliar ground; she chose her way with care. She knew she was going to remain in this area for a long

time, even though her senses were aware certain dangers
awaited her. This small gathering place of the humans
and the undulating land around it, with the warmth in
both the times of light and darkness, touched something
in her brain with vague remembrances of the ancient
lands. She shuddered; her brain had not as yet lost its
horror of the vile crowded places where the humans
gathered, marking no difference between the light and
dark hours.

She moved through the jungle growth, her senses
tuned to the whispers of the night.

As it had always been, in all times, she required a
private place of her own removed from the pathways of
the humans. A secret nest, a hideaway where she could
relax in safety free from her woman body and return to
the ancient ways for a little while.

The river was dark-watered, unmoving and shallow.
It swallowed the moonlight. She moved along the low
river bank, searching, searching.

Finally she found it. An area twice the length of her
body across, a small cave of interwoven branches and
entwining creepers. Water plants along the bank hid it
from the flat openness of the water.

Slowly, eyes glinting, she circled it several times,
flattening the high grass, feeling it rippling along her
body. Her nostrils flared as she acquainted herself with
its peculiar scents.

Soon she was satisfied with the arrangement of the
grass. She lowered herself to the rank-smelling earth
and slowly pulled her body in upon itself until it coiled
neatly, protectively. Once, twice she hissed. She had
claimed her area, and she would do battle for its
possession.

She would rest here until just before the light, when she'd return to the woman body.

As sleep began to drift into her senses, contentment moved deep within her, almost warming the eternal chill. It was a good place.

# CHAPTER 2

An earth-warmed breeze struggled through the cabbage palms and long-leafed pines, rustling the dry fronds and branches, sounding like falling rain. Shafts of sunlight, filled with whirling motes of dust, were gold and yellow in the blue-tinted shadows. But in the small irregular clearing the sunlight spread into a flood. The colorless glare splashed on the crumbling sugar mill ruins, turning the remains of the coquina stone walls into sharply dimensioned angles and planes of black and grey.

Ludlow's Mill was a portion of a half-forgotten past. When debris of modern civilization littered it, the wild foliage obliterated it within days. The clearing hacked from the forest was constantly in jeopardy. Relentlessly nature was determined to reclaim what man had wrested from her.

They had driven out to the ruins after lunch. Jeff had no desire to make the trip, but he and Jennifer had agreed to come with Karen. Karen was glad to be there. She wanted to escape the incomprehensions of the previous day; she knew the tranquil ruins would cleanse and calm the dark workings of her mind. But what she had really wanted was to make the trip alone, to sit

silently and allow the peace to uproot the tendrils of
doubt coiled in the recesses of her mind.

Throughout the morning, and on the drive out, she
had seen no shadow trailing her sister. In the cab of the
old Dodge, Jennifer had been the vivacious woman she
remembered. Whatever it was she thought she had seen
in Jennifer the day before was gone. There was still an
aura of detachment about her sister, but Karen marked
it off as the impassive cocoon of all city dwellers. Yet,
now, as the three of them walked along the weed-grown
lane to the ruins, she knew she could not write off yesterday's feeling as hallucinations. Something had been
with her sister, following her, moving with her. Something hidden in shadows. Something without a soul.

She found herself walking slower than Jeff and
Jennifer, and they pulled ahead. She didn't mind; she
had always considered herself an alien here and approached carefully, step by step, with respect.

Jennifer and Jeff disappeared around a bend in the
narrowing lane and in a little while she heard their
laughter, Jeff calling something and Jennifer answering
back. Their voices were as out of place in the pastoral
silence, as an off-key whistle in the midst of a subdued
chamber recital.

She rounded the bend. There was the clearing, the
filtered sunlight in which she walked ricocheting from
the earth as glare. She reached the edge of the trees and
stopped, suddenly feeling she was standing on the edge
of a vacuum. A chill webbed through her like tiny cold
wires enmeshed under her flesh; she felt her hands
clench and pressed them tight against her thighs to keep
them from trembling.

Above the treetops a crow cawed, bold and full of

empty fury. Flapping its wings, it swept over the clearing; somewhere nearby a ground creature took fright and scurried for its burrow.

Jeff and Jennifer were almost at the ruins, walking slower now along the meandering path.

The afternoon breeze made a curious whimpering in the treetops. She didn't like the sound, and, because she didn't, realized she was standing stiffly and half-hidden in the shadows of the trees, hiding herself like a person playing hide-and-seek. The sound was too much like a moan, as though somewhere up in the dark net of branches a terrible pain was being inflicted. It touched deep, wordless terrors in her. Her heart began to pound.

On the east side of the clearing, the clumsy vine-entangled ruins of the old sugar mill rose from the foliage like a battered old rock. Amber afternoon light splashing in and out among depthless black shadows gave the ruins a sinister appearance which she knew—surely she knew—was utterly misleading.

Slowly, over the frantic pounding of her heart, she became aware there were none of the sounds one expects in the middle of a forest—no whine or hum or darting insects, no chirping or rustling of tiny ground creatures. Nowhere did a bird call to its mate. Silence was building upon silence, and she suddenly felt these precise moments in time had no fitting into history. It was an orphan interlude.

As much as she tried to turn her mind from it, she felt great danger lurking within the crumbling walls. Even out in the weeds and brambles of the clearing, she sensed fear and anger hovering. At that instant the humid air beneath the trees became heavy and thick, and she gasped for breath.

Her fear increased. Everything—sound, emotion, even perception—had moved out of perspective.

She forced herself to suck in a mouthful of sultry air, filling her lungs with wet syrupy dampness, then slowly shook her head and asked herself half-aloud, "What kind of damned nincompoop are you?"

She stepped out onto the path. The sun's full force struck her, pricking her eyes as it bounced up from the dry earth, pressing an intolerable weight on her shoulders. She gasped and bent slightly forward. Her body suddenly seemed four or five degrees hotter, and she wished she had worn her wide-brimmed hat in spite of Jeff's abhorrence of it. He called it her "granny hat."

Jeff and Jennifer were waiting for her in the shade of a wall.

Jeff was watching her, grinning. She saw with a tiny shock that he was turning into a smaller facsimile of Jason. He had her green eyes, and his brown hair was under-tinted with her auburn coloring; but all the rest of him was Jason—the big frame, the square jaw showing through adolescent roundness, the direct way of looking at people. He ate with the appetite of a fifteen-year-old, of course, but she saw to it that he ate healthy food, not junk, and there was a litheness and solidity about him more appropriate to a boy a year or two older.

She was so damn proud of him. Giving birth to him was the greatest thing she'd ever done. Oh God, if only Jason had lived to see the teenager he had fathered.

"Something worrying you, sis?" Jennifer's voice was low and touched with concern around the edges.

"No. Why?" Karen looked at her sister and saw how closely her blue eyes matched the blue of the sky. Then she said, her voice light, "I'm one of those people who love the heat, but never get used to it. Maybe it's beginning to show."

She was beginning to wish she hadn't suggested they come out to the mill. She felt strangely unprotected and vulnerable. Something was oppressing her mind as the sun was weighing down her shoulders, and she knew that there would be no peace for her here today.

"Mom, I know all the things here. Can I go and see if there's anything left of my old tree platform?" Jeff moved towards a vine-draped pine.

"Go ahead, but if it's too dilapidated don't try to get up on it. Remember, you've put on a few pounds since your father built it for you."

"Okay."

When Jeff had disappeared behind the pine, into the forest, Jennifer turned to her. Karen could not bear to have her sister sense her feeling of vulnerability. She turned away and studied a little pepper tree inching its way between two stone blocks near the base of the wall. Could she have experienced some kind of psychic trauma at the edge of the clearing? She felt very frightened. This was the place she came to heal life's multiple lacerations of mind and soul. If her nerves were fraying, and she could not heal them, what might not happen? Goblins in the shadows, behind trees, under the bed? She'd live in a great curve in reality!

She drew a deep breath and turned to face Jennifer. "What do you think of my hideaway place?"

"It's as good as you told me it was. I like it. It makes me think of Camelot and the Canterbury Tales."

"I think you're as incurable a romantic as I am."

Jennifer shook her head. "No, I think it's identification. Everybody identifies with certain things—you know, times and places. I've always felt out of step with time, somehow; so I identify with places. Besides, it's easier. There's too much to take into consideration when you try to relate to time."

"Whoa! Wait a minute, kid sister. Remember, this is a small-town gal you're talking to—not an Ohio State philosophy major sipping sherry at a soireé. Don't go into relativity, please."

Jennifer laughed. "You're right. That's Cleveland 'in' group talk." She looked around. "Do you know the history of this place?"

"Certainly. Well, at least some. What kind of guide would I be if I didn't have a spiel to give?" She looked at the ruins; they looked shoddy, uninteresting. And the wild vegetation smelled rank. "It's owned by an old fellow named Homer Ludlow, and not many people ever see, or even know about, these ruins. Old Ludlow won't open them to the public, even though the county and state historical societies have been after him. They want him to allow them to designate the area a historical site. They've done that at New Smyrna and the area south of St. Augustine. But he's adamant, and to tell you the truth, I don't know if I blame him. I suppose it's a heritage and people should have the opportunity to visit; but on the other hand, the dirt bikers and the four-wheel-drive freaks would probably churn the road into a shambles overnight.

"The mill was built by the Franciscans sometime in the late sixteen hundreds, not as a mill, of course. It was a mission. Then, when the English moved in around seventeen sixty, it was a portion of a huge land grant given to Ludlow's ancestors . . . something like sixty to seventy thousand acres. They converted the mission into a sugar mill to grind the cane they grew. When the Seminoles rose up in the eighteen thirties and attacked this area, it was destroyed. As was the town of New Smyrna to the east. I guess it was a very bloody and dark time in our history . . . and one not written about very often.''

For almost ten minutes Karen walked Jennifer through the ruins, showing her a row of rusted, crumpled boiling vats, the heavy rollers and gear wheels of grinding machinery lying on their sides, saplings thrusting through wheel spokes and vines wreathing the rollers.

When they had made a full circle and were back at the arch from where they had started, Jennifer plumped down on a block of masonry and let out her breath in a long sigh. "That was the grand tour.''

"Sorry. I guess I got carried away.''

"No. No, I'm glad you gave it to me.'' Her eyes moved slowly around the area. "I'm very, very happy you brought me here.''

Was there a hint of amber hue behind her eyes? Did they slit ever so slightly?

Karen said, "This is my get-away-from-it-all place. When I come out here, I'm able to get all my problems back into manageable proportions.''

Jennifer's head continued to swing ever so slowly from side to side. "It would be a good place for a lot of things.''

Karen didn't want to look at her sister's eyes. She wasn't certain what she wanted. She continued talking. "There're times when I really have the feeling I'm derelict as a mother . . . that I've too many self-centered interests. When that feeling gets too heavy, I come out here and get my act together. It's as if I can reach inside myself, right into the center of my brain, and sort out whatever problems I have and toss them away or, at least, index them."

"I envy you."

"That's silly, Jen! You've got so much going for you, I'm sure. Do you have a boy friend? You've never written about one."

"Well, a fellow named Eliot, but I'm not certain he offers what I want to spend a lifetime sharing. He's so mod, so 'in'. I sometimes think he's a creation of the giant marionette manufacturer who has populated the world with disco-goers, skiers, and water bed wallowers. There's never anything new with him. Never any resolution."

"I'm sorry, but he sounds dull to me."

"He is."

They both laughed.

"But really," Jennifer went on, "it's all right, because I'm in no hurry to get married. Believe it or not, I like being a career woman. I got promoted, you know. Now I'm Assistant Public Relations Manager at Neutronics." After a pause for Karen's congratulations, Jennifer added, "And I enjoy having my own apartment, and the freedom living alone permits. And Karen, I'm realistic enough to know that I might be too selfish for marriage, because I've formed my own life patterns." She shrugged her shoulders. "I guess that makes me sound like the perfect candidate for spinsterhood."

"No. It just shows you're independent."

Jennifer leaned back on her elbows, her voluptuous body thrusting upward in a langorous arch. "You haven't mentioned Patrick, Kar. What about him? Your letters have said great things about him, but you haven't talked about him since I got here."

She looked carefully at Jennifer, but the blue eyes were noncommittal, the striking face expressionless.

"I hope you'll like him, Jen, because there're so many ways in which I need him. I know that's a nice solidly trite phrase, but sometimes you've got to use one to express yourself. I can handle the day-to-day routines of life, and most of the not-so-routine affairs, but over all I'm finding I need help. You've set up a happy life style living alone, but when I began to live alone it was among the fragments of a destroyed married life. Oh, I've coped, Jen. I can do that; anybody can, if they have the will. But I'm still relatively young, as you know—thirty-four—and I'm healthy and I have wants of the body as well as of the mind. With those, I can't help myself—I can't cope. I need help, and Patrick is giving it to me. Maybe it's basically physical, I won't say it isn't because I can't, because I'm not certain; but we are compatible and we have our common interest in art."

There was a moment of sun-drowsy silence as Jennifer returned her stare, then said, "Sis, I'm all for it. I'm a woman, too, remember, so don't try to explain to me. I'm in your corner and I'm in Patrick's corner. You and Jason had a beautiful thing for eight years. Now, I think, you have the chance to experience beauty again. Take it. Grab the brass ring."

"Thanks." She could think of nothing else to say. There had been such sincerity in Jennifer's voice, such concern. She was ashamed of her earlier thoughts.

"Just one question, though, Kar. What does Jeff

think?"

For a moment Karen felt shocked, and then she laughed. "The relationship between Jeff and Patrick is so solid I didn't even think to mention it! I believe, well—I believe he loves Patrick, Jen. Actually he accepted Patrick before I did, really and truly . . . and that's made it so damn easy for all of us. There's absolutely no jealousy between competing males. And it's not a dependency relationship of any kind. I'm certain there've been times when Jeff's missed Jason a great deal, but it's been four years, and what seemed so permanent when we were a complete family is now only a memory. No, I feel safe. They've evaluated each other and both like what they've found."

"Mom! Aunt Jennifer!" Jeff's voice came from around the corner of a wall.

"Over here," Karen called. "What is it?"

Jeff emerged running, stumbled over a root, almost fell, and thrust out his right hand against the abrasive coquina rock of the wall. Karen winced, thinking of the burning pain on the palm of his hand, but Jeff seemed not to notice. When he reached them, he came to a dramatic halt. He was obviously carrying momentous news. A thick lock of his reddish-brown hair fell down his forehead, over his left eye. He pushed it out of the way with an impatient gesture.

"You know Sue Ann Miller who works at the Quick Stop store?"

"Yes, of course. What about her?"

"She's down at the big stone . . . you know, the one Patrick lays his paints on when he works out here?"

"What's she doing?"

"Nothing really, I guess. She was lying on it when I

first saw her, but then she saw me and sat up and kept looking at me.'' He gave a little grin. ''She has a kinda sexy way of looking at you.''

''So I've heard.'' She turned to Jennifer. ''Sue Ann has somewhat of a reputation. You know the type, no bra, the tight T-shirt and tight jeans.''

Jennifer arched a brow. ''How old is she?''

''Oh, nineteen, I'd say. She graduated from high school last summer and has been working as a night clerk in the convenience store down the road from us ever since. She's a physical person, somewhat primitive, if you know what I mean.''

''Physical?'' Jennifer turned her head and gazed out across the clearing.

''She is that. And almost disgustingly healthy.''

At that moment there was a sudden rustling of leaves on the far side of the archway, followed by the sound of shuffling foot falls. All three turned to look. There was a slight pause. Karen and Jennifer rose. Then a girl stepped through the arch. She stopped a dozen feet from them and looked at Karen, then Jeff, and finally Jennifer. Her hazel eyes, in a rather full face, lingered on each in turn, seemingly placing them in order of importance. Beads of perspiration glinted on her forehead and arms. The T-shirt she wore was damp, its thin cotton material molding tightly to the full round flesh under it, emphasizing the curves and hollows.

How long, Karen wondered, had the girl been standing on the other side of the archway? Had she followed Jeff from the stone and stood out of sight listening to them gossip about her? She smiled, feeling tight and embarrassed, and said, ''Hello, Sue Ann.''

Sue Ann Miller turned to face her with a hollow stare.

"Hello, Mrs. Sommers."

"Sue Ann, this is my sister, Jennifer Logan. She lives in Cleveland and is spending her vacation with Jeff and me. She'll probably come in to the store frequently."

"That's nice. I'll help you all I can, Miss Logan."

Karen looked at Jennifer, expecting her to say something. Her sister's attention was completely focused on Sue Ann. And suddenly Karen was certain she saw something strange underlying the intent expression on Jennifer's face. She moved a step to her right, to get her sister's entire face into a better perspective, sure that her impression was wrong. She saw in the blue eyes what she could only think of as a want so big it was a consuming greed. She was about to say something to break the lengthening silence, which she knew could become ugly if it stretched on much longer, when Jennifer said, "You're very healthy, Sue Ann."

It was an odd, unexpected thing to say. But it didn't appear to take Sue Ann by surprise. "Thank you, Miss Logan. It's nice of you to say that. I exercise every day."

Sue Ann was not the docile child her answer suggested. Karen sensed a terrible oddness forming. These moments were turning into something untrue; unreality seemed to be replacing reality.

Sue Ann was standing in an area of open shade looking at Jennifer's narrowing stare. It was as though she was mesmerized. Karen stood stiffly, trying to control her thoughts.

Jennifer stood with her legs slightly spread, her head tilted somewhat to the right. "Do you come out here like this very often, Sue Ann?"

"Oh, yes. It's nice and peaceful." Her voice was low,

and seemed to speak words formed by a heat-blurred mind. Then she looked at the deepening sky. "What time is it?"

Karen looked at her watch. "It's ten after three."

"God, I didn't know it was that late. I've got to leave. I'm supposed to be at work at six." She started backing away. "It was nice seeing you and Jeff, Mrs. Sommers—and meeting you, Miss Logan."

Without another word, Sue Ann turned and went through the archway. They heard her going into the underbrush a few yards behind the wall, listened to it rustle for a moment and then hiss into silence. She had gone as quickly as she had come.

Karen felt drawn in upon herself. Had she been the only one to see the smudging of personality in Jennifer's face, or was she so tied up in psychological knots that all her thoughts were darkened with unreal dismay? Around them, the shadows were lengthening, relentlessly swallowing the clearing, reaching for the ruins like a creeping stain. Somewhere in her, plangent nerves quivered, sending a tremor through her, but she braced herself and the spasm died unborn.

"I think it's time for us to go," she said.

"Me, too," Jeff said. "I'm hungry."

Jennifer only nodded.

They walked back along the path across the clearing, Jeff a little ahead of his aunt and mother. The trail was narrow, and Karen felt the cottony heads of weeds brushing her bare legs. They felt like creepy insects on her skin.

"Hey, mom. Can I ride in the back of the pickup on the way home?" Jeff had stopped and was waiting for them.

"Yes, I suppose, if you sit up behind the cab."

"Great! I'll meet you all there."

"You'll do nothing of the kind. You'll walk right along with your aunt and myself."

"Awwww—" Jeff kicked at a clump of grass.

When they reached the trees, Karen hesitated and looked back at the ruins. She wondered, as she did it, if Lot's wife had harbored the same feelings—of wonders brought to an end. Nothing was different, yet something had changed. It was like looking into innocence and finding a nightmare. A thing unholy had incubated back there in the heat. For a time it had surrounded them, spreading throughout the ruins on the sun's warmth as it sought dark crannies in which to spawn its evil. She shuddered and looked away from the ruins. The old stones had changed. Everything had changed.

She moved swiftly across the fields away from the river, a pale darkness gliding through the murky night. There was no moon, no stars; no light at all outlined the trees and shrubs. But her darting tongue sensed the trembling of their leaves and her eyes delineated them. She moved through the stubble and weeds as swiftly as she would during the hours of light. She had no need to concentrate on landmarks; her senses would return her to the placé she had left the woman body in its coma.

Even though she was not hungry, the urge to gorge herself had pushed her close to a frenzy throughout the afternoon. Since seeing the wholesome body among the ruins, the longing for its blood had become a great need.

Perhaps no more than once in ten moons did she encounter a human brimming with such perfect health. And never was she able to resist that very special feeling.

A ditch lay across her path. She slowed her pace and slithered down its side and then part way up on the other bank. She raised her upper body above the tangled weeds on its brink and moved her head from side to side. Her eyes scanned the darkness ahead; her tongue tested the heavy air.

Beyond some distant trees there was a brilliance marking the place she wanted to go. It made the darkness disappear in the way it melted away when the time of light came upon the land . . . only this brilliance was white and glaring. Immediately she sensed the possibility of danger.

She waited. Nothing came to her on the night air. The urge to taste the blood of the healthy body became a coal of heat searing inside her. A tremor ran the length of her body. She could wait no longer. With a hiss, she moved out of the ditch and across the field in the direction of the light.

She slithered slowly into the row of ornamental bushes ringing the parking lot of the building and coiled beneath them. As her eyes ran back and forth across the area, seeing the impossibility of crossing the smooth paving between her and the building in which the girl was, a savage fury erupted in her. Her muscles tautened, and her scales rattled thinly. She coiled herself tighter and stared at the invulnerable building.

She waited. The darkness would be on the land for a long time, and she was safe here beneath the bushes. Waiting was a thing which she had done for as long as she could remember . . . from the ancient times when she had hunted these humans in their first tiny settlements.

A car, rattling and coughing, pulled into the smooth

place and stopped at the side of the building. After a moment, a young man climbed out. For a time he stood beside the open door looking up at the low-hanging clouds and then at the area around the building. Finally he gave a shrug and entered it.

Some of the tightness left her body, and she uncoiled slightly. An amber hue slipped over her vision; the scene foreshortened into tighter perspective. Now the fury was gone from within her, replaced by a new excitement. Within the building lay the appeasement of her two consuming hungers. There would be a way to cross through the light.

She extended her head out through the small branches of the bushes and stared more intently. Her tongue darted out. There were no vibrations. All was well. She hissed and slipped back into the darkness, beyond the reach of the illumination.

# CHAPTER 3

Karen woke with a start. She looked straight up into darkness, knowing her eyes were open, seeing nothing in the thick blackness. She blinked and stared upward again. And again she saw nothing. Heat pressed down upon her, setting its great soggy weight on her breasts and belly and thighs like a huge beast spawned in the eternal night. It squeezed the juices from her body, trying to turn it into a dried shell of shriveled flesh. She lay very still, brutally cornered between fragments of a forgotten dream and a lost reality. Perspiration ran from her in sticky rivulets. From within, from the separate darkness that was her memory, eyes glared at her with an amber hue and hideous lips curved in an unholy smile. She wanted to cry out at these shards of horror.

Then she saw, not too far away, a pale grey oblong floating in what she slowly realized was the darkness of night . . . a window between two lightless worlds beckoned her. She rolled to her side. The sweat-dampened sheet and pillow case pulling at her, trying to suck her down into a swampy morass.

With a tight little moan, she rolled off the bed and stood swaying in the dark heat, struggling to bring her-

51

self back from the cold terror-churned place into which she had wandered; trying to orient herself to the strangeness of what should be her familiar bedroom. Slowly, placing one bare foot carefully before the other on the warm hardwood floor, she walked to the window.

A skim of clouds covered the moon like a thin veil, as though hiding something in the sky from human eyes. On the lawn diffused light was vague and ashen-colored. In it, shapes and non-shapes moved eerily through the shadows. The jasmine and gardenia blossoms drugged the humid air with their over-heavy perfume, and for the first time that she could remember, the fragrance revolted her. It was cloying and burdensome, hinting of decay, and she was reminded of the aromas of funeral flowers left too long in a warm room.

Somewhere in the direction of the town a dog barked, a furious authoritative warning, that it's territory was being trespassed upon. The sound tore at the night with its rasping harshness. Then, as suddenly as it had begun, it stopped. Silence like that of an empty cathedral lay on the night. But then there came a yelp, followed immediately by a howl of fearful terror. Karen shuddered and drew a deep breath, the howl rose to a scream and ceased. Now a silence of horror lay out there in the night, empty of animal sounds and all other noises.

Karen shivered, a cold fear raising her skin in goose flesh beneath the sheen of perspiration. A tear parted the veil of cloud cover and the moon shone through it like tarnished silver.

She started to turn from the window, putting her back

to whatever unnatural horror was out there. But as she
moved, from the corner of her eye, she saw a paleness
gliding along before the darkness of the jasmine bushes.
She turned back and looked down at the mosaic of dim
patterns. At first there was nothing definite . . . only
what her imagination created there. Then, towards the
rear of the lawn near the old toolshed, she saw
movement, a swift blurring of something light-colored
moving from the line of jasmine bushes toward the
black cube of the shed. It passed through a moth-hued
area of moonlight like a thing uncoiling. There was
nothing definable, no real shape, only fragments of an
eerie nimbus moving rapidly through the disturbing
darkness. But she knew it was a living thing answering
the commands of a thinking brain. As she stared, her
heart hammering with racing beats, the swift figure
reached the shed. Before it moved to the door, a portion
of it which might have been a head turned towards the
house and lifted so it pointed directly up at the bedroom
window.

"Dear God!" Karen fell back a step.

Two glowing red eyes glared up at her.

The Sunday morning paper carried a photograph of
Shirley Simpson on the first page of the local news
section. It was the standard department store portrait,
flatly lighted from basic lamp positions with the subject
posed at a three-quarter angle, her head turned too
stiffly on camera, but crisp and showing the dead girl's
dimple. Accompanying it was a scanty history of her
short life. So few words, Karen thought, to describe the
ending of the world for a young life.

She had finished two cups of scalding coffee since

coming into the kitchen. Dawn had been little more than a scratch of pearl along the horizon when she had gone out to the toolshed. Everything had been as she remembered it in the shed. Nothing had been disturbed. Now she realized she had had no clear idea of what she sought.

Jeff came into the kitchen as she was washing out her coffee cup.

"Aunt Jennifer not up yet?"

"Not yet. When you're on vacation you get to sleep late. You ought to know that from the sack time you've been putting in since school's been out."

He went to the cupboard and got out his box of cereal.

"Don't you want something else this morning?" she asked.

"No. This is okay." He got a bowl out of another cupboard and stood holding the box in one hand and the bowl in the other. "I didn't sleep too good last night."

She was aware of a sudden shifting of her senses. "What?"

He shrugged. "I didn't sleep too good."

"Why?"

"Mom, I don't know." He opened the box and started to pour the cereal flakes into the bowl. "Maybe I was dreaming. But I can't remember."

"Did you hear any noise—like outside on the lawn?"

"No. Maybe I heard a dog howling. I don't know."

"Okay." She got the jug of milk from the refrigerator and poured some over the flakes. "What time's the clinic this afternoon?"

"It's been called off. Mr. Pritchard went to Tampa."

He gave himself a dramatic slap on the forehead. "Damn!"

"Jeff! Watch your language."

"Yeah . . . I'm sorry."

"Okay. Now, what's wrong?"

"I forgot to oil my glove."

"All that drama because of that?"

He shrugged. "I guess I got carried away."

"I wish you'd get carried away that much about mowing the lawn."

He mumbled something under his breath and took a mouthful of cereal. Around it, he asked, "Do you have anything special planned for today?"

"I don't know. Don't talk with your mouth full. You do remember, don't you, that Patrick's coming this afternoon?"

"Yeah, hey—that's right!" He swallowed the cereal.

She felt herself moving away from the conversation, as though, somehow, it was an extension of what had occurred during the night. And, dear God, she didn't want to associate Jeff with that. "Look, I've got to do some work this morning," she said. "When Jennifer gets down here and has finished her breakfast, maybe you can find something for her to do until noon. Okay?"

"Sure."

Leaving him to finish his cereal, his elbows firmly planted on the table, she went upstairs to the bedroom she had converted into a studio. She felt no excitement in approaching her work. A certain diminution had occurred while she had stared out of her window into that world without light in which something alien prowled. Much of her self-awareness was gone.

The drawing table stood before the wide bay window opening to the north. On it was a row of small jelly jars in which she mixed her paints and a Maxwell House coffee can in which she kept her brushes. As she approached it, she thought how forlorn and deserted the table looked. In front of it, the old bar stool picked up at a garage sale looked oddly dilapidated.

Without much interest she stood looking down at the preliminary sketch taped to the table—a lily pad and a frog. It was a trivial subject, and she wasn't at all certain the book would sell. It was missing the sophistication even the children of today possessed; and although mothers and aunts and friends did the purchasing in the childrens' book market, she felt even they were no longer interested in frogs and lily pads and smiling fishes. Yet, she chided herself, she knew nothing of the world of marketing.

She looked out the window. On the far side of the sky, a single puffy white cloud roamed across the morning blue. Its aloneness made her feel a sympathetic smallness. She stood with her left hand resting on the drawing table, looking at the cloud, and felt the dimensions of the room shriveling in upon themselves, moving in on her, threatening to squeeze her tight. The old house creaked around her, its dry timbers protesting the strain laid upon them for over fifty years. The noise reminded her of a wooden ship under sail; and as she watched the cloud drifting from one side of the window to the other, she had the uncanny impression that the house was moving through the morning light.

The telephone rang. Its jangling drove deep into her, splintering the wandering thoughts turning in on themselves in her mind. She picked up the handpiece quickly.

"Karen? Sorry to phone you this early in the morning." It was Joseph Waingard, publisher of Tiny Tales Books, the successful series of children's books which she had been illustrating for almost five years.

At the sound of his business-like voice, the shadows scurried from her mind. "What in the world are you doing in the office so early? My lord, the ground down here is still wet with dew."

"I'm not at the office, love. I'm still home, but I wanted to talk to you before you got away for the day. I truly hate to bother you like this, but we need to talk about *The Little Yellow Frog*. We've had a shift in schedules up here, and the frog is being pushed forward six weeks. Can you make it?"

Rapidly, images of the completed illustrations formed in her mind. "Yes, I see no reason why I can't. I've eleven completed and over half done on the twelfth. That leaves me two and a half to go. But don't tell me you want them next week, Joe."

"No, no, Karen. I'm only going to ask you for a miracle, not the impossible."

She sighed. "Joe, I'm not sure I know what your definition of a miracle is. Remember I can't walk on water—I can't even water ski."

His metallic chuckle came through the earpiece. "How about August first instead of September fifteenth?"

"Joe, you sure love throwing a woman curves."

"Sorry, but can you do it?"

"I can do it, yes; but I took this assignment because it had such a fine lead time. My sister came down from Cleveland two days ago to spend a couple of weeks, and I was planning to get in a lot of chit-chat with her."

"Oh." The phone line hissed for a moment. "I'm sorry, Karen. But listen, there'll be a bonus in it for you."

"I'm not asking for that, Joe. I'll get them up to you by the first of August, and then you owe me one. How's that?"

"You are a sweet and wonderful doll, Karen Sommers. It's a deal."

"Damn and double damn!" she said to the empty studio after replacing the handpiece in its cradle.

Again she looked out the window. The lonely cloud had vanished. In its place a thunderhead was commencing to build up in the northwest, a grey and white mass of vaporous cotton blotting out the blue, rolling upon itself as it spread across the northern horizon.

If there was thunder connected with it, it was so far away no rumbling could be heard, but over the hedge she could see the tops of trees starting to wave. High up in the thunderhead a unicorn formed, tossing its horned head as its hooves pawed at the blue sky beyond its reach. Then its proud horn melted and slowly its head fell to its chest. In a moment it was gone—like so many of the lovely myths of the past.

She went to work on the sketch. It was mechanical with her. The blending of the acrylics and the detail lining with ink on the board held no creative excitement for her. She had approached it as a job. Now she looked upon it as a burden.

Then the sketch was done. She pulled it free from the tape, turned it over and blackened the back of the tracing paper with graphite. She pulled an eleven-by-fourteen illustration board from the stack on the credenza, taped the sketch to it and traced it onto the board, lifting the paper occasionally to make certain the graphite lines were forming. When she was finished, she pulled the sketch free and laid it on top of the others on the floor. Then she leaned the tracing against the coffee can and stepped back to examine it, seeing whether she had retained the freedom of line which she had in the sketch.

Jeff's voice came to her through the open window. "No, Aunt Jennifer. You've got to put more twist into it—you know, roll your shoulders and arch yourself. Now watch—like this."

She heard a thump, followed by feet trotting on gravel and shell.

"All right. Now watch me this time, Jeff, and tell me how I do."

Karen went to the window. Jennifer was trying to dribble Jeff's old basketball in the driveway, running with short steps towards the hoop hung above the garage doors. She straightened and leaped upwards in an arching reach for the hoop. Stretched in a long taut arc, muscles pulled and flesh flattened, she was like a ballerina in a pirouette. Sunlight glowed around her.

God, she is a beautiful woman, Karen thought.

The ball passed through the hoop without touching it. Jennifer looked at Jeff from her semi-crouch and laughed.

"Geez, that was great, Aunt Jennifer! You were only fooling me about not being able to shoot baskets, weren't you?"

Jennifer straightened. "Just a little, Jeff."

"I bet you can do a lot of other things, too. Can't you?"

Jennifer smiled at him. It was a slow smile, moist and brazen and tantalizing, filled with ancient wisdom and physical intimacy. "Yes, Jeff, there are many things I can do. Maybe while I'm here I'll show you some of them."

"Yeah." Jeff stood staring at her. The ball had bounced away and now lay out on the lawn.

Lunch was hurried, thrown-together tuna sandwiches and iced tea. If the interplay Karen thought she'd seen had actually happened, no residual emotions sat with them now at the kitchen table. Neither showed more than normal interest in the other. Yet during the light conversation, Karen found herself watching and waiting, dreading an expression or movement that would bring back the shadows of apprehension.

While she and Jennifer were washing the dishes, a quick job, Jeff asked, "What time does Patrick come, mom?"

"Around three."

"That gives Aunt Jennifer and me time to walk down to the river and back."

She drew a deep breath. "That's pretty far."

"We've got plenty of time. Almost two hours."

"Well—" She looked at Jennifer. "Maybe your aunt would like to stay here at the house. I think you gave her quite a workout this morning."

If Jennifer saw her silent appeal, she ignored it. "Oh, I think we've got time, Kar. Jeff says it's only a half a mile . . . and he does make it sound like a beautiful place." She gave her a sideways look. "We'll be back in plenty of time, I promise. You know I'm anxious to meet Patrick."

She didn't know what to do. She couldn't refuse. She was defeated. "All right."

She went up to the studio, but all desire for work was gone. The tracing, still leaning against the coffee can, was no more than a webbing of grey lines. And while she stood staring at it, a great helplessness descended on her. Suddenly she missed Jason with an agony she had not suffered since the days immediately following his death.

The loneliness turned to fear. Instinct was trying to whisper something to her. A warning. But of what? It was like a strange cry from muffled lips. And then she knew it concerned Jeff, because she saw a mental image of him and it was blurred.

She grasped the drawing table with both hands and leaned over it, head drooping. If she admitted her fears, they would destroy her. To acknowledge them filled her with a deep dread.

*Dear God, where are my thoughts going?*

She wanted to run out, find Jeff and pull him to her as she had done when he was a baby. Then he would be safe again, the advancing nightmare world pushed back.

"Damn it! Stop it!"

She pushed herself erect. No more, damn it! It was all a fantasy, an evil fantasy.

She looked at her watch. It was twenty minutes until two. In an hour and a half, Patrick would arrive. Anticipation knew no age limit, she thought, but it took on a very special kind of meaning as the years passed.

After a last look out the window, she went to her room. A shower and discreet application of cologne were in order before Patrick's arrival.

She undressed slowly, carefully laying her blouse and

jeans on a chair. After the shower there was a tan blouse
and skirt combination she'd put on for Patrick. Her bra
and panties, she dropped into the small laundry basket
behind the door.

While she was taking a clean bra and panties from the
dressing table drawer, she glanced up and saw an
auburn-haired, blue-eyed woman staring back at her. It
was herself, in the wall mirror.

She straightened and looked at her reflection with an
interest she had lost between the time of Jason's death
and the coming of Patrick. She knew what she was; a
big woman, structured to an Amazonian scale, the kind
Dior and Pucci turned their backs on in utter horror,
and female novelists disregarded entirely.

The hair, cut in a frothy hairdo, framed the face like
deep-hued flames. The face could not be called beautiful, but it was striking, with prominent cheek bones and
a wide jaw which triangulated into a firm chin. The
mouth was firm and full and the eyes were clear,
sparkling just a little bit with the anticipation of
Patrick's arrival. They seemed perfectly compatible
with the vigor of the statuesque body.

Her extravagant breasts were round, and firm,
countering the powerful hips flaring out from a waist
that was perhaps too slim for perfect proportion. From
the arch of her hips, her legs tapered down in firm
potent thighs, melting into strongly muscled calves.

She turned to her right, and then to her left, watching
the drawing of muscles along her sides and flanks—and
was content with what she saw. With a little grin, she
gave herself a slap on her left flank. Then she ran for the
shower.

At two fifty-nine, Patrick turned his three-year-old

Chevy station wagon into the driveway and stopped in front of the garage. He gave the horn one blow, and unfolded his way out from behind the wheel.

"Hello! Anyone at home?" His voice was a deep uninhibited baritone booming around the corner of the house.

He stood with one arm leaning on the roof of the car, big, powerfully built man with a mane of yellow, sunbleached hair and a neatly clipped golden beard that could easily have become a bush of wild sawgrass. He was dimensioned for out-of-doors living; his tawny eyes seemed especially designed for squinting at the horizon's curving shoulder. His tightly muscled legs, sheathed in form-fitting khaki slacks, seemed meant for striding passionately towards far places with his beard bristling and his yellow mane flying in cool Aegean winds. He was a man who gave the impression of not being interested in the unimportant things of life; a man meant for heroism.

Performing the completely feminine gesture of patting her hair into place, Karen rushed across the veranda and down the steps.

"Hi! You're right on time."

"Of course." He put his hands on his hips and assumed a lofty stance. "Patrick O'Shawn is in tune with the milliseconds of the universe."

She laughed. Already he was diverting her, reaching out to her with his masculinity, seducing her with his looks and presence. She stopped a step or two from him and placed her hands on her hips, arms akimbo, and said, speaking an old, old cliché, "'Tis full of the blarney you are, Patrick O'Shawn."

"Aye, that it could be," he answered in vaudeville

Irish, "But if it is, it's the sight of you, me darling, which fills me with the old sod's blarney."

They both howled with laughter. He closed the distance between them in one great step and wrapped his massive arms around her shoulders, pulling her solidly against his chest. He didn't have to lower his head far to reach her upturned lips. The kiss was long, leaving her sagging even tighter against him at its finish.

Finally he loosened his hug and moved back half a step. Slowly, in gentle strokes, his big hands slipped down her back and rested on the swelling of her hips. He pressed his lips softly against her cheek. "We've got a date tonight, Karen Sommers."

She nodded.

He released her but still held both of her hands in his. "Where's Jeff? And that sister of yours? I'm very curious about her, Karen."

"Oh?"

"To see if she's a real human being. You've always made her somewhat larger than life when you talk of her.

She felt her hands tremble inside his. "Oh?"

"What's wrong?" He'd felt the trembling of her hands, and a scowl furrowed his forehead. His hands tightened around hers. "Someone walk over your grave?"

She shook her head and lowered it, unable to look into the concern flooding his tawny eyes.

"Do you have a problem?"

"No. Really I don't." She looked up at him again and forced the wooden muscles around her mouth to curve into a smile. "I'm just tired. Joe Waingard set my deadline on the frog illustrations up six weeks, and I've been slaving on it all day. I guess I'm kind of headachy."

He cocked a brow. "Aaaah. So, is the excuse being formed to call off our date tonight?"

"No, you ox!" She stepped forward, pressing herself full length to him, feeling the wonderful security he always brought her.

He began unloading molding from the station wagon. "I'm going to make us some frames; come on, give me a hand?" Together, they carried it to the shed where he would make the frames. They had taken in two armfuls when Jeff and Jennifer came through the opening in the hedge at the rear of the lot.

"Hey, Patrick, when did you get here?" Jeff ran up to them.

"Just a few minutes ago." He touseled Jeff's hair, then looked at Jennifer. "And you are Jennifer, I'd say."

Jennifer nodded and smiled. It was the smile of primal sensuality that Karen had seen turned towards Jeff at the basketball hoop. "Yes. And you must be Patrick."

He nodded, then deliberately ran his eyes up and down her. "On first sight, you seem to be everything Karen says you are."

"Oh?" The smile became mischievous. "Big sisters have a habit of exaggerating when they speak of younger siblings."

His eyes locked onto hers. "Perhaps. But Karen is a level-headed person; so I'll accept her evaluation."

Jennifer slightly lowered her head and looked sidewise at Karen. "That's nice of both of you. I could become embarrassed."

"Patrick, can I help?" Jeff was standing at the wagon's tailgate, looking in.

Patrick turned from Jennifer and grinned. "I'll go you one better. Why don't you finish taking the molding into the shed and stack it with what we've already taken?"

Jeff nodded and began pulling out a bundle, happy; he was a part of events again.

For a moment they watched him, making certain the task wasn't too much for him and that he was doing it correctly. Then Patrick said, "Ladies, the drinks are on me."

In the house, he poured each of them a sherry and mixed himself a gin and tonic. They sat around the kitchen table. Through the open windows a faint breeze stirred the curtains and ruffled a stack of paper napkins on the table.

"So," Patrick said, after taking a long sip of his drink and setting the glass down with a small thump which rattled the ice. "How long are you planning to stay, Jennifer?"

"Maybe until my welcome runs out." Her eyes drifted away to the window. "No one could have convinced me this peaceful way of life existed—the life Karen and Jeff possess here."

"I'm sure they won't hurry you."

A quick glance from Jennifer to Karen went ignored. "I hope not, but then this is only my second day."

Karen knew she should make a statement about Jennifer staying just as long as she wished. She said, "You know this place is yours for as long as you want to stay, sis."

"Thank you, big sister." Jennifer's eyes sparkled,

and she got up and made a little dancing turn in the middle of the room. When she flopped back in the chair, she said, "I think I'm going to take you up on that."

Patrick laughed and began talking of the upcoming art show in Palm Beach. He had been invited to exhibit. From there the conversation moved in several directions. Yet, once or twice, when he asked Jennifer direct questions involving her work, her answers were lengthy and wordy but, Karen noted, actually told nothing of her job. It was very much like listening to a politician's speech and then, afterwards, when you allowed your mind to pick at the words and phrases, discovering there was no framework beneath them—that they were hollow, set in a vacuum. She wondered if Patrick sensed the ambiguity, too. Or was she being unnaturally critical?

When the drinks were almost finished, Jeff came in. Getting himself a Pepsi from the refrigerator, he came to the table and stood beside Jennifer.

"All the molding in the shed?" Patrick asked.

"Yes, and I closed up the station wagon."

"Great. Tomorrow we'll start making the frames."

"Can I work the saw, Patrick?"

"I don't see why not, if you're careful."

"I will be."

Three days before, she would not have noticed and, if she had, would have given it no thought; but now Karen saw Jeff's hip pressing against Jennifer's arm. She, in turn, almost appeared to be pressing against his leg. The apprehension coiled within her stirred. She shot a glance at Patrick hoping he noticed the abnormality. Patrick was looking at the window.

What *was* it that was making her want to reject her sister?

Making sure her voice was steady, she asked, "What did you and your aunt do down at the river, Jeff?"

Jeff shrugged. "Oh, not too much. We just walked along the bank for a ways until we found this real neat place. The trees kind of make a cave, and it's real quiet and nice. You know . . . peaceful, I guess."

"What did you do there?"

"Just talked." There was no guile in his expression. "Aunt Jennifer told me things about history and how the world was a long, long time ago. She said the river and the place we found was how the world was before there were so many people on it."

Patrick lifted a brow. "Are you a student of history, Jennifer?"

"Oh, no. Not a student. Merely a light reader. Mostly I'm an escapist. How wonderful it would be to live in a less hectic time."

Patrick shook his head. "This is a magnificent time to live! All the wonders of all the civilizations have funneled right down to this day and age. And we're adding more. This is a gutsy time to live, Jennifer. Exciting. We've crossed over thresholds nobody knew existed two or three decades ago. No, these times aren't hectic—they're thrilling."

"You have your art, Patrick," she said. "You can lose yourself within the creation you're developing on a canvas. That's escaping, whether you admit it or not. Your art is a world removed from the real world, and when you enter it you leave the strains of this one behind. Now truthfully, isn't that right?"

He turned his gin and tonic slowly in his big hands,

staring down into it. Then he looked up at her from beneath his brows. "Some of what you say is true, yes. I
admit it. But the world in which I live affects my paintings, is carried over into them, so it's not a whole
escape. It's more of a blending of the two. And besides,
the time I spend without a brush in my hands is as
exciting as the time I do. Lord, coming here to Karen
and Jeff is big excitement for me. Watching television is
a thrill. It's an electronic marvel. Reading of a new cure
for a dreaded disease sends a shiver up and down me.
The other things—the drugs, the crime, the bush
wars . . . well, I've the feeling they've always been with
humanity, in one form or another; so it's not too different now, really. Which still leaves me thinking it's an
exciting time to live."

"I envy your ebullient philosophy," she said.

He finished his drink. "It's good to live with." He
patted his shirt, then his pants pockets. "I'm out of
cigarettes."

"Here." Karen pushed her pack towards him.

"How many do you have?"

"This and another pack."

"That's not enough for the both of us. I'll run down
to the Quick Stop and get a carton."

"Oh? May I go with you, Patrick?" Jennifer looked
sideways at him. "I'm going to need some skin lotion."

"Me, too?" Jeff asked.

"Not you," Karen said. "You stay home and help me
fix something for dinner."

"Awww."

"Come on, Jeff. Don't be that way," Patrick said,
turning a look of disappointment in Jeff's direction.

"Well . . . okay."

While Jeff set the table, Karen made hamburger patties and sliced several tomatoes. When he was finished with the table, she put him to shucking six ears of corn while she tossed the salad. Neither said much. She, because she didn't want to say anything which might sound irrational. He, because he was sullen, about not going to the store with Jennifer and Patrick.

As the evening wandered through conversation and TV, Karen became slowly aware that Patrick seemed remote. Actually, she thought, it was more that he was reacting passively to his surroundings. Not withdrawing; there was no tension about him at all. In fact, it was more as if he was uncharacteristically studying the evening's life. Only if you knew him well, were intimate enough to share many of his private thoughts, would it be a thing to be noticed.

What had happened? It must have been something on the trip to the store, something beyond his immediate understanding. She gazed at him. Patrick indeed gave the impression of someone studying a new discovery, skeptical until its worthiness should be proven. Had it been an act of Jennifer's or a word she had spoken? He did seem to have backed away from her sister, to have erected a subtle barrier between them. But, she sighed to herself, she would probably never know, because she knew she would not ask him.

There was no coolness in the night. In her bedroom, she stood naked, a step or two back from the window, and felt the perspiration beading on her body. Down the hall she heard the shower splashing, and now and then the sound of blowing lips and exhaling of breath. Patrick was the only person she'd ever known who could make showering sound like a ride on a surfboard. Only because Jeff and Jennifer were in bed did he refrain from yodeling; but, even so, she found herself waiting for the customary blasphemous yowl when he managed to turn the hot water faucet too far to the left and the needle-sharp water scalded his chest.

It didn't come.

Outside, fireflies pricked winking holes in the night, their tiny points of yellow illumination like clusters of lost stars whirling through an endless universe. Crickets chirped. Beyond the hedge a night bird cried. Nowhere was there a hint of last night's horror. No unmentionable things were out there, slinking from dark shadow to dark shadow. Perhaps, she thought, nature was ashamed of what she had permitted the previous night and was filling this one with charm and grace.

"You're a magnificently beautiful woman."

She hadn't heard him coming down the hall or crossing the room to her, and she jumped in surprise.

He stood behind her, slipping his hands under her arms. She allowed her breasts to be cupped in his broad palms. "Where were you?" he asked.

She leaned her head back, seeking his shoulder while pushing her breasts against the roughness of his palms. "Not as far away as I was before you came."

"I don't understand."

"I was hoping you would."

His left hand wandered from her breast and moved down her side, his blunt fingers digging ever so softly into her flesh when they reached her waist. "You're being evasive, I think."

She gave a little sigh. "Not intentionally. It's just that . . . that rational thoughts are evading me."

He moved around to her right side, leaving his arm encircling her, and gazed out into the blandly innocent night. "Now you've become esoteric."

She turned her head and looked at his profile. How much its bearded ruggedness resembled the warrior profiles found on ancient coins! She wondered if he had ever seen his profile; and, if so, did he see the same thing? Or did he see the side view of a stranger's face, as so many of us do? No matter. Whatever he thought, she drew strength from him.

She drew a deep breath. Her mind was wandering, playing hide and seek, the great escape game, with the problem it didn't want to face. But she couldn't permit herself to hide from it. If she did, it would be forever a terrible memory. She asked, "What do you think of Jennifer?"

His fingers dug deeper into her sides. "What do you mean, honey?"

"Just what do you think of her?"

"Honey, she's your sister, so in my book, she has to be one of the best."

She turned within the circle of his arm. "Now you're the one who's being evasive. If you thought she was 'one of the best', you'd say so."

"I did, Kar."

"Not very convincingly. You sounded like you said it because you thought you had to—because she is my sister."

"God Almighty!" He dropped his arm from around her waist. "You've gone female on me. What do I do? Rent a billboard and erect it across the road saying, 'I think Jennifer Logan is one helluva fine woman'? Would that be convincing enough?"

Something was coming loose inside her, something that kept her emotions from falling apart. She felt an awful loneliness threatening her, and she reached out and laid her hand on his arm. "I'm sorry."

His irritation had faded away. "So am I, honey."

He encircled her again with his arms, and this time drew her to him. He leaned down and kissed her, his mouth gentle on her lips. As his lips touched hers, she felt a trembling within her that might have been a fear suppressed. She knew this man would bring her fully to life again.


She moved down the hallway with slow undulations. Half way down it one of the bedroom doors was closed, but there were sounds coming from the other side, guttural gasping sounds. She nudged against the wooden panel and listened to the stumbling, rambling noises. A man's panting breath, a woman's moans. Assault and response. Assault and response.

"Ooooh . . . oooh . . . "

Gently she pressed the long slenderness of her body against the door, listening, feeling the discontent mounting within her. Slowly she rubbed against the door frame until a tingle squirmed through her muscles and beneath her scales the flesh prickled.

Not much longer. Not long.

The young one's door was partially open. The boy was lying on his left side in a milky puddle of moonlight coming through the window. He wore only a pair of undershorts. Her tongue flicked out. Through the amber mist she watched the slow rise and fall of his chest in tempo with his placid breathing and the fleeting succession of expressions crossing his face. Her heart began to race.

She hissed softly, turned away, and slithered down the hallway.

Outside, in the garden, she glided slowly in the darkness of the shadows, staying away from the moonlight pools.

Although it would be different, she would drink the blood of the girl from the store during the hours of light. She would feast at the place of tumbled stone in the forest. But only this once, only this one time, would she feed without the protection of the darkness. Then, with the richness of that blood warming her, the mating would be as nothing to accomplish.

She coiled herself in a shadow deeper than the others. The old house loomed in a huge fretworked bulk above her. A place where one could live long. Undisturbed.

Her tongue flicked out.

# CHAPTER 4

On the flat top of the fallen block of masonry located on the western side of the mill ruins, Sue Ann Miller lay stretched out, full length on her stomach. With a slow languorous movement, she increased the pulling of her long strong muscles under her hide. They were so taut they strummed, and she delighted in the tiny prickly sensations the heat caused on her smooth skin. Still stretching, with her belly and breasts pressed against the stone, she worked her thighs and loins in a slow rotating movement against the masonry in a bizarre dialogue between flesh and stone.

Around the edges of the clearing, the creatures of the forest ignored her and went about their individual affairs, making their daytime sounds: chirpings and rustlings and short sharp cries. In turn, Sue Ann paid them no attention and made no fast move which would startle them and send them fleeing. She liked them surrounding her.

The morning sun lay heavy on her shoulders and back and thighs. The white T-shirt she wore darkened along her sides and her shorts became a richer hue of blue from the perspiration on her flanks. Her breathing slowed. All up and down her sturdy body, the stretched muscles relaxed. Her mind drifted, moving into an un-thinking warm contentment.

Soon, she told herself, Terry would arrive. Last night when she had left the store at the end of her shift, and he had come in to begin his, he promised to meet her here this morning in the old mill ruins—and had given her a breath-sucking kiss to seal the date. She ran her tongue over her lips, as if the passion of that kiss still lingered there. She shivered. God, he was really something good. He sure knew how to use what he had. And, in a real nice way, he made her work hard and use what she had so she enjoyed the whole sex act so much better. Goose flesh rose on her as she remembered some of the subtle things he'd done to her. Maybe, she thought, he'd bring a cold six pack of Heinekens with him; or, even better, a joint of Columbian Gold. If he brought either one of those, and if he did the things to her he'd done the last time they met out here, she'd never want to go back at all. Not that she ever did want to go back to work. That Quick Stop was for the birds. Yet, she had to admit it was a good job for meeting some swinging guys. But just as soon as the tourists started arriving this fall, she was definitely heading for Daytona Beach. Maybe even Fort Lauderdale. Shit, a smart girl, using what she had with style and discrimination, ought to make herself a bundle at either one of those places during the season. Then this dumb dumpy town could kiss her ass. Again she stretched herself, slowly, luxuriously, and once more rubbed her belly and loins against the masonry.

There was a sound behind her. She didn't bother to look up. But she lifted her rump slightly and gave it a wriggle. Why not give him a little show—a little thrill? "How's that, Terry."

But nothing happened. He said nothing. There was only silence, an all-around silence, she suddenly realized, with no bird songs and no insect noises. Involuntarily her muscles tautened and she felt hotter than she should, even under the fierce sun. She was suddenly frightened, and when she tried to sit up found she couldn't move. She lay motionless, like an animal hiding from a hunter.

Then, over the beating sound of her heart, she heard something in the weeds behind the stone. It was a traveling sound, a sort of slither; it was coming closer and closer. She held her breath to hear it better. Then right beside her, something hissed. Her fear exploded into terror. With a cry, she rolled to her right side, clawing with her fingers at the rough ungiving surface of the stone. She started to push herself up into a sitting position.

Something heavy landed on her shoulders, driving her back down against the stone, knocking the air from her lungs so she couldn't breathe or scream. Something cold and slippery lashed across her face and wrapped around her head, covering her eyes and mashing her lips against her teeth. Blindly she kicked, but encountered nothing more than empty air. Then there was a second hiss, and the thing entwined around her yanked her head up and back. For an instant her eyes were free and she saw blue sky and a white cloud; then next her head was slammed down against the stone. Pain exploded inside her; darkness rushed at her. She didn't know how, but she managed to fight back. Her head was pulled up again. She cried out. The coils tightened around her head, squeezing, moving in on themselves, until pain was crushing against her brain and the skin on her forehead

split and blood smeared her face in a sticky mess. A
scream filled her throat and she tried to force it out, but
it turned to no more than a guttural moan.

"No . . . no . . . . " She didn't really know she was
whimpering. It was only sound. She was dizzy; the
blackness was trying to claim her.

She felt sharp cold fleshy ridges rippling up and down
her neck, seeking like fingers. She knew what they were
feeling for and tried once more to heave herself up and
roll away. But before she could, they found the nerve
centers they sought and squeezed. The blackness rushed
in on her from all sides now, and she felt herself
tumbling down into a bottomless chasm where a terrible
coldness waited her.

The lamia, coiled around the girl's head, looked
down along the naked body, sprawled helplessly half on
and half off the piece of masonry. Hunger and excitement flowed from the amber slits of eyes; throat already
haunted by the taste of the rich blood awaiting her.

The girl moaned again, a low continuous sound in
which pain and terror mingled. She clawed at the rock
and fought for solid footing on the sandy soil, frantically arching herself above the ragged edge of the stone
block cutting into her back. Her feet made harsh
scraping noises in the dry weeds. The straining muscles
cording beneath the tanned skin, the sweat running
down the belly and the bucking haunches intrigued the
slitted eyes. There was so much health and strength
there.

The lamia hissed in pure delight.

Sue Ann heard the hideous sound, and somehow
knew it was the sound of approaching death. Desper-

ately, her haunches thrust and bucked. Her ripe belly
heaved like a bellows, ballooning out and sucking in
beneath her jutting rib cage, the heavy mounds of her
breasts quivering. The amber eyes watched; they had
witnessed similar movements in wanton dances performed in ancient times.

"Please . . . ." Sue Ann's voice was muffled by
squeezing coils. "Whoever you are, please . . . I'll—
I'll be good to you . . . I'll do whatever you want . . .
anything . . . . But please . . . please let me go . . ."

A hiss answered her.

Minutes of pain and terror and exhaustion crept past.
Sue Ann grew still. Only her belly heaved in accompani-
ment to her sobbing pants; the muscles quivered with
tension in her widespread legs as she braced herself
against the stone's sharp edge.

The lamia could feel the body heat emanating from
the sweaty flesh. A red ant was crawling back and forth
over the slippery wet belly. Around the edges of the
clearing birds darted through the shadows of the trees:
grackles and crows, and the occasional flash of a
dancing bluejay. A wayward breeze tripped through the
branches and over the taller weeds. Nature was no
longer taking notice of the struggle on the block of
masonry.

Finally the lamia stirred. The shadows had lengthen-
ed. The red ant had reached the girl's left breast and was
crawling around its base. Inside her the hunger was
ravenous, tearing at her like angry jaws.

She tightened her coils. Sue Ann moaned, but lay
still. There was no more will in her.

The lamia shifted, pulling the head back until her
throat bulged upwards in a rich arch. Sue Ann squealed

in agony; a violent tremor shook her.

Bending over slowly, her breath hissing through her flared nostrils, she placed her mouth against the hot flesh. The tang of salt spiced her tongue. Then slowly, carefully, she sank her fangs deep into the straining throat.

Biting the tip of her tongue, and holding her breath, Karen drew a long sweeping line down the illustration board, forming the stalk of a cat-o-nine-tail. As she lifted the brush, she let out her breath and studied the line. There came a nod of approval. After a moment she dipped the brush into the paint, pointed it on a scrap of board, and drew in another stalk.

Since mid-morning she had been in the studio working on these silly illustrations for the dumb frog book. Although her technical sense told her the illustrations were good, she just couldn't bring herself to think of them as more than reasonably satisfactory. She supposed it was her distaste for the story.

She was about to lay down another stalk when Patrick entered. He was dressed in shorts and a tank top, his feet shoved into frayed thong sandals. Sawdust sprinkled his forearms. It looked like tiny flecks of gold against the tan of his skin.

He came across the studio, laid his hands on her shoulders, and stroked them gently. He brought the smell of sawdust with him, clean and spicy and evoking a scene of deep rich loam and cathedral pines. She bent her head and rubbed her cheek against the hardness of his knuckles.

"You smell good," she said.

"Sweat? You like the smell of sweat?"

"No, the sawdust. A sawdust smell goes with a man."

He leaned forward and placed his lips softly in her hair. "I love you, Karen Sommers."

"And I you, Patrick O'Shawn," she said.

"Let's take a walk, Kar. We've been working all morning. We owe ourselves a break . . . just you and me."

She stared out the window. "And do what?"

"Oh, a walk—or a short drive."

"To where?"

"I was thinking about Ludlow's Mill."

"And about something else, as well as a stroll?"

"Perhaps."

She laughed. "You're oversexed, Patrick O'Shawn."

"Perhaps."

They both laughed, and he walked around to stand at the side of the table. "Last night was good, Karen. Being together like this is good. What we have is becoming bigger than any word to describe it. Do you feel it, too?"

She nodded slowly. The passion she had known in the past was returning to her. "Yes, I feel it, darling."

He cocked a brow. "Then, the mill?"

"Where's Jeff?"

"A kid named Billy Porter came by, wanting Jeff to go with him and see something about baseball. I told him it was okay, and they rode off on their bicycles. Was it all right?"

"Yes. Billy's a good kid. He's Cynthia's son. You know her."

"The school teacher whose husband's a supervisor, or something, at the citrus processing plant?"

"Yes." She looked down at her brush and turned it in her hand several times. "And Jennifer? Where's she?"

"I don't know." He was gazing out the window. "I haven't seen her all day."

"Well, at least Jeff's not with her."

"Does that make a difference? They get along so well together. I'd think you'd be happy to have her here to look after him while you're working."

"That's the way it should be, I admit."

"But it isn't." He turned from the window and looked at her for a moment. "What is it about you two? Before she came, she was damned near a goddess to you —Jennifer wrote this, and Jennifer did that, and Jennifer's the pretty one. Now you act confused and worried whenever she's involved in anything, and sometimes, it seems to me, you want to govern my thoughts concerning her." He turned back to the window. "You've got my curiosity aroused, Karen Somers."

She didn't answer. What she really wanted to do was to stop thinking. To do something so uncomplicated her mind could relax while her body reacted purely by instinct. Then whatever was occurring around her would be like events happening on the other side of a locked and bolted door. But if she did that, if she managed to isolate herself, would she lose the peace she was gaining with Patrick?

She looked up at him. The sun coming through the window was a fine etching light on his features, touching the crow's feet at the outer corners of his eyes and accentuating the thrust of his cheekbones. A couple of hairs curled out from his beard and looked like loops of thin golden thread. He was so much man! But it would have taken a man of his proportions, physical and mental and emotional, to vanquish her memories of Jason—to enter her life as he had.

Suddenly she got up. "Let's go to the mill," she said, and wasn't in the least bit surprised to hear how throaty her voice sounded. "I have to go there."

"*Have* to? What do you mean?"

Looking out the window, watching a sparrow flit among the jasmine, she said, "I was frightened out there yesterday, Patrick."

"Frightened? At Ludlow's Mill? Karen, love, that place is as close to the bucolic as you can get. It's innocuous—it's nature's gift of peace and comfort to us. What in heaven's name could have frightened you out there?"

"I don't know." She drew a deep breath, willing her voice to be calm. "I had the feeling there was danger there, that it was lurking among the shadows of the walls. The whole area was evil and ugly."

"Holy Christ, Kar! That place is as free of evil as a Baptist meeting ground."

She shook her head, remembering the little shivers running up and down her spine as she stood on the edge of the clearing. "I said I don't know what it was, but I do know the entire place was enshrouded in some kind of malignancy. It was so potent I could almost feel it as a physical thing, Patrick . . . like a cold autumn wind blowing on me."

He looked at her, his face betraying the mixed emotions playing with his mind. "Something had to cause it. You've got no idea what it was? None at all?"

She ran the palms of her hands, which were becoming sweaty with the remembering, down the sides of her thighs. There was no rational way, at least for the moment, to tell him of the strangeness she had seen on Jennifer's face; no way for her to be sure whether it was a cause or a result of the fear she had known. "One, maybe. But I don't want to talk about it; not yet, anyway."

He frowned. "It must be big, Kar, because you've always told me everything. You've always trusted me to help if I could."

"I know. And that's the way it still is, darling; but those things have always had . . . substance. They could be worked out with logic. This isn't like that. What I was aware of out there yesterday was . . . well, unreal. It bordered on the supernatural." She turned and faced him squarely. "I have to get it all together in my mind before I can, before I will, talk about it."

He reached over and put a hand on her shoulder. "I don't like this, Kar. I don't like it one bit. I've never thought of you being frightened, and I sure as hell don't like thinking about it now. Are you certain you want to go?"

"Yes."

He sighed and squeezed her shoulder. "Well, my reason for wanting to go was different—but I'll help you. You need to climb back up on the horse after you've fallen off."

"Climb back up on the horse! Block that metaphor, Patrick!" She was grinning.

He slapped her lightly on the rump. "Come on, Dale Evans. Let's get going!"

As was their custom, they took their sketching pads, felt-tip pens and charcoal pencils. The ruins were forever changing as shadows shifted and sunlight reached into nooks and crannies. Sometimes they were all a great grey smoothness; sometimes the vine-festooned archways were entrances into times long past, or shadowy openings into worlds still darkened by the future. Sometimes the chimneys were silhouetted fingers beckoning at the blue sky's idling clouds, and sometimes they were nothing but crooked, disentegrating masonry. Tomorrow she and Patrick could stand there and the scene would be different than it was today, though the walls were as they had been a dozen years ago and as they would be a dozen years from now.

Karen stopped short on the path across the clearing and drew a sharp breath. Beside her Patrick also halted. Ahead, on the fallen masonry block Patrick used as a work bench, lay Jennifer.

She didn't see them. She was lying on her stomach, her left cheek resting on the hands folded under her head. Her face was turned away from them. She was dressed in snug shorts and a halter, the strings untied so the sun would brown her sweeping back without any demarcation. All up and down the long curves of her back and thighs a thin sheen of perspiration glinted on her healthy skin. She was breathing placidly, in the rhythm of relaxing slumber.

She looked utterly at ease. At home in this wilderness.

Karen and Patrick moved slowly towards her; neither, for some undefined reason, wanted to awaken her. Then, when they were perhaps fifteen feet from her, they heard a hissing noise. It stopped them short.

"There's a snake somewhere by the stone," Patrick whispered. "You stay here, and I'll go wake her." He moved nearer the stone.

Again the hissing sound.

"Jennifer, wake up!" Patrick called.

She stirred, then quickly turned her head toward them. For the briefest of moments, her eyes were the narrow amber slits Karen had seen the day before. Then she blinked and smiled. "Hello."

"Jennifer, don't move. There's a snake by the stone. Just stay still and let me find it." Patrick circled the stone, scowling down into the weeds tangled at its base. "I don't see anything. It must be gone."

Jennifer gave a little laugh and sat up, her heavy breasts swinging. She looked brazenly female, all voluptuous thrusting haunches and breasts, sweeping soft flesh and toned muscles. But if she intended to attract him, she failed, Karen was glad to see; Patrick glanced only once at Jennifer and then turned his eyes towards the shifting light on a coquina wall. He made Jennifer the outsider.

Jennifer leaned forward in a lazy arching movement, reaching behind her to tie her halter strings, and watched him with a dewy sleepy-eyed expression as she rebound her breasts in cloth. "Thank you, Patrick, for coming to what you thought was my rescue. It was very brave and kind of you."

Good lord, Karen thought, she's acting like a melodramatic heroine in a nineteen thirties movie. Or was she? Karen could not stop the dark thought. Was she coming back from . . . someplace else . . . and having difficulty in refocusing her mind and senses?

Patrick shrugged. "I'm happy there was nothing there to rescue you from."

"I could take that two ways," she smiled, seductively. No, Karen scolded herself. It had been a friendly smile, nothing more.

"Yes, you could." There was no expression on his face.

For what seemed a long time, Jennifer sat looking directly at him, studying him, eye half-hidden behind lowered lashes. Sunlight buried itself in the thick gold of her hair and shimmered deeply there. Her nostrils flared as if seeking an elusive scent on the still air, and in her throat a pulse began to beat visibly. Suddenly the woman sitting on the stone looked like a creature of the wild.

Bits of dark loam and torn leaves stuck to her elbows and the undersides of her forearms, and her knees were stained where earth had been wiped away. She must have been down on her knees and forearms not too long before, Karen thought. For what reason? Crawling? Digging? What other explanation could there be? She remembered slitted amber eyes in a tautened face; greedy stares at a young boy's body. Violently she pushed the image away. It was too incongruous.

Jennifer pushed herself off the stone and stood between them. "I should be going. I guess I've lost most of the day already; you were both so busy at the house I decided to take a walk and stay out of the way." She looked around the clearing, then at Karen. "I like it here, Kar. I hope you don't hold me too rigidly to staying only two weeks."

Karen laughed, but it was forced and sounded tight. "Just as long as you want, Jen. You know that."

"What about your job?" Patrick asked. "How long can you stay away?"

Jennifer laughed and gave them an exaggerated wink. "I've got an 'in' with the boss."

"I've heard of that situation," Patrick said. "It must

be a comfortable feeling.''

At first Jennifer did not seem to know how to take the comment, but the open smile came back to her lips and she said, "And a secure one too. But it's probably only vacation talk. You've heard people on the first and second day of their vacation say they're going to find a way to stay longer . . . or maybe never go home again. I guess that's me.''

No remoteness hovered in Jennifer's face when that big smile curved her lips. She became the very beautiful woman Karen remembered, a vital, healthy person who was so full of life she seemed charged with electricity which touched those around her and filled them with excitement. Looking at Patrick, Karen saw he was less withdrawn; whatever had distressed him last night was gone. If anything *had* disturbed him last night— suddenly all her misgivings seemed idiotic.

"I know what you mean," Karen smiled. "I've felt that way myself. It's too bad it can't work that way."

Jennifer gave her heavy hair a toss. "Maybe this time it can, who knows. I'm going to give it some thought, Kar, because there's really nothing holding me in Cleveland.''

"There's your job, Jen. And Eliot."

"There's always jobs to be had, Kar. And Eliot?" She gave an eloquent shrug. "Someone else will find his strings and, puppet that he is, he'll go dancing off with them.''

Resolving to make it true, Karen said, "Well, you're welcome to stay and try."

Jennifer looked from Karen to Patrick and back again. Then she broke into a mischievous grin. "I think I'd better be going and let you two do what you planned to do when you came out here." She started off, waving once over her shoulder.

They stood watching her stroll across the clearing, her hips swaying.

Patrick whistled slowly under his breath. "You Logan women are every inch woman, I'll say that."

"You have an evil mind, O'Shawn."

He leered at her. "Appreciative, my dear. Appreciative. Not evil."

A bank of clouds moved indolently in from the west, rolling across the sky like a frothy wave. It covered the sun with a misty fog, for a moment changing it to a moon-like disc, pale and vacant and very lonely. All the shadows melted in upon themselves until the clearing and the ruins became no more than variations in a field of monochromatic grey. Karen looked around and thought how much the area resembled a ruined castle— a romantic chivalric castle. The fantasy of the mill was returning. She shook her head and closed her eyes. How could she ever have turned this place into a breeding ground for terror?

"Kar? Come over here, will you?"

Patrick had laid his sketch book and pencils and pens on the stone and was bending over it, scratching at a something on the edge.

When she reached his side, he pointed with his forefinger and asked, "What does that look like to you?"

Brownish-red flecks of a dried substance caked under his nail. She looked carefully where he was pointing. At first it was no more than some kind of rusty material gathered in a crevice in the coquina stone. That's what it looked like, but instinct told her what it was.

She looked into Patrick's frown. "It's blood."

He nodded. "It hasn't been here long, either. It's still liquid down in the crack."

She stood stiffly, looking at his finger fixedly, feeling herself sliding away from herself, from Patrick, tumbling into a stark and naked darkness. Time and movement were slowed. From far away, from somewhere outside the twilight world, she heard the sounds of something terrible advancing.

"Kar?" Patrick reached out and grasped her upper arm. "What's wrong?"

She sensed rather than felt his grasp, but knew it was good and vital. She turned her head to look at him. Slowly he came into focus, moving out from the lightless area, frowning with worry. She shook her head.

His frown deepened. "You're frightened. By God, you're frightened!"

From somewhere words came. "Yes. But I—I don't know why."

"Come on, Kar! Get hold of yourself." He released her arm, pulled out his handkerchief, and began wiping the blood from his finger. "You sound ready to go round the bend."

She leaned against the edge of the stone. Its sharpness across her buttocks was comforting; it helped clear her mind. She kept her head down, staring at her feet. "Does that imply I'm going crazy."

"Oh, Holy Christ!" He threw his arms wide, windmilling. "No it doesn't mean that!"

"Well, don't you think finding fresh blood on a stone in the middle of nowhere is odd? Especially when my sister has just been lying on it?"

"I do, love. I agree one hundred percent with that. But allowing a tiny spot of blood to throw you into a tizzy is a bit much.''

"That's what frightens me, Patrick. Why should your showing it to me so completely terrorize me? It's abnormal.''

A new understanding seemed to settle on his face. "I'm sorry, Kar. As usual, I was using my tongue when I should have been using my ears.''

She looked up at him. Even though he wasn't that much taller than she, he seemed a colossus above her. Yellow and gold sprinkled his hair and lay along his ruddy cheekbones.

"I don't want her to stay here," she said.

"Come on, hon. Just take it easy. Something's weird here, but we'll figure it out.''

She drew a deep breath. The air tasted bitter.

"I'm going to talk with her tonight after dinner," she said. "I want to find out who, or what, my sister really is.''

"Oh, come on! She's your sister, Kar!''

*"No, she isn't!"*

"Kar! I don't know what's gotten into you. You're being irrational.''

"Maybe so. But do you think finding your sister lying on a bloodied stone is a thing to pass off with a shrug of your shoulders? I don't!''

"So, what are you going to do? Yell and scream at her after dinner, upsetting everyone's digestion?''

She wanted to strike out against him with a torrent of words, but under her growing hysteria she realized he was possibly right. She began to feel sheepish. She shook her head. "No. I don't want to direct false accusations at her.''

"Then you'd better calm yourself down, darling.''

She moved to him and leaned against his chest. "Oh, God. I'm becoming so erratic. I can't seem to think straight. Please keep me from being reckless."

He folded her tightly in his arms. "Count on me, Kar."

But at dinner she could make no room for her questions. And immediately after dinner Cynthia and Don Porter dropped in with Billy and their eleven-month-old baby, Susy. Jeff had told Billy so much about his aunt that they wanted to meet her.

They were a couple who, when first met, seemed totally unmatched. Cynthia missed being plain only by the brilliant green of her eyes, which were magnified by the great circular glasses she wore a third of the way down her small nose. Her hair, of nondescript brown, was cut in ragged bangs across her forehead and hung helter-skelter to her shoulders, bordering her face like a nest. What with the big round glasses, she gave the impression of a piquant owl staring out at the world. If she knew how to coordinate clothing, she had never bothered to use her knowledge for as long as Karen had known her. Her clothes always looked like pick-ups from the racks of the Goodwill or Salvation Army stores, or borrowed from someone else.

She was perhaps five foot five or six, slender and well-proportioned, rather awkward in her movements. But she was a direct thinker and an understanding listener, and thus an ideal conversationalist. No one left her company feeling cheated in the exchange of ideas, and her careless appearance was soon thought of as a charming feature of her delightful personality.

Don was the opposite. Perhaps three years older than Cynthia's twenty-nine, he was pudgy. Don was always carefully groomed as if hoping to counter his wife's carefree dress style. His Penney and Sears slacks were always wrinkle-free, and both his sport and dress shirts, though wash-and-wear, were starched militarily stiff.

Don was a line supervisor at Grove Center's major business, the Golden Harvest Packing Company. The job was seasonal, giving him time during the late summer and early fall to pursue an avocation which he hoped to turn into a vocation—selling wholesaling fishing gear to the hundreds of tackle stores and fishing camps of central Florida. However, though he was an avid sportsman and knew his products very well, his friends doubted he would succeed. A normally quiet man, almost reclusive, he didn't have the drive to battle opposition in that competitive field. Aggression was not part of him, although he had a persistence which might substitute for it. Because of his doggedness, no one advised him to give up his dream, and Cynthia quietly made plans to continue teaching for the foreseeable future. She wasn't bitter or disappointed. She loved Don with every bit of herself. Karen was sure their affection would never fray.

While Jeff and Billy Porter went outside to do whatever it is fifteen-year-old boys do in twilight on a large lawn, Patrick fixed drinks.

"I suppose," Cynthia said, turning her owlish eyes on Jennifer, "you find our life rather quiet after the bustle of a city."

"On the contrary. It's exhilarating. For the first time in I don't know how long, I'm able to . . . oh, move off from myself and contemplate life. It's marvelous."

Cynthia nodded. "Perhaps that's so. We who live here probably don't appreciate what we have."

"I honestly don't think you do. You take it for granted; you probably don't even realize there's a dog-eat-dog life just over the horizon."

"We know, Jennifer," Patrick said.

She raised her glass to him. "Some of you do, yes." Her eyes lingered on him, her lips pursed.

"Karens tells us you're in public relations," Don said into the silence.

Jennifer turned away from Patrick. "Yes."

"That sounds interesting," he said.

"It's nerve-jangling."

He gave a deprecating laugh. "I don't believe we've a job in the whole town that jangles a single nerve."

Cynthia grinned. "We're kind of a big sanatorium here."

"You have peace here," Jennifer's voice was so low it barely carried to the others. "Time moves slowly in Grove Center. You are fortunate people."

"Yes, maybe we are," Cynthia said, slowly. "Sometimes one doesn't recognize the bluebird when it's in his own garden."

"But sometimes a hawk swoops down," Patrick said. "And then there's trouble in that lovely garden."

Once more Jennifer looked at him. This time he returned the stare, his lips compressed under his beard, until it was she who dropped her eyes, taking a sip of her drink.

Don said, "Why don't you extend your vacation, stay a while, Jennifer?"

She took so long to answer that Karen thought she was ignoring Don's friendly question. Then she spoke. "To tell you the truth, I'm thinking seriously of moving here. Two days, and I'm in love with the place."

"Oh, that would be wonderful, Jennifer. I know it would make Karen happy," Cynthia said.

Jennifer looked at Karen, her eyes sparkling. "What would you say, sis? Can I bunk here, until I find a place?"

Karen felt a sudden blankness claim her mind. She forced a smile to form on her lips, and said, "Of course, Jen."

All of Jennifer's big ripe beauty glowed as she laughed. "I'm going to do it. I'm really going to do it! I just know I can find a job in Orlando or Daytona Beach. Don't you all think so?"

"With no trouble at all," Don said.

"Do it, Jennifer." Cynthia leaned forward in her chair. "We'd have fun, I know. You'd bring some new ideas to us, new ways of looking at things."

Jennifer laughed with delight, the fluting laugh of an excited young girl. "Thanks, Cynthia. You're making me want to go out right this minute and start looking for a place. But I warn you all, I'm a party-pooper. And as for excitement—I'm approaching the age of spinsterhood."

"I'm with Cyn," Don said. "If you move here, maybe we'll have some parties for you to poop."

They laughed.

Conversation ebbed and flowed, but Karen wasn't a part of it, at le)st she didn't feel she was. Theapprehension coiled within her was threatening to take control; she was absorbed in her inner battle with it. Jennifer was her sister. She loved her.

Cynthia looked at her watch. "Good lord, Don! Do you realize it's ten after ten?"

Don glanced at his, then smiled at Jennifer. "You

see, you've already made us almost miss our bedtimes."

Jennifer laughed. "Flatterer. But I thank you. I guess I can always say that I didn't poop out on our first get-together."

"That's right," he answered. "You've now got a credit of one."

Patrick started moving towards the door. "Let's go out and round up the young ones, Don. We might have to do some searching. I haven't heard a noise out there for the last half hour, and to be quiet together is just unnatural for those two."

When they were gone, Cynthia picked the baby up from the sofa and snuggled the blanket around her. "What do you two have planned for tomorrow afternoon?"

"I think I'm going to start my big act of settling-in in Grove Center," Jennifer said. "You know—getting really familiar with the area. Maybe visit a real estate agent. Now that I've got my mind made up, I want to do it all fast."

Cynthia nodded. "I can understand that. What about you, Kar? Any great plans?"

Karen shook her head. "No. Only working on those damned frogs. Why?"

"All the stores are having all kinds of sales—you know. Midnight Madness, Inventory Reduction Manager's Sale, Assistant Manager's Sale. The kind when they bring out year-old stock, dust it off and put it on tables in the middle of the aisle so we can fight over what we turned our noses up at last year. I thought you two might want to join me in the fracas."

"Oh, I'd love to, Cynthia," Jennifer said, "but I'm going to be very single-minded about this moving. I'm not going to allow myself to be distracted."

Karen nodded. A shopping trip with Cynthia might hold back some of the darkness moving around the edges of her mind. She really had no desire to go shopping, but she had less to stay in the house. "I'm not that single-minded. What time?"

"Well, what about one o'clock?"

"All right. I'll come by and pick you up."

Cynthia shifted the baby in her arms and started for the door. "I hope Patrick and Don have the boys corraled."

In answer, they heard the voices of the four of them out in the yard, laughing over something. It was a good sound to Karen, a sound of wonderful normalcy. But would the normalcy last? Or would it slip away by degrees?

When the Porters had gone, Patrick suggested a Pepsi to Jeff, but he shook his head and held out a stack of catalogues. "Billy gave me these, and I think I'll go read them."

As he went up the stairs, Karen said, "I don't think I'm believing what I'm hearing. Going to bed? At ten-thirty?"

But she was relieved; because, for a reason beyond explanation, she felt more comfortable to have him out of the room and away from his aunt.

Jeff gave her a crooked grin. " 'Night, Mom." He headed up the stairs.

Whether out of a need for protection or the desire to be near a loved one, Karen moved closer to Patrick. Jennifer stood across the room smiling at them, again examining them, waiting, as it were, for them to do something. Somehow, she reminded Karen of a three-dimensional shadow being cast into the room by a creature in another time.

Jennifer was holding the last of her sherry. She made little tilting movements with the glass so the wine sloshed around the bottom and up the sides. In the light from the table lamp beside her, the liquid appeared heavy and warm. Dark shadows moved within it, transparent stickiness webbed the inside of the glass. Still watching them, she raised the glass to her lips and drank thirstily, her blue eyes staring at them over the rim, unblinking, reflecting the wine's amber hue. All of her spontaneous gaiety was gone.

She ran her tongue slowly, hungrily, around her lips licking the wine from them. "Cynthia Porter is a very good friend of yours, isn't she, Kar?"

"Yes."

"You seem very close."

"Yes."

"You never mentioned her in your letters." It was a rebuke.

"No, I guess I didn't." She raised a brow. "You never mentioned Eliot in yours, Jen."

"We do have secrets from each other, don't we?"

"I wasn't aware of it. Cynthia's no secret, Jen. There was never a need to mention her."

Something flickered in Jennifer's eyes. "It seems there's a lot we have to learn of one another."

"I guess there is."

Patrick rattled the ice in his glass. "Well, that's not unnatural, you know. You two have lived separately for a long time and not even seen each other in the past three years. Getting reacquainted is called for."

"What he says is right, Jen."

Jennifer continued to look at her. Then she nodded, and, without another word, carried the wine glass to the kitchen. They heard the water running in the sink. In a few moments, she came back into the living room, and said, "Well, good night. I'm off to bed."

Karen watched her mount the stairs. When her sister disappeared around the first landing, she felt some of the knots within her commence to loosen. But suddenly she was tired, terribly, terribly tired. All up and down her body muscles ached with exhaustion. She wanted to roll herself up into a ball and close in her consciousness so nothing could possibly touch her.

"I think you were railroaded, darling," Patrick said.

"I didn't know what to say, I just stood there big and dumb, didn't I?"

"I don't agree with the dumb, but the big—" He put an arm around her waist and pulled her to him. "The big, I like."

She leaned her head against his shoulder. "I'll remember that the next time a sales clerk intimates they don't have dresses for Amazons."

"Why don't we go to bed?"

"So you can show me your appreciation of big women?"

"One big woman."

She arrived at the outer edge of the parking lot, but waited among the shadows until the human heart had slowed.

Traveling acr;ss the fields within the burdenöf the woman body was tiring and slow, particularly tonight.

The sexual drive was sweeping her like a cosmic storm. She stood for a moment within the protection of the trees on the edge of the convenience store's parking lot making certain she had complete control over the woman body.

Then she crossed the asphalt and opened the door. Air-conditioned air swirled past her into the humid night, making her shiver as it brushed against her hot skin.

The young man was sitting behind the counter. He looked up slowly from his *Playboy*. Mechanically, he asked, "Can I help you?"

She arched herself, thrusting forward the deep luxuries of the woman's body, and moved toward the counter volutpuously swaying. The rich blood she had drunk that morning was a molten stream racing through her veins. She felt her cheeks flush and parted her lips to allow some of the fiery heat to escape.

"I think you can," she said, the want in her making the words come slow and husky in her throat.

He was on his feet now, the magazine lying beside the cash register. He opened his mouth, then closed it without uttering a sound.

She leaned across the counter towards him. The upper slopes of her big breasts bulged above the skimpy halter she wore beneath her unbuttoned shirt. He looked boldly at them, then moved his eyes up to hers.

"What do you want?"

"Can't you guess . . . Terry?"

"Yeah." Then he frowned. "How do you know my name?"

She pushed the open shirt from her shoulders and down her arms. "I've made enquiries."

"Oh. Why?"

"Because I've seen you and I want you."

"You mean . . . just like that? Here? Now?"

She smiled. "Here. Now. Or any other place you know where we can have privacy."

"Holy shit . . ." Suddenly his face tightened and he became wary. He moved back a step, his eyes darting towards the door. "What is this? A new form of hold-up? Are you supposed to get me with my pants down half-way—and then your boyfriend comes in and zaps me? Is that it?"

Irritation rose in her, and she hissed gently. But she hid it from him and managed to smile. "If that's what you fear, lock the door. Certainly at this hour few customers come in, and no one will try the door while we spend . . . a half hour . . . together."

He relaxed. "Yeah . . . yeah, I can do that."

"Do it, then, Terry. Do it."

He took the store keys from beneath the tray in the register drawer. "There's a little office back there, through the door beside the cooler. While I'm locking up, why don't you go there and . . . and get ready?"

He possessed her with the eagerness of youth, shunning foreplay, not knowing what to do when the coupling was finished. During the act, he had not been gentle, but neither had he made undue demands, though she had rather wished he would. What she sensed in him was a kind of awe. It told her that she was the first mature woman he had ever had. She had performed several of the ancient acts with him which left him gasping and unbelieving. There would be a great need for him later, when she was established here in Grove Center.

Later the door was unlocked and they stood on their respective sides of the counter. He asked, "Will you come back tomorrow night?''

"Can you wait that long, Terry? I'm not certain I can."

"What do you mean?"

"What time do you get off work?"

"Eight o'clock in the morning."

"Why not meet me at Ludlow's Mill?"

"In the morning? This morning?"

"Yes. Can you do it?"

"Sure. Hell, yes, I can do it. I was supposed to meet Sue Ann there this morning, but she never showed up—the bitch. She didn't even come to work tonight."

"Sue Ann?"

"The chick who works here from six to midnight—when she's not off trying to earn a buck on her back."

"I'll be there, Terry. I will be there."

# CHAPTER 5

It was dark in the bedroom. Patrick did not know whether he had been asleep and awakened by an alien noise, or if he had not been asleep at all. Everything seemed to be just a little bit jumbled. It was an uncomfortable feeling, like being lost in a maze, unable to get out. He drew a deep breath and let it out slowly, feeling his chest muscles stretch and contract and is heart thump steadily inside his rib cage. And, amid the disruption in his thinking, he recognized fear. But of what? He had no idea.

Beside him Karen was sleeping quietly, her daytime competence replaced with a soft innocence and vulnerability. There was an almost childlike frailty in the lavish curves of her vuluptuous body, he thought, and wondered how deeply womanhood penetrated. Looking at her in the feathery light of the moon entering through the window, he thought how damnably lucky he was. Few men were fortunate enough to meet a woman such as this one. He felt like one of the special favorites of the gods to be so anointed. Once again he resolved to do all in his power to make himself worthy of the trust this very special woman placed in him. Love her. Respect her.

Protect her.

Sleep was impossible for him now. Too many things were building up inside him, too many shadows without form moving through his thoughts. He felt tense. He felt as though an unseen piper was fluting a tune of savage and merciless rhythm to which he had begun to dance. Whatever was happening, he didn't understand it. If he lay here any longer, there was no telling what horrors might gesture at him from within the nightmares he'd create.

Moving very gently so as not to awaken Karen, he slipped out of bed and padded to the window.

Night was still out there on the land, but in the east the anemic grey of first dawn laid its ribbon along the horizon. As always it had the cold dead look of another world. In spite of the warmth pushing in upon him through the open window, he shivered; and he knew it for what it was—a sudden chill caused by the winds of wisdom. He wanted to go out, to walk through this breaking dawn and meet it face to face.

He threw on jeans, T shirt and sneakers, and trotted down the stairs. For one brief instant, he felt a little bit ashamed, as does one when making ready to perform an uncalled-for, aggressive act. But he shrugged it off. He wanted to meet the dawn, that was all. There was nothing aggressive about that.

Out on the lawn, he stopped. There was nothing alien in the weakening darkness. No faint sounds carried on the dampness of the dew-heavy air, no shadows moved within shadows. There was only the smell of the jasmine and, overhead, the moon withdrawing through the silhouettes of the pepper trees and pines, before the rising light in the east.

He strolled slowly down the driveway to the road, hesitated, then turned left, walking towards the groves and pasture lands. The asphalt felt hard through the thin soles of his sneakers; he became aware of a tiny pain in the arch of his left foot. He grunted. Off to his right a bird called, and was greeted by another and then another. The world was beginning its ritual of daily rebirth.

He was not thinking, not creating conundrums nor unraveling self-made nightmares. He was simply walking, aware only of the pleasant physical exercise. So when he came to the lane leading back towards Ludlow's Mill, he was astonished to realize he had come so far. And as he paused there, he remembered Jennifer saying that she, too, had walked the three miles without being aware of it. An absurd inconsequential injection of memory. Why did it flash through his mind? A growing paranoia?

He stood still, gazing across the fields to the east of the road. The young light touched the dew on the grass tufts and bracken, turning it to silvered drops. Something was attempting to make itself known to him. He tried not to force it. Once, then, twice, it came within reach of his consciousness, but slipped away before he could grasp it. What it was, for certain, he'd never know; but he knew he should go to the ruins. It was not a thought, not an explicit command of brain to muscles, just a feeling coming from that ancient part of himself that was deeper than conscious thought.

He walked along the lane. Under the arching branches darkness still held tightly to the earth, and he had to take his steps with care. Despite the early hour, sweat rolled down his cheeks and the T shirt stuck tightly to his shoulders.

The clearing was desolate in the murky light, a brooding crescent scar slashed into the silent forest. The ruins were black and shapeless forms. It was a lifeless place, an empty shell upon which the foliage crept.

He moved slowly across the clearing, the dew-soaked weeds dampening his jeans up to his knees. Around him there were rustling and rattling sounds as the night creatures scurried for their burrows and the day ones came forth cautiously. From the distant interstate highway the muffled roar of a hurtling eighteen-wheel truck told him he was not alone in this twilight world. For a reason he didn't want to evaluate, it made him draw a deep breath of relief.

He stood in one of the vine-draped archways and again sought the elusive thought his mind had tried to grasp at the outer end of the lane. But this time it remained hidden and came nowhere within reach. He began to wonder why he was here. When he had left the house, he'd been so damned certain; he had simply wanted to meet the dawn. He began to feel silly and childish. What the hell was he doing out here?

"You're a fool," he said out loud.

He pushed himself away from the cool stone of the arch, took one final look around, and began to head back toward the lane.

That was when he saw the movement at the far side of the clearing. He hesitated, watching the darkness gliding against the black tree shadows. Very suddenly he didn't want to be seen by whatever it was. He turned and ducked through the archway, heading for the opposite side of the ruins. There he took shelter behind a wall. To his surprise he felt his heart beginning to accelerate, and his lungs were suddenly empty of air; he sucked in mouthfuls of the damp morning air.

He looked around the corner of the wall. A dark-clad figure was coming across the clearing, approaching the ruins with a slow and swaying walk.

It moved leisurely along the path in the growing light, stopping several times to examine a particular blooming weed or ground vine, or raising its shapeless head towards the brightening heavens where the sun was forming pink fans across the emerging blue. Finally it straightened from the delicate whiteness of a Queen Ann's Lace and walked on towards the flat-topped stone.

Patrick moved a half a step around the corner. Something about the movement of the figure seemed familiar. It rounded a small bush and came into full view.

It was a woman. She was dressed in a dark and hooded raincoat, or something like it, the hood raised to cover her head like a monk's cowl. Now that he saw her for what she was, the movements of her body beneath the black material seemed very sensuous. A moment later the familiarity became a certain knowledge.

Even as she reached the stone and threw back the cowl, allowing a mane of golden yellow hair to cascade into view, he recognized her.

Jennifer.

She stood beside the stone, slowly turning her head

from side to side as she looked around the clearing. For a moment, when she looked in his direction, her eyes hesitated. He stood very still and found himself holding his breath while her gaze roamed the walls around him. Inexplicably he felt like an intruder who had crossed some line of privacy and good taste; he felt like a voyeur. He felt dishonest, as if he was stealing something pure and simple. Then the embarrassment turned to annoyance. There was no need to be ashamed. Jennifer was a trespasser as surely as he, and no apologies would be called for when he stepped around the corner.

He was about to do that when she started away from the stone. She was heading toward the northern edge of the clearing. At a large oak she stopped, turned, and once again scanned the clearing. He wasn't certain, it could have been a bit of wayward light combining with his imagination, but as she looked through the brightening light he thought those blue eyes became glinting amber for an instant. Apparently satisfied, she turned, ducked under a low-hanging bough, and disappeared into the underbrush.

He waited. In the still air he could hear the rustle of foilage from the shrubs and saplings bordering the clearing. His curiosity arose along with his perplexity; he stayed where he was.

Perhaps ten minutes passed before Jennifer reemerged from the trees. When she did, he saw that all her caution was gone; she returned to the stone without looking around. Whatever it was she had done back there among the trees, it had plainly satisfied her. She moved with total confidence.

The sun was well up now. The morning coolness was giving way to a sultry day. The dew was drying. Half of the stone was in sunlight, and the tiny sea shells embedded in the coquina rock made sharp little shadows, so the flat surface looked like a bed of rusted nails. On the far side of the woods, branches were beginning to stir; a morning breeze was starting its journey over the land.

Jennifer laid the palm of her left hand on the sunlit area of the stone and moved it back and forth across the rough texture as if testing its warmth. Apparently satisfied, she straightened, looked once more around the clearing, and began unbuttoning her coat.

Patrick didn't watch her. Instead he watched a chameleon scurrying and stopping, scurrying and stopping on the wall. Yet his mind was not on the lizard; he was thinking hard. Why was Jennifer here? No answer presented itself, at least no answer that felt solid.

He turned back to look at her. The coat was lying in a dark heap on the ground. Jennifer was standing beside the stone, her arms clasped behind her neck, legs together, arching herself upwards, towards the young sun. She was totally nude.

He stared. He knew he should turn away, that his behavior was on the level of a ten-year-old half-wit; yet he could not. The artist in him told him no crime was being committed, that he was looking at far more than the magnificent body of a handsome woman. He was seeing a painting waiting to be transferred to canvas, a poem of flesh and stone and vegetation.

She was the earth mother at her shrine. She was the

giver and the taker of life. The receiver of the seed and the giver of the milk of nourishment. She was the first woman, the eternal woman. She was all of womankind.

While he watched, she arched herself backwards with her arms outstretched, welcoming the sun. Her belly pulled flat and taut beneath her thrusting rib cage, and her heavy breasts rose upwards, offered to the warm sunlight. Then she thrust her pelvis forward, offering the brown-haired triangle at the apex of her thighs to the light, spreading her legs apart very slightly. Loins and belly and breasts were wantonly directed at the sun. She stood like that for a long, long minute, surrendering herself to the morning. Then suddenly she broke the spell with a high giggling laugh and fell on her belly across the stone.

Patrick drew a deep breath. He had the feeling that time had collapsed around him, that for the minutes just passed he had been a visitor in two separate worlds. One an ancient sunlit past, the other a dark and brooding present. Perfection and imperfection.

Very carefully he moved away from his hiding place, away from the stone toward the surrounding forest. As he picked his way through the underbrush, moving almost silently, he found his thought sequences splintered. When he tried to focus on a particular subject, it would suddenly dissolve like a dream, leaving him with empty and groping. But there was one thing of which he was very certain. This afternoon, or as soon as he could arrange to return to the ruins, he was going to go behind that oak and find Jennifer's secret.

He had circled through the forest and was within sight of the lane when he heard a car turning onto it from the county road. He moved behind a tree. A dilapidated VW bug rattled along the ruts in the direction of the ruins. A young man was at the wheel, staring straight ahead intently. Patrick watched until the thin plume exhaust smoke rounded a bend and disappeared. He had seen the driver more than once. He couldn't think where.

For a moment, he thought of following the car down the lane to see what the driver would do when he found the ruins already occupied by a nude woman. But he knew. He knew there would be no surprise. He knew the boy was going to meet Jennifer.

He was almost halfway to the house when he remembered where he had seen the boy. He was a night clerk at the Quick Stop Store. Terry, his name was. Very ordinary. A feeling bordering on disgust rose in him. All his disarrayed thoughts were suddenly reassembled, and Jennifer's strangeness became abhorrent.

When she got up, Karen found there was no one in the house but Jeff and herself. When Patrick had arisen, and where he'd gone, she had no idea. As she passed Jennifer's room a complicated curiosity touched her, and she opened the door a crack and looked in. The bed was empty and unmade. If she read into coincidences, a rapid succession of queries would race through her mind, but nothing of the sort occurred. She went down to the kitchen and put the coffee pot on.

While it was perking, she walked down the driveway for the morning paper. Today the plastic bag was intact, the paper neatly folded within it. On the way back to the house, she took the paper from its sheath and glanced at the headlines. They were the usual; on-going corruption and tension, and man's eternal inhumanity to man. She refolded the paper and tucked it under her arm. Each morning she was becoming more and more convinced of the world's gradual disintegration.

She was on her second cup of coffee, thinking about the frog and the lily pad she'd work on that morning, when Patrick came through the kitchen door from the veranda. He paused inside the threshold, stared at her, then rubbed the back of a hand across his brow.

Something was wrong. She felt it just as she would have felt a draft of chilled air, and the distance between her and the rest of the world increased.

"How was the worm?" she asked, setting her half-empty cup gently on its saucer.

He shook his head. "I don't understand. I'm missing something, I guess."

"Early bird? Worm? There's an old adage—"

"Okay. I get it." He went to the cupboard for a cup, and when he had taken it from the shelf filled it with coffee. "Sorry. I'm not with it right now."

He sat down across the table from her. Restlessly his eyes moved across the newspaper lying beside her elbow, then out the window, and finally to hers. "What has happened to all the good things in life?" he asked. "Honor and honesty and kindness. Where have they gone, Kar? Or are they still here, but we don't recognize them any more?''

She frowned, disconcerted at the depressing echo of her own thoughts. ''They're still here, darling, but sometimes they have to be searched for.'' She sipped her coffee.

''Then we'd better start searching.''

The coffee suddenly tasted bitter. ''What do you mean?''

He sat staring over her shoulder through the window. Finally, he said, ''You didn't speak with your sister last night. I think you should today.''

''Why?''

''I believe it's imperative she leave—at least this house, Kar. There's something not right in that woman, and, I think, a great dishonesty.''

''What makes you think so? What's happened?''

She sat quietly as he described what had occurred at the ruins. While he talked, in a low monotone, she began to feel a great fear. She had hoped that Patrick would see that Jennifer was not as she should be, and yet, now that he had, she realized that she had hoped even more strongly that he would laugh her out of her doubts. And she also felt the pinch of anger. Why should this happen to her and those she loved?

''She's not the sister I knew,'' she said. ''Sometimes I think she's no more than a shadow.''

''No, she's real, Kar.''

She nodded. For a moment she didn't want to carry on the conversation any longer. She was afraid to.

''I want to go with you when you go back to the ruins,'' she said.

''No, I don't think that's wise.''

"Why?"

He shrugged. "I just don't. Believe me, it's a really bad idea."

"You know something you're not telling me."

"No."

She looked straight into his eyes. There was no duplicity in them; she knew he wasn't lying to her. She knew, also, that he was absolutely against her going to the ruins. And she realized she was grateful for his determination. It was a calmness in the center of an emotional tempest. At the same time, he was taking it all so seriously that it increased her fears. After all, what had he seen? Simply a woman taking a sunbath.

"You won't hold anything back from me, will you?"

"No. I won't do that. I promise," he said.

"Good God, Patrick! You're making my skin crawl."

"It might be worse, love. It might be worse." He got up and took his empty cup to the sink and rinsed it out. "I've several more paintings to frame. I'll be out in the shed."

"When are you going back to the ruins?"

"When it's safe. When she's here at the house and well occupied."

After he was gone she washed out both their cups. As she put them in the draining basket she felt completely disoriented, as though listening to a surrealistic play unfold, voices screaming in horror and disbelief and disgust.

"Damn it all! Damn her for coming here!"

"Who, mom?"

She whirled. Jeff was standing in the doorway leading from the living room.

She shook her head. "Nobody. I think this is going to be one of my frustrated days."

"The kind when it's best to stay far away from you?"

"That kind. What do you want for breakfast?"

"I'm not hungry, honestly. Just orange juice and milk."

"Sure."

He was about halfway through both glasses, as she finished bagging the garbage for him to take down to the road for the county truck to pick up. He asked, "Were you talking about Aunt Jennifer?"

She looked up at him from her bent position. "When?"

"When I was coming in the door. Is she the one you damned for coming here?"

"Why would you think it was her?" She closed the plastic bag and straightened up. She scowled at him. "There're other things referred to as 'her'."

"Yeah, I guess. But I think it was her."

"For heaven's sake, why?"

"Because I don't think you really like her."

"She's my sister, Jeff. What you just said is almost unholy. Sisters love each other. Why do you say that? What makes you think I don't like Jennifer?"

"You look at her funny. Real strange looks, mom, as if you don't . . . well, you know, trust her."

She could think of nothing to say. If Jeff, in his unsophisticated self-absorbtion, could see through her attitude towards Jennifer, then her sister, with the unnatural awareness she seemed to possess, would surely do so. Her questions of the previous evening had just been answered. She was transparent.

Not wanting to ask the question, but knowing she must, she asked, "What do you think of her?"

"I think she's neat."

"Oh? How? In what way?"

He gave the universal shrug of young boys trying to express themselves and dropped his eyes. He looked embarrassed, as he did when talking to her about girls. "Well . . . she's good looking and she— you know, knows how to get along with me. She doesn't seem as old as she is, and she makes me feel kinda older and . . . and, oh, you know, good, I guess."

Karen sat down opposite him. He squirmed in his chair, watching her with ill concealed apprehension in his blue eyes. What she was about to say had to be worded delicately.

"I think I know what you're trying to say." She spoke slowly, watching his face carefully. "Jennifer has been very good with you, probably better than the other women of her age you know. There's no doubt she has a knack for young people, and that's wonderful. Too many people our age, hers and mine and Patrick's, look on kids as necessary evils. But there are two ways, Jeff—particularly for a woman —to relate to a boy, and I think Jennifer is being too intimate with you in some ways." She took a deep breath. "Do you know what I'm trying to say?"

"I think so." He was moving his orange juice glass around on the table top forming designs with the dampness clinging to its bottom.

"Okay. I don't want that intimacy to go any farther than it has already. Understand?"

"Yes, ma'm." He hurriedly drank the rest of the orange juice. "Can I be excused now?"

"Certainly. Patrick's in the shed, framing, if you want him." She pointed at the garbage, "Don't forget this."

"Oh, Mom! I'll get it later!" The kitchen door slammed behind him.

She stared after him for a moment, then shook her head, and got up. She put the garbage bag on the side veranda where he couldn't miss it. The entire episode had been irrationally unsettling. Had the time so suddenly arrived for Jeff to leave the age of innocence?

When she reentered the kitchen, she saw it was nine fifteen—forty-five minutes past the time she'd planned to be in the studio working on that damned frog. She wished that fate—or Joseph Waingard—should have allowed her an assignment she liked.

It was as she entered the studio that the idea struck her. From where it came, or for what reason, she had no idea. Suddenly it was there.

She went to the telephone book laying on the floor beside the wooden stool on which the phone extension squatted. She looked up the area code and dialed directory assistance.

"May I help you?" The operator's voice was without intonation, machine-like.

"Yes, please. I'd like the number of Neutronics, Inc., in Cleveland. I think it's on St. Clair Street."

The wire hummed over a background of musical computer peepings. The remote voice came back and precisely enunciated Neutronics' number. She thanked the woman—or the mechanism—and hung up.

She dialed again.

"Thank you for calling Neutronics. May I help you?" This voice was definitely a young woman's, cheerful, lively.

"Public Relations, please."

While the switchover was made and a telephone began to ring, she tightened her grip on the phone. This had been very impulsive. Perhaps it was a bad mistake.

"Holscomb speaking." The voice was hurried and brittle, like steel being tapped with a small hammer.

"Mr. Holscomb, my name is Karen Sommers. I'm phoning concerning Jennifer Logan."

"Oh, you're the sister she's visiting in Florida. Nothing's wrong, is there?" There was concern in his voice.

"No. No, not really." She was suddenly embarrassed, feeling like an intruder.

"What can I do for you . . . is it Ms, Miss, or Mrs. Sommers?"

"Mrs."

"Then tell me why you're phoning about Jennifer, Mrs. Sommers."

His precise speech was making it difficult for her. She imagined office lights glinting on rimless eyeglasses while a tight mouth spoke words through unmoving lips. She wondered if her hastily thought-up explanation for the call would be transparent.

"Well, I suppose I'm being foolish, Mr. Holscomb, and I assure you, Jennifer knows nothing about this phone call. But . . . well, is she in good health, do you know?''

"Jennifer? Good Lord! She's as healthy as the proverbial horse, Mrs. Sommers.''

"Oh.''

"Is she sick or something?''

"No.'' She felt defeat closing in on her, but there was so much more she wanted to know, and now she felt foolishly inarticulate.

The man on the other end of the line must have sensed her discomfort, because when he spoke again much of the hostility was gone from his voice. "You sound somewhat at a loss for words, Mrs. Sommers. Is there something you want to ask me, or tell me?''

"Maybe I'm a little dismayed,'' she said. "It's been three years since I last saw Jennifer, and she was so vivacious at that time. Now she's so remote and withdrawn, I began having notions she was holding something back from me. But to your knowledge, she isn't doing that?''

"Not to my knowledge, and I think I'm knowledge-able enough about Jennifer to speak with certainty. We've worked together five days a week for several years. I'd know if there was any physical problem, believe me.''

"Mental?'' It slipped out before she thought.

"Mental? Mrs. Sommers, why have you phoned? What are you trying to find out? Jennifer Logan is one of our prized employees. She does an excellent job here, always doing that little bit more than the job description calls for, and has never complained about an overload of work. We can't give her enough, it seems. And before you ask, her relationship with her fellow employees is remarkable."

"No remoteness?"

"None whatsoever." He paused, and she thought she heard fingernails tapping a desk top. When he spoke again, some of the sharpness was back in his voice. "I think I've talked enough, Mrs. Sommers."

"I appreciate what you've told me, Mr. Holscomb. I guess I'm just imagining things."

Again Holscomb's voice softened and became human, the voice of a public relations man. "I'm sure you had a reason for phoning, and I can tell you are worried about Jennifer. Can you tell me why? I do really want to help if there's a problem. We all think so much of her up here."

She hesitated, looked out the window, and saw only the empty yard. "The woman here is not the sister I remember, nor the woman you described."

"I'm afraid I don't understand."

"I don't either, Mr. Holscomb. I don't either, and that's why I'm troubling you. To look at her, she's the same person she was three years ago—blonde, handsome, and sparkling. But inside, there's something different, as if her mind was occupied with something unrelated to what is going on around her —preoccupied, I guess would be the word for it. She never used to be that way, and it's rather shocking to me."

"Well, she does get that way now and then, that I have to admit. There are times when she seems to be gathering wool, but we all do that. Sometimes we have to tune out the world so we can come up with a solution to a problem. There's certainly nothing to worry about there. That happens to most of us, doesn't it?"

"Yes. Perhaps I should be doing that now instead of annoying you. But . . . but when she woolgathers, there's no facial change, no specter of another personality?

"Are you asking if she could be schizophrenic?"

"I guess I am."

"That's absurd! If you're talking about the woman visiting you, then you're right, Mrs. Sommers. That woman is not Jennifer Logan."

She was suddenly ashamed and contrite, and her ego was bruised a little bit, too. She said, "I think you've just answered my question, Mr. Holscomb. You've been very gracious and understanding with me, and I appreciate it more than I can say."

"Well, to tell you the truth, I'm not at all sure what this was all about, but if it's helped you, I'm happy. You tell Jennifer to have a good time and get back here as soon as her two weeks are up. Her desk's piled ceiling high."

What would he say if she told him Jennifer wasn't planning to return, that she had decided to stay here in Grove Center and bring her strangeness to its quiet streets? "I'll do that."

She was hanging up when Holscomb's voice came from the telephone. "Mrs. Sommers! Are you still there?"

"Yes."

"I did happen to think of something. I doubt if it has any bearing on whatever it was we have been talking about, but. . . . About ten months ago Jennifer became ill and stayed away from the office for almost three weeks, some kind of a cold bug that caused her to feel weak and run a high temperature. When she did come back, she was disoriented for a short time, maybe a day or two. But that's the only break in her routine since she came to Neutronics.''

"There were no changes in her?"

"Only the disorientation, which lasted no time at all."

Suddenly the rimless glasses didn't glint in her mind's eye. A human warmth in the eyes behind them softened their hard glare.

"Thank you again."

She hung up and, determined not to think, went to her desk. For the next hour she worked on the illustrations, finishing one and transferring the sketch of another to illustration board. Meeting the deadline was going to be difficult, she knew. Obstacles which she did not know how to overcome were turning the miracle of meeting the date into the impossibility of meeting the date. The realization pressed in on her with such force she stopped work for a moment and stared out the window, wondering if a gradual nervous collapse would be the end result. Another half hour passed and, looking at the illustration, she saw nothing added to the scene, only a spot in the lower right-hand corner where a drop of perspiration had fallen from her chin. It was grey on the white illustration board, fluted and veined; a rounded blossom of ugliness. Looking at it, she wanted to cry, though she knew it could be corrected with a few dabs of the paint rag. Her stretched nerves demanded relief. She sat staring dumbly at the spot, waiting for the tears to spill from her eyes and mingle with the perspiration on her cheeks.

Possibly that was why she didn't hear the footsteps climbing the stairs. Only when a board creaked in the threshold of the studio door did she become aware of a person standing there. Watching her.

Jennifer was leaning with her left shoulder against the door frame, her arms folded under her breasts and the voluptuous curve of her right hip pushed out in a deep thrust. All the clean wholesomeness which had been an intregal part of her charm was missing. Standing in the doorway was a woman who knew and offered all of sexual desires and perversions. This was a woman who lived beyond the borders of the acceptable.

The heavy mane of her yellow hair fell in tangles about her face to curl in knots on her shoulders. Her lips were puffed full, as though they recently received long, demanding kisses, and her lightly applied eye-shadow had been smeared around the eye sockets, forming a mask-like stain.

She stared at Karen arrogantly; a mere hint of a wise smile curling the outer corners of her lips. The heavy sexual aura emanating from her dominated the studio.

For the first few seconds Karen felt intimidated. Then she picked up her paint rag and wiped the brush she was holding.

"I want to talk with you, Jennifer. Now, while we're alone."

Jennifer didn't move. "Not now. I'm tired, and everything I say will be no more than automatic responses. I don't think either one of us wants that. Nothing would be settled. Nothing permanent, that is."

"This is the time. I want it to be now."

Jennifer pushed herself away from the door frame and stood at her full height. Under the mounds of her breasts, her fingers dug deep into the flesh of her upper arms. "Don't try to force me, sis. I don't push easy. Right now I'm tired and I want to take a nap. When I awaken, then we'll have our discussion."

She turned and walked into the hall.

"Where were you?" Karen called after her.

"Walking."

Karen heard her close the door of her room. The bolt slipped into place.

Karen threw down her brush and got up. Patrick— she had to see him.

In the shed Patrick was daubing glue on the ends of two pieces of molding before puting them in a vice. In a far corner Jeff sat on a wooden crate. When she walked in she met that special silence which comes when the person who is the subject of a conversation enters a room.

Patrick grinned at her. "Hi."

She wanted to respond to his affectionate off-handedness, but she had lost the prescription for easy joviality.

"When you get that corner joined, may I speak with you?" she asked Patrick.

He looked at her sharply. Instantly, she knew, he saw in her eyes what she was hoping he would. "Just give me a half a minute." He looked at Jeff. "You'll excuse me, won't you, tiger, while I talk with your mom?"

Jeff gave a shrug. "Sure. Go ahead."

"Don't forget the garbage," she told Jeff. "You

could take it down now, you know.''

"Yeah, I could." He went out of the shed almost eagerly, as though happy to get away.

Patrick looked at her. "She's home?"

"In her bedroom, taking a nap. With the door locked.''

"Fine. Then I'm off. What are you going to do?"

"Remember? I promised Cynthia to go shopping with her this afternoon. I'll take Jeff over to the Porters to see Billy.''

He reached out and pulled her to him, tight, so her breasts were heavy on his chest and her loins were thrust against his. She helped him, planting her feet solidly on the floor and offering the full length of her body, driven by a surprising desire to be taken by him, here, now, in the sawdusted and shadowed room.

"We don't have time," he whispered.

"I know." Her need was pulsing in her loins and swelling her breasts; it was the sexual desire which comes sometimes at moments of high stress. "Later.''

He kissed her, working his tongue into her willing mouth, and then drew back slightly, stroking her left flank. "Later.''


Karen did little actual shopping on the shopping trips she made with Cynthia. She knew there was no sense in her friend's approach to marketing, but accepted the invitations for the pure enjoyment of the hours they spent "on the trail," as Cynthia said.

Cynthia Porter was fun to shop with. She made it an adventure, going through stores with the same

carefree abandon as she used in dressing herself.
Dashing to an establishment sponsoring a coupon
sale and discovering she'd forgotten her coupons,
criticizing the next "hawker's" merchandise in all
too audible terms, pouncing on her "finds" with
delight, she'd stride on her slender legs in the regal
manner of a tribal princess whirling through a
bazaar.

Today was no different.

"I've got to have coffee," Cynthia said as they
came back out into the heat from the false coolness
of a hardware store. "Hot, black coffee!"

Within a half dozen steps she stopped and took off
her glasses. "Look at the fog on these lenses! I've
told Don more than three dozen times, if he'd invent
something to put on eyeglasses so they wouldn't fog
when you come out of an air-conditioned building,
he'd be a millionaire! So much better than selling
fishhooks and bait buckets." She took hold of
Karen's arm. "Guide me to The Soup and Nuts. The
coffee's on me."

The Soup and Nuts was one of the original down-
town restaurants and, like many of the retail busi-
nesses in that location, was desperately trying to
improve itself without the expenditure of nonexistent
cash. It was one of the ones not succeeding.

Hanging greenery, mostly philodendron, failed to
conceal blistered paint. Discount-store art hung
between the vines, garish splashes of orange where
umber would have sufficed and electric blue instead
of ultramarine. Within the last decade vinyl tile had
been laid, but had faded into an earthy grey-brown.
Karen sometimes thought the color was original; it

was ideal for hiding stains. Lunch was still being served. Local businessmen leaned over the daily special, talking of the past and the future of Grove Center, but very little of the present.

A fat young woman, moving with something between a waddle and a sway, took their orders.

When the coffee was in front of them and Cynthia had replaced her glasses, she asked, "Can I maybe tread on forbidden territory?"

Karen smiled. "Where have you ever found forbidden territory, Cyn?"

"Well, now and then, I do crawl over the wrong fence."

"I've no fences—not with you, anyway. You know that."

"I hoped that was so. Okay. Last night Don and I were talking when we got home. Are we right, or are we wrong; but it seemed to us that you and Patrick were standoffish with your sister. Distance, the more the better, between you two and her seemed to be the order of the evening. And here you are today without her." She tilted her head owlishly, "Private territory?"

Karen played with her unused spoon. Fact and fear, knowledge and speculation, fought within her, making an answer very nearly impossible. What she said here and now might at some future time prove idiotic. "She seems to have different interests than we do."

"Big-city ideas versus small-town convictions?"

"No. It's more than that, Cyn. It's like the clash of two faiths, two worlds even. No communication. No way to try exchanging ideas."

Cynthia pursed her lips in a silent whistle. "That's not good."

"No. Not good at all."

"Boy! Did Don and I blow it last night suggesting she stay! I'm sorry."

"You didn't know. Don't worry."

Cynthia's round glasses aimed directly at her. "But you're worried, Kar. You're badly worried. Some place behind your eyes, there's a big dose of uneasiness. I saw it last night, but I didn't recognize it. I thought you were only weary." The green fire in her eyes seemed to reflect in the lenses of her glasses. "You want to talk, Kar?"

Suddenly she did. She wanted to lay the whole terrible mess on the table between them for everyone in the restaurant to see. She wanted Cynthia to become aware of the fear prowling within her.

She pushed the coffee cup away and leaned towards Cynthia. "It's terror that stands between Jennifer and me, Cyn. I'm afraid of her, and I'm afraid of having her in my house. I think more and more that she came here with an evil purpose directed towards me and, maybe, towards Jeff—and I feel so totally alone."

"My God, Kar! Do you know what you're saying?"

"I know, Cyn. God help me, I know. And I want so very much to be wrong. I'd even welcome your telling me these are the imaginings of a neurotic. But I'm not that. You know the way I can stay on an even keel."

Cynthia turned her coffee cup slowly on its saucer, with a forefinger hooked in its handle. "There's no denying that, Kar. Everyone admires your spunk—and your determination. It takes a very level-headed person to do what you've done since Jason's death.''

"All that's changing, Cyn. More than once in the last few days I've felt I've lost the handle on things—even the little things have become huge baffling problems which seem beyond my ability.''

If there had been a mild tolerance on Cynthia's face, it was now replaced with genuine concern. The bond between them was drawing her into an appreciation of what Karen was telling her. She asked, "When did it start?''

"The second day she was here. I took her out to see Ludlow's Mill, because it's been a very special place for Patrick and me; and, I guess, I wanted her to feel the tranquility of it. There aren't many places you find that kind of peace anymore, and I was certain she'd enjoy it.''

"Did she?''

"Yes. In fact, she seemed at home there in the wilderness . . . as if she actually belonged in a forest. But then we met Sue Ann Miller, the clerk in the convenience store down the road from us. The way Jennifer looked at that girl, Cyn, I'll never forget. There was lust and greed in her eyes. Not sexual. It was worse. Like an insatiable hunger. It was ugly, Cyn. She was like a carnivore studying its next meal.''

"Dear God.''

"That's not all. If it was, I'd put it off to my imagination.'' She could taste the bitter flavor of what she was about to say. "She's attracted to Jeff and attempting to make him aware of her as a woman. Not as his aunt, but as a woman.''

''Karen, that's unimaginable!''

It was until you saw it, she thought. Until you saw what was within her sister behind those speculative eyes. Very slowly she told Cynthia of the way Jennifer watched him with a hungry look in her eyes. The way she managed to rub her body against him, apparently innocently. And the almost erotic dance she had turned the basketball shooting into. After she started to talk, she found that the words came easier than she had imagined. Some of the bitter flavor melted from her tongue. The sharing was a help.

For a long moment after she had finished talking, a silence lay between them on the table. Karen wondered whether she had talked them into an emotional corner, and whether her friend was trying to decide on a way to extract them.

Cynthia spoke. ''She sounds sick, Kar. Maybe what she needs is help.''

''I thought of that, Cyn; so this morning I phoned the company in Cleveland where she works and talked with a Mr. Holscomb. According to him, she's one of their best employees—liked by both management and co-workers. So, whatever it is, it's a thing she kept hidden up there or which has happened to her here.''

''And she seems so nice.''

''When she's herself.'' She looked directly into Cynthia's great oval glasses. ''After all her talk last night about starting the settling-in process, she went out early this morning on a long walk—and the woman who returned to the house was not Jennifer."

"What do you mean?"

"I was working in the studio. She came and stood in the doorway. But it wasn't my sister standing there. It was a slut, Cyn, a creature which was a denial of everything decent in womanhood. I had made up my mind to tell her I wanted her out of the house; that, for that matter, I didn't want her to stay here in Grove Center. But I couldn't. She defied me, then locked herself in her room." She hesitated, knowing that what she was going to say next might turn Cynthia away from her. "The person I was talking to wasn't Jennifer, Cyn. She wasn't my sister. The woman in the doorway was someone else. Someone *other*."

Cynthia sat staring at her. Shifting, formless things moved in her eyes and across her face. Finally she drew a deep breath. "There's no place to turn for you, is there? Not even to Patrick."

"I can only get rid of her."

Cynthia reached across the table and laid a hand on top of Karen's. "You know the three of us will help, Don and I and Patrick."

"I know."

The lamia was uneasy. She should have kept a tighter control on the woman body: her own desires had been witnessed in the actions of the woman. She felt danger.

She was coiled well back from the bedroom window, in the deep shadows of the room. On the bed the nude woman sprawled, arms outflung and legs spread wide.

A noise outside; she raised her head from the shadows and peered over the window sill. She saw the man's car. It stopped. He got out, then turned and reached back into the front seat. She rose a little higher and leaned forward. He pulled out a stained white cloth and then one of blue and stood looking at them turning them over in his hands, examining them.

She hissed. It was wild and savage and filled the room.

The man carried the garments of the girl whose blood she had drunk at the stone.

She had disposed of the body where it would never be found, under the black waters of the river, but the clothes she had buried in a shallow hole near where she had feasted. Momentos of that most savory of meals.

Her tongue flicked in and out.

The man approached the house.

He had seen her going to them while she was in the woman body. The sense of danger grew.

She turned from the window and again looked at the body sprawled on the bed. It had to be protected. It had to be carefully controlled.

# CHAPTER 6

The deputy sheriff was a puffy man. Karen
received the impression his body was in reality a
series of balloons strung together inside the grey-
green uniform; it bulged so with completely out of
places curves. The underarms and back of his shirt
were sweat stained; under a magnificently pneumatic
belly, his belt buckle was tarnished and the gun
holster on the belt dull and cracked. As Karen
watched him push the T shirt and shorts around on
her kitchen table with a pudgy forefinger, her heart
sank. This was the local law enforcer? She knew what
Lois Rutherford had meant the other morning.

"I know who belongs to these," he said in a deep,
gravelly voice. "I seen them on her enough at the
Quick Stop Store. They're Sue Ann's."

"I understand no one's seen her for several days,"
Karen said.

He nodded. "Yep. The kid who works the
midnight shift at the store called us, but we didn't
take much heed. Sue Ann has a habit of going off for
a day or two now and then. She's one who sure loves
to party and doesn't much let work interfere if she's
on a good one." He picked up the T shirt and studied

the stains. "This here puts a different light on it, though, I'd say."

"Particularly since they were hidden in a shallow hole and covered with brush," Patrick said.

"Yeah, yeah, you're right. But, if they were so well hid, how come you stumbled on them, Mr. O'Shawn?"

"Curiosity, officer. I was out there and heard noises coming from behind some shrubbery. When I went to investigate, I saw the T shirt and shorts partially exposed, as though an animal had been rooting around in them."

"Hmm. Well, I reckon. Strange things do happen." He bundled the two garments together. "I'll take these in to the office and put out a missing persons report on Sue Ann."

"Let me know if there's anything I can do to help," Patrick said.

The deputy nodded. "You can count on that, Mr. O'Shawn." Then he was gone.

"Patrick, why didn't you tell him the truth? Don't you think in the long run that would have been better?" She shook her head. "He didn't really believe you, you know, about an animal rooting."

"I think you should have your talk with Jennifer before we go public with this."

She turned away. She had already gone public when she told Cynthia and phoned Neutronics. Had she been like some careless medical assistant, opening the wrong test tube and allowing a virus of unknown destruction to seep out? A throb began in her head, pulsing in her temples in such a way she knew it would become pain before too long.

It was dinner time. She could occupy her mind with the preparation of the meal and permit her subconscious to try and unravel the twistings of her thoughts.

"Anything special you want for dinner?"

He shook his head.

But she couldn't think of a thing to prepare; her mind refused to be distracted that way.

Patrick perhaps sensed her confusion. He said, "How about me going to get us all some Wendy's?"

She smiled in gratitude. "I'm not functioning. I'm like a person who tries to keep going but is wading through big fluff balls of cotton. The way I feel when I have the flu."

"Where's Jeff? Maybe he'll want to go with me."

"I think he's up in his room. He was going to take a shower when we came back."

"Okay. I'll see if he wants to tag along."

"I'll make some iced tea while you're gone."

Patrick took the steps two at a time, his big frame shaking the old timbers so they groaned in protest. He was one of a kind, she thought, watching him bound up to the second floor: a young, excitable boy was always lurking within his heroic proportions and once in a while the boy would take command, dashing with intensity and passion into the moment.

A moment later they both came pounding down the stairs, Jeff emitting screams of delight as Patrick thundered after him. Neither saw her as they raced through the foyer and out the door. She watched them circle the station wagon once before scrambling into it, howling with laughter. At that precise moment she was very much aware of the full meaning of love, and everything took on a deeper dimension.

She turned from the door. Jennifer was standing at the foot of the stairs.

She was knuckling her eyes like a small child. She looked very clean and brisk and competent. "God, did I sleep. I must have been exhausted."

Karen said nothing. This Jennifer seemed totally unconnected with the sluttish one who had stood in the studio door.

"Did I hear something about dinner?" Jennifer asked, running her tongue exaggeratedly over his lips. "I'm starved."

"Patrick and Jeff have gone to Wendy's to bring back hamburgers and fries."

"I hope they get doubles." She pushed herself away from the newel post and headed for the kitchen. "I heard you tell Patrick you'd fix some iced tea to go with the burgers. Come on, I'll help you."

In the kitchen Jennifer didn't help; she did it all by herself.

While she mixed the pitcher of instant Nestea, she said, "I'm not going to go to work as soon as I find an apartment."

"Oh?" In spite of herself, Karen was apprehensive. "What are you going to do?"

"Visit Disney World. Everyone at work told me I simply must make a trip there. I *must* see Mickey. And then there's Sea World and Daytona Beach— miles and miles of beach—maybe I'll buy a kite. And I might go over to the Space Center. It sounds sort of way out. Maybe I'll stow away."

Karen chuckled. "You sound like a kid going on vacation."

It was Jennifer's turn to giggle. "I feel like a kid, sis. This whole idea is becoming such a wonderful adventure! But tomorrow, I'll be practical long enough to rent a car and go apartment hunting."

This was the Jennifer Holscomb insisted existed, the Jennifer who was her remembered sister—the fun-lover, the young woman who lived with an edge of perpetual excitement. The woman who was not what she appeared—or appeared to be what she was not. God, it was confusing. Yet, maybe it was confusing only to her. Maybe Patrick, too. No one else —not Jeff, or, until she had told her, Cynthia and, of course, not Don.

The meal almost got by without tension. But Patrick was wary of Jennifer, and Jeff was withdrawn because of the discussion he had had that morning with his mother. Or at least that was what Karen thought; he acted as if he wasn't certain how to behave.

Trying to keep the conversation neutral, Karen asked Jeff, "What are you doing at the clinic now?"

"Starting batting instruction. That's really what I like."

Patrick laughed. "Only the romantic part, eh?"

"Well—no. The other things are important, too. But I like the batting."

"Well, don't let the rest of the instructions slip by. If you can't do them, you'll never get to bat."

"When I get settled," Jennifer said, "I'll come to watch your games."

"We aren't playing games. It's a school."

"I'll come anyway," she laughed.

When dinner was finished and they were sitting at

the table smoking cigarettes, Jeff looking everywhere but at Jennifer, Patrick asked, "Are you really planning to move to Grove Center, Jennifer?"

"I really am, Patrick. I feel so good here, so free. There's none of that sense in the big city."

He nodded and looked at Karen, who was studying her cigarette tip. "What about your apartment in Cleveland?"

"I'll send for my things. It's a furnished apartment; there isn't much."

Karen had the overwhelming urge to get up and throw her arms around the handsome blonde sitting across from her, and cry, "Welcome, sis." But instead she said, "I'll drive you around. I can show you the better areas of town."

Jennifer shook her head. 'Nope. I'm doing this on my own, and on my own I'm doing it all the way."

Karen did not insist, and felt a little ashamed of herself.

Jeff asked, "Can I go with you, Aunt Jennifer?"

"No, but you can be my first visitor."

Patrick gave Karen a quick glance. "Mom, can I be excused? I'm gonna shoot a few baskets before dark." Karen nodded.

"I'll join you," Patrick said, jumping up and following Jeff out. He had avoided Karen's eyes.

Karen and Jennifer washed the dishes and glasses, Jennifer again doing most of the work, saying she had to pay for her keep somehow. When they were finished, she wandered out to the veranda and stood watching Jeff and Patrick dribble and shoot their baskets.

Karen went out and stood beside her. She knew

that Patrick was expecting her to talk to Jennifer, to tell her not to move to Grove Center. But how could she? This Jennifer was the lovely, and beloved, sister she had always been. She shrugged and spoke. "Does that answer how they get along together, sis?"

Jennifer nodded, then said slowly, "Maybe I made a mistake, Kar. Maybe I should have married. When I'm working and doing all the things associated with it, it seems to me it would be terribly stifling; but watching Jeff, I know what I've missed."

"Oh?"

"A child. Bearing children is one of the reasons we women are here, isn't it?"

"Don't ask a women's libber that, Jen."

"Never." She reached over and took Karen's hand.

From the kitchen the sound of the radio gained in volume as a rock band shredded the stillness of the evening. It was a disjointed, orphaned sound, very much like the cry of an unwanted, wounded creature.

Patrick gave the ball a final toss to Jeff. "That's enough for me, tiger. I'm bushed."

"Aw, Patrick, we've got light enough for a few more shots."

"But I don't have the stamina, Jeff."

Jennifer went down to the driveway. "I'll shoot a few with you, Jeff."

"Okay." Then he remembered what his mother had told him, and glanced at her. Karen scowled and turned away.

Patrick came and stood beside her. "What the hell's going on, Kar? That's the woman out there with Jeff who picks up guys in a convenience store."

"What am I going to do, call him away from her?"

"No." He made a helpless movement with his hands. "I guess not."

"Patrick, maybe we're wrong. Have you thought of that? She's so damned normal now, so sweet. And no one else but you and I have misgivings about her."

Cocking his head he looked at her, obviously baffled. "I saw her at the mill, remember? I saw the kid driving the wheels off his VW to get there. I found Sue Ann Miller's clothes buried out there, remember that? We found blood on the stone on which she was lying—just fifty feet from the buried clothes. Do you recall that? Is it a sweet and normal woman who gets herself in situations like that?"

"No! Goddamnit, no!"

She turned and ran into the kitchen.

A few moments later, Patrick came in and stood by her side.

"Sorry," he said. "I was just trying to keep things in perspective."

"I'm sorry too. I flew off the handle too easily."

"Come here."

She smiled and leaned against him. It felt good in an earthy, feline way. His protection right now seemed bigger than life.

Some of what was going through her was transmitted to him, and he moved his arm so it brushed the outside of her right breast. "What are you doing later on tonight?"

"Oh . . . I've nothing definite in mind, but I might be open to suggestions. Do you have any?"

"Mmmm, yes, you might say that I have."

"Like what?"

"Well, we could go out to the Golden Dove for a drink or two and a few stumbling dance steps; or, we could cut out that waste of time and just meet in the bedroom."

"God, you're bold. But that's one of your endearing attributes. It's one of the reasons I've somehow grown to be rather fond of you. I think I'll choose meeting you in the bedroom."

They went back out to the veranda.

Outside, the final light of the day had faded into orange and then mauve beyond the trees on the back of the lawn. For a long moment the haunting color hung in the sky, then a grey veil moved across the heavens, and night was upon the land.

Jennifer and Jeff came to the veranda steps, walking closely as people who share an intimacy sometimes do . . . almost, Karen thought, as if they were wanting to hold hands. Both were sheened with perspiration and breathing faster than normal. Several times their eyes met with that special good humor physical closeness brings, and for a dreadful moment, she saw them as a couple returning from an intensely private affair.

Just before they reached the steps, Jeff said, "You're really terrific, Aunt Jennifer. Can we do it again?"

The wording of the question flustered Karen.

"I don't see why not, Jeff." Jennifer's voice carried an undertone of huskiness.

He looked at her and smiled.

In an attempt to recover her composure, Karen

asked, "Anyone for lemonade?"

Jennifer made a negative motion with her hands. "No, thanks, sis. I'm going to head for the nearest chair and flop! This aging body needs recuperation. You know, it's not as resilent as it was when we used to play hopscotch."

Jeff, it seemed, took his cue from her. "I don't want any either, I'm not thirsty."

"Well, okay." She felt strangely defeated, all out of proportion to the occurrence. "I just thought something tall and cool might be needed."

Patrick said, "Jeff, let's go in and see if we can find a baseball game on TV. There must be one somewhere on one of the channels."

"Maybe forty-four. It's the independent station."

They went into the house. When the door slammed behind them, Karen turned to her sister. "Are you sure you don't want me to drive you tomorrow?"

Jennifer shook her head, "I'm sure, Kar."

"Well, at least you'll let me drive you to the car rental agency, won't you? We have only one here, and it's a little hard to find."

"That I'll allow you to do."

As much as she didn't want to do it, Karen found herself attempting to look through her sister's blue eyes, searching for the other Jennifer. They weren't there. All she saw was an affectionate and self-reliant woman. No indication of a teetering on the brink, no sign of the strange creature existing beyond the borders of society. She felt shoddy and ashamed, and knew she had taken the first steps toward despising herself.

Jennifer walked to the edge of the veranda and

looked out into the night, drawing deep breaths. "God, smell that. It's like living in the Garden of Eden. In Cleveland, if you dare open your window, it's exhaust fumes and factory smells that come in." She turned. "Oh, Kar, I honestly believe I'm approaching the happiest days I've ever known."

"It couldn't happen to a nicer gal, Jen."

When Jennifer turned to face her, there were tiny sparkles of tears in the corners of her eyes. "I love you, Kar."

Karen went to her and put an arm around her waist. "It's going to be good having you near, sis."

Jennifer nodded. "I need a family. I need something more than acquaintances and friends."

"You have a family. Jeff and me—and Patrick."

"I know." She drew a deep breath, and said in a lighter voice, "You know, we're heading for a maudlin discussion here. I think I'm going up to bed."

Karen laughed. "You're right. See you in the morning."

When her sister had gone up the stairs, she stood staring off at nothing. Everything was jumbled. She loved her sister, and she was afraid of her sister. At least she had been fearful of her until these last few minutes. Now she wasn't certain. Blood was certainly thicker than circumstantial evidence—and everything, except, maybe, the stares at Jeff, was just that. Patrick hadn't actually seen Jennifer with the clerk from the Quick Stop. The sun had been hot and the stone warm, so the blood in the crevice could have remained fluid for hours. It might have been by accident that Jennifer had gone in among the trees near where Sue Ann's clothes were buried. She and Patrick were constructing a monster out of an innocent and, it seemed, lonely woman. And standing there, she began to feel ridiculous, like a do-gooder who finds there *is* no great offending evil. The sword of righteousness she carried was rusty.

She laughed with the pure new joy of the moment, and, suddenly feeling girlishly soft, went across the lawn to the jasmine bushes. She picked several blooms and fastened them in her hair above her left ear.

Just as she returned to the veranda, the sound of the television ceased. She heard Jeff and Patrick talking. A moment later Patrick came out the door.

"How did it go?"

"Fine."

"She is definitely going to stay in Grove Center?"

"Yes, and I don't think it will be the horror we thought."

Patrick drew in his breath. He fished in his pockets and brought out a package of Benson & Hedges. He lit two of them and handed her one. "Tell me what you mean."

"I think we've been over-reacting. I think we've been like two new lawyers who have built an entire case on very little circumstantial evidence." She glanced at him and saw bewilderment in his eyes. Resolutely, she continued. "One or two out-of-the-ordinary occurrences took place, and we allowed ourselves to blow them all out of proportion. Couldn't that have happened?"

He nodded. "It's possible."

"Darling, she's so damned normal now, so like the

sister I grew up with that that has to be the explanation. She's very affectionate and self-reliant—you've
seen that tonight. I just can't condemn her yet,
Patrick. Not on a daub of blood and an . . . interlude . . . with a younger man. I'm not sanctioning
the latter, but I'm willing to overlook it. I think she's
a lonely person."

"Perhaps. You do what you want. You know I'll
go along with it."

She refused to hear the remoteness in his voice,
and said, "I know. Thank you. I must try to accept
her. If I don't, I could become an emotional cripple,
dreading what might happen in the future so much
that I miss out on the present. I just want to push
these days way back in my mind where they can get
lost."

He took a deep draw on the cigarette and allowed
the smoke to dribble from his nostrils and mouth.
"If your rationale is right, they will. You know that.
If things go as they seem to be going, in time all the
details will be lost and only a blurred memory will
remain."

"Time the healer."

"Something like that."

"Has Jeff gone to bed?"

"Uh-huh." He ran a hand through his beard.
"The kid has a big feeling for his aunt."

"I know. I hope time will take care of that, too."

"It will."

He hooked a forefinger under her chin and lifted it
so her lips neared his, then kissed her long and hard,
his tongue darting inside her mouth and caressing the
soft warmth there.

She moaned and put her arms around his neck, fighting for breath as delicious quivers ran up and down her belly and thighs.

He pulled his lips away. "I think we should have a small drink in celebration."

She only nodded.

"What do you want?"

"Something soft and gentle."

He gave a guttural chuckle. "The drink, perhaps. But no promises for what comes afterward."

"No . . . not what comes after." She pushed tight against him, seeking to brace herself against the great tugging of the orgastic tides moving through her. "Make me work after the drink. Make me work hard, Patrick."

He kissed her again, his hands roaming over her, then pulled away. "I'll fix you a sherry."

She sat on the veranda steps waiting. The night was warm and sticky and fecund. Time was nonexistent. She became more and more aware of the primitive readiness of her body. She waited docilely for his return, trapped within her aroused womanhood.

When he came back, he sat beside her and handed her a goblet half full of sherry. He had a gin and tonic for himself.

He pointed at the moon just now rising over the tops of the pepper and pine trees. It was a fat crescent, somewhat like a scimitar. "It's too fine a night to spend in a hot bedroom."

"Yes."

"When was the last time we walked by the river and made love?"

"Too long."

He led her by the hand down the narrow path from the rear of the lawn, through an overgrown field, to the black silent waters of the narrow river. It was named the Little Sandy, but people around Grove Center just called it the river. White moonlight lay like milk on the opaque water, and the hyacinth and lily pads were green-touched stains. Cat o'nine tails pushed their slender silhouettes above the water. And over it all hung the silence of the primeval earth, the ancient time from which came the desires driving their two bodies.

A dozen yards or so down the river, he stopped in a small area where the grass was thick and almost knee high. Sweet-smelling shrubbery surrounded them, and a few overhanging branches partially sheltered them from the inquisitive moon.

Very slowly he undressed her, then undressed himself. She stood quietly, unmoving, waiting for him to take her flesh in his big hands and make her cry out in desperate ecstasy. Wanting him to pleasure her in such a way that, in turn, she could please him in ways he had never known.

At last he faced her. He reached out with his right hand to entwine his fingers in the thick auburn curls at the junction of her thighs. Slowly, enscribing curling arabesques on the soft flesh, he moved his hand up her belly, smiling as she shuddered and moaned, and spread his palm over the heavy mound of her left breast. Almost immediately the thick nipple hardened and thrust into his hand. She leaned forward slightly, pushing the flesh against his palm. Her breathing became faster. Then his other hand reached out and took hold of her right breast.

Holding tight to both of them, he pulled her down after him as he lay on his side in the sweet grass. She lay next to him, her arms partially behind her, as he still held tightly to her breasts.

She felt her heart moving into her throat with a wild pulse beat.

Breathing was becoming more and more difficult, her lungs straining for air. She threw her head back in the deep grass and moaned out loud.

He released her breasts, put his arms around her shoulders and pulled her to him. He found her lips and kissed them very hard, shoving his tongue deep into the moist cavity of her mouth. After the first assault, she returned the kiss, eagerness for eagerness, dueling with her tongue with hot desire. And during the kiss his hands roamed over her, exploring the lushness of the firm curves, tantalizing nerve ends with butterfly fingerings.

Then he was rolling her over on top of him, his hands spread on her flanks, his fingers digging slightly into her quivering muscles. He didn't say anything. He didn't have to. She knew what he wanted, and she moaned softly in anticipation.

She straddled him on her hands and knees and arched herself so the heavy mounds of her breasts brushed their thick nipples across his lips. Slowly she rocked forward and backward so her swaying nipples demanded to be caught between his teeth and sucked.

Then his hands moved down her sides and gently lifted her.

"Now," he said.

She pushed herself erect, moving her hips in a rotating motion as she sought his up-thrust manhood. He guided her, playing softly with her as he did.

"Slow," he whispered. "Do it slow and nice."

She nodded, and began. He fondled her jutting breasts and stroked her tautened belly and slapped her flexing buttocks.

"Keep it slow, baby. Keep it nice and slow."

"Yes . . . yes. . . ."

She spread her legs wider, lowering herself, and bent forward over him. She pressed her mouth against his chest, taking little nips at the curls of hair, licking the tang of salt from the sweaty skin.

He grinned and took her nipples between thumbs and forefingers, sending a tingle through her torso. "Just a little faster, honey."

"Like this?"

Sweat was running down her in rivulets, plastering her hair over her face, making her skin slippery and shiny in the misty light.

"Maybe a trifle faster."

She grunted. She was beginning to labor. Muscles and flesh were being taxed. He stroked her knowingly.

She knew she was reaching exhaustion, but there was no memory as to what exhaustion was; there was only desperate flesh crying out for relief.

"Now faster. Faster."

She drove her loins down hard, twisting, pumping, feeling the explosion building up within her.

When it came it was sound and sight and taste, a great flickering waterfall of sensation moving her from dimension to dimension until she lay sprawled on top of Patrick whimpering into his chest, quivering with after-tremors.

He was stroking her back. "You had a great need."

"Yes." She sniffled, and didn't know whether or not to be ashamed of sounding like a young girl. "I had a terrible need."

"You are wonderful, Karen Sommers." His big hands hesitated in their stroking. "I love you very much—very very much."

"Oh, Patrick, I'm going to cry, and I don't want to cry."

"Go ahead, cry. That's one thing I am here for."

She giggled. "You sound so quaint sometimes, so old worldish."

He rolled her off him and cradled her against his shoulder. "It's a magnificent night, Kar. Let's stay here and play at Adam and Eve until the sun comes up. We can make love off and on, nap off and on, and think of only the consequential things—namely you, and Jeff, and me."

She nodded. Suddenly she felt terribly sad.


Jeff hadn't been sleepy when he came up to his room, but he could tell that his mom and Patrick wanted to be alone. He knew what they did when they were by themselves at times like that, and he knew that they knew he knew—but they all pretended something else, and he went along with it. To him it was a kind of an interesting game.

He was lying on his stomach across the bed leafing through a catalogue from an Orlando discount store. Just the other day he and Billy had been talking about buying a walkie-talkie set, going in together on

it. But even at discount prices the sets were pretty
expensive, anywhere from twelve to forty-five
dollars. Maybe they'd have to wait a while. But it
sure would be great to get a set before the summer
was over.

"Can't you sleep either, Jeff?"

He rolled over, surprised, and stared at the
doorway. His Aunt Jennifer was standing just inside
it. She was right on the edge of the light pool from
the high-intensity lamp he was using, and somehow
she seemed only half real, being kind of in and out of
the shadows as she was.

"I haven't tried to go to sleep," he said. "I was
looking through this catalogue."

"Oh." She moved a step towards him. It brought
her more into the light, and he saw she was wearing a
nightgown of some kind that ended just below her
hips—and was almost transparent. "Did you find
what you wanted?"

"Yes." He swallowed. "I guess."

She walked slowly toward the bed. Under the sheer
material of her gown, shadows moved over her
flexing skin like dark caresses. Jeff stared transfixed,
knowing he was seeing what he shouldn't be seeing,
but unable to turn his eyes away from the smooth
belly and swaying hips and quivering breasts. Now he
felt a molten fire at the bottom of his stomach, and
he wanted to jam his fist into himself to stop the
ache. He sat up on the edge of the bed.

She sat down beside him. A pulsing warmth came
from her, along with an elusive smell he couldn't
place, heady like perfume but deeper, too; something
that made him think of a big warm animal.

She looked straight at him, then, her eyes mere slits
and her lips parted and glistening from the tip of her
tongue. "You know, I'm going to get my own
apartment, Jeff."

"Yes."

"I'd like to have you visit me." Her voice dropped
so low he had to strain to hear the words. "I think we
could learn to enjoy one another, Jeff. We could
show each other all kinds of . . . of things."

"What . . . what kinds of things, Aunt Jennifer?"

A tiny smile hovered on her lips. "Have you ever
played show me yours and I'll show you mine with a
girl, Jeff?"

He shook his head. Inside him was confusion.
Astonishment mixed with cold splashes of fear. God,
this was the real thing, not a night-time fantasy. He'd
had them, too. Of Aunt Jennifer. Since she had
arrived and he had found how nice she was, he'd
twice had fantasies about her. In them she had been
almost as naked as she was now. For a fleeting
instant, he tried to remember how he acted when he
imagined scenes like this, but couldn't. Geez, this
was too different. His fantasy never included the
warm fragrance, the mysterious smile, the veiled eyes
which confronted him now. This was real . . . but it
was unreal, too. It was weird.

"Would you want to play it now?" Her voice was
husky and strange. It didn't belong to his Aunt
Jennifer.

He couldn't find is own voice to answer. It was lost
in the sudden tightness of his throat, and that made
him feel silly. Like a damned kid. Through the
gossamer gown, he could see the dark shadows of her

nipples and the dark triangle in her lap. He looked up into her eyes. They were watching him. Inviting him. Oh Christ, what was he to do? After mom had had her say in the kitchen, he'd been very careful to keep Aunt Jennifer out of his thoughts. Now here she was, offering him more intimacy than he had ever dreamed of.

Before he really knew what she was doing, she reached down, caught the hem of her nightgown, and pulled it quickly up over her head, dropping it on the floor beside the bed.

Breasts, belly, hips, legs. Dimpled, provocative flesh filled his whole field of vision. He stared.

She laughed, stood up and faced him, arching her voluptuous nakedness at him.

Still laughing she moved her shoulders so the big round bowls of her breasts quivered and swayed. "Do you want to touch them, Jeff?"

Still he stared.

"Have you ever felt a woman's breasts?"

He shook his head. "No . . ."

She arched herself more, towards him. "Take hold of them, Jeff. Put your hands on them."

He stood up, and slowly, unsure of himself, he reached out and laid both hands on the firm curves. Although he had often lied to Billy, it was the first time he had ever touched a breast. He moved his hands around the plump breasts, squeezing a little with his fingers, until he felt her nipples engorge and push against his palms.

A soft murmuring was coming from her parted lips, and he saw that her belly was starting to move in and out. He watched her face tauten and relax, and stroked her breasts harder. She hissed in her throat.

His heart was pounding so hard he could hear it against his eardrums, and his hands were starting to shake.

"There's more of me, Jeff. You can put your hands other places."

He looked at her. Maybe he could understand better by seeing what was in her eyes, but they were almost closed. He left his hands where they were.

"Do you like how I feel?" Her voice was so low he could barely hear her.

He nodded, not trying to speak. He knew his voice would come out in a squeak if he did.

Then he felt her hands at his waist and moving around to his back, her long slender fingers moving up and down in skin tingling strokes.

"God. . . ."

Her arms wrapped around him and pulled him tight to her.

"We can be good for each other, Jeff."

Suddenly he was terrified. It was all wrong doing this with Aunt Jennifer. She was almost like . . . almost like his mother!

"Oh, geez—Aunt Jennifer . . ." He pulled away from her. "This . . . this isn't right."

She dropped her hands to her sides but made no move to cover herself. She stared at him, first amused, then concerned, and then a little angrily. He stepped back, and bumped against the bed. And as he stared back at her she began to change. She was not his aunt, but another woman, another woman who wasn't exactly a woman, who was something strange. It excited him and repulsed him all at the same time, made him feel childish at the same time it made him want to do to her whatever it was she wanted him to do to her.

She saw is confusion and smiled. "There is nothing to be ashamed of, Jeff. I'm a healthy woman and you're a healthy young man. Because we're related makes no difference when people feel as we do toward one another. We're beyond that, don't you see? Let others worry about control and understanding—let us worry only about obtaining pure enjoyment, each from the other." She reached out and ran her fingers down his cheek. "You do understand, don't you, Jeff?"

He didn't, but he wanted to. He felt himself becoming excited again. He nodded.

He reached forward and touched her breast. She did not move. She stood very straight and still, her golden hair cascading around her face, her slitted blue eyes watching him carefully, and her rich lips quivering on the verge of a smile. On her face was an expression of infinite patience, the teacher leading an exceptional student into a very special realm of knowledge where reverence for life played no part.

He leaned forward to kiss her, to show her he knew how to french kiss.

Downstairs a door slammed. His mother and Patrick came into the kitchen. Their laughter floated up the stairwell, taut and nervous like the laughter when adults drank too much wine and were controlling emotions which wanted to escape, to be free.

Jennifer gasped, pushed his hands away, and stood, swaying, looking down at him with what he at first thought was indifference but then realized was regret.

"Be careful," she whispered. "Do not tell either
your mother or Patrick I was here."

He nodded, thinking that it was a dumb thing for
her to say. In no way would he tell them. She picked
up the nightgown and hurried to the door; then she
was gone. He flopped across the bed, opening the
catalogue once again and leafing hurriedly through it
to the section on electronics.

She lay beside the river looking at the dark water.

The boy would be easy to control and make her
own. And then. . . .

Her tongue flicked in and out.

She moved along the bank in the direction of her
nest.

# CHAPTER 7

Wednesday morning was brilliant, sparkling with the vivid, colors usually seen only on postcards. A breeze, which would soon fade away under the sun's heat, was blowing from the northwest, stirring the air and giving the trees and bushes something to nod and whisper about.

Karen was the first one up. She took her time walking down for the newspaper and returned to the house even more slowly. The morning was beautiful, and she wanted to savor it, minute by minute, bit by bit, for there would never be another one quite like it. It was the first morning of a new beginning. A terrible fury had gone away during the night, and she felt a great relief like a warmth around her heart. The four of them would make a good family . . . a real family.

When she returned to the kitchen, Jennifer was putting the teakettle on and Jeff was setting the breakfast table. From upstairs came the sound of the shower. Patrick would be down soon.

As she was unfolding the paper, she glanced at Jeff. He was watching his aunt. On his face was an odd expression—one, if she didn't know better, of almost sexual longing, though diluted with bewilder-ment. She looked away hurriedly, refusing to give credence to the thought.

"I feel like a big country breakfast," Jennifer said. "Have we got the makings?"

"Only the eggs and bacon."

"Then that's what we'll have." She gave Jeff a pat on his backside as he was bending over the table. "When you finish there, take over the duty at the toaster and fix us each two slices."

"Only one for me," Karen said. A fleeting look of near panic had skipped across Jeff's face.

She was not going to read anything into it! She was not. Only that her sister was a good-looking woman and Jeff was a boy in whom awareness had awakened. That was it, and that was all it was.

Patrick came into the kitchen. His great, tawny bulk seemed to fill the room with safety. Without being aware of it, she moved closer to him.

He looked at the eggs and bacon on the drainboard and the skillet warming on the stove, and said, "Jennifer, if this is your idea, I forbid you to leave here for your own apartment."

"Doesn't my sister feed you?"

"Oh, yes, yes, she does that. But she fears terribly that I might get a two-inch roll around the waist."

Jennifer broke an egg into the frying pan. "Well, when I get my place, Patrick, you'll be welcome to slip over for a good hearty meal."

"How about me, Aunt Jennifer? Could I do the same?"

"I expect you to, Jeff."

"Thanks a whole lot, you two!" Karen laughed.

"It's TV dinners around here for the next week."

Both of them gave the appropriate, expected moans.

When breakfast was over, Patrick helped Karen clean up while Jennifer went to her room to dress. He asked, "Still feel the same about her?"

"Still the same. You weren't so tightened up, either."

"No. It's possible, hon, we were hasty."

"Very possible." She hung the tea towel on its rack. "What are your plans for the day?"

"Oh, work some more on the frames and maybe wander out and do some sketching. I've a couple of ideas in my head; I'd like to try to put them on paper. Nothing definite, just nebulous abstractions right now."

"I guess I'll work on Mr. Frog when I get back from taking sis to the car rental office. Jesus, those boards have become a drag."

"It's a mind occupier."

"I'm ready when you are, Kar." Dressed in a blue dress and white shoes, and carrying a white purse, Jennifer radiated competence, self-assurance, and beauty.

Karen looked down at herself, at the white shirt she wore tied at her waist and the paint-spotted blue jeans. She suddenly felt irredeemably sloppy, and asked, half to herself, "Where has my feminity gone?"

"Nowhere, sis," Jen asnwered her. "You do more for those jeans and that shirt than most women can do for a Gucci original."

"You're a good person to have around, Jennifer

Logan.'' Karen found she meant it, that she didn't
have to pretend the goodwill she felt. ''When you get
your own place, I'm going to insist you come by at
least once a week to work on my ego.''

Jennifer chuckled. ''You might insist that I *don't*
come around so much. Now that I've found what it's
like to have a family, I could make a pest of myself.''

''No way. You're part of that family.
Remember?''

On the way to the rental agency, which was on the
east side of town, Karen said, ''You know, we're not
too bright.''

''Why?''

''Well, for long-range planning, that is. If you had
driven down here, you could have saved yourself the
expense of a car rental.''

''Oh, I don't have a car any more, sis. I sold it
some time back. I've never been much on cars, and it
was so decrepit it would have taken a bundle to fix;
so I sold it to a fellow in the mailroom. He said he
could make it like new. I've been using public trans-
portation and taxis, and I find it isn't so bad.''

''Not here. We have no public bus system, and the
taxi runs whenever the driver wants to answer a call,
which I think is when he needs money for a new
bottle.''

''That's part of the charm of Grove Center.''

''It's not one of the things I'd include in the list.
But—what about tonight? Are you going to spend it
at the house?''

''Oh, yes. Even if I find a place today, I'd be with
you tonight. There'd be all those things that have to
be done to a place before you move in. I'd need at

least a day to do them.''

"If you need help, I'm available.''

"I know. But it's going to be mostly running around—you know, laying in soap, towels, mops. . all those dandy little things that make a house a home.''

When they parked in front of the car rental agency, Karen thought briefly of offering Jeff's services for the moving of furniture or carrying of boxes. But little alarms went off in her mind. She instantly pushed the idea away.

Once Jennifer was dropped off, Karen found that there was a remoteness about the remainder of the day.

She came home, went up to the studio, and worked on the illustrations—disliking them more and more with each brush stroke. She had to fight the impulse to slap paint wildly from one corner of the illustration board to the other in order just to finish them.That she was turning the completion of them into such a problem was as infuriating to her as the abhorrence she'd built up for the subject matter.

Outside, Patrick loaded the back of the station wagon with the paintings he was going to take to the Palm Beach art show the following day.

Halfway through his task, he came up to the studio. "Kar, why don't you and Jeff come with me tomorrow? We could have ourselves a three-day holiday.''

She jabbed a forefinger at the illustration taped to the drawing table. "That's why. That damn dumb frog.''

"Well, you're ahead of schedule—''

"No. Don't tempt me. I'm ahead of schedule, true, but I'm going to need all the minutes I can cram into it, because it's going slow."

He pulled a package of cigarettes from his shirt pocket, held it up, and when she nodded lit one for each of them.

"You given any more thought to becoming just a fine artist?" he asked, looking out the window.

"Yes. And then I give thought to the supermarket, Florida Power and Light, gasoline, and those odd little outlays like clothing and dry cleaning and Jeff's allowance."

He turned from the window and dropped his eyes to hers. "You don't have to be so independent, you know. You can let me help with the expenses. I'm using up my share of some of the bills you mentioned, you know." He sighed and took a deep draw on his cigarette. "But that would be a threat, wouldn't it, to personal liberty and self-reliance?"

"What do you mean by that?"

He knelt down beside her, cupped her chin with his left hand, and said very slowly and very solemnly, "It means, by God, Karen Sommers, that I want to marry you."

"Oh, Patrick . . . Patrick?" She felt very sweet and tender towards this big man. "You really want to make an honest woman of me?"

"A fine artist. One who has the talent and the guts to turn out wonderful work, and can do it if she has the time."

She kissed his wrist and smiled up at him. "You mean it's all altruisitic, then?"

He scratched her gently under her chin with the tip

of his forefinger. "No, not all."

"What else?"

"Sex!"

They both laughed.

He dropped the hand from under her chin and took hold of one of hers. "Well, Kar? Do you have an answer?"

He seemed so hesitant she felt a sudden tenderness towards him. "You know I do."

He leaned a little forward. "So?"

A thin mist formed over her eyes and something very thick filled her throat. She couldn't trust her voice, so she nodded.

"What does that mean?" he asked.

She wanted to laugh and she wanted to cry, but this was not the time for either. "It means yes, you big lummox. Damn it—it means yes!"

A few moments later, when they pulled back from their embrace he asked, "When?"

"As much as I don't want to be, we do have to be practical. Weddings have all kinds of little side effects. Like moving in together. Like telling Jeff. Like changing the name on the Florida Power and Light bill. . . ."

"For God's sake, don't become that practical."

She smiled, but said, "There is one thing we've got to think about seriously . . . probably the most important."

"What's that?"

"Jeff."

"Oh." He sat back on his heels and looked away. "Do you think that's a problem, Kar?"

"No, not really, but it's something we've got to

consider. There's no doubt in my mind he loves you, darling; but when we get married you'll—well—you'll suddenly be replacing Jason in the father role. It could be some kind of a shock for him—I don't know."

He looked back at her. "We get along great."

"I know. But there'll be differences. Discipline, for one. When you become his stepfather, you'll have to give orders. Can you do it, Patrick? Can Jeff accept them?"

"Yes, I think so. Jeff and I respect each other. I wouldn't be bossy, and I'm certain Jeff wouldn't take advantage of me." He took one of her hands in his. "Besides, darling, I'm not trying to replace Jason. I couldn't, and I wouldn't try."

She reached out and ran her free hand through his hair. "That's all true, but let's not tell him yet. Why not wait until you come back from the show? Maybe the vacation trip will be a good time to do it."

"Let's not make a problem out of it, Kar. But if you think it best to wait, then that's what we'll do."

In mid-afternoon, Jennifer drove up the driveway in a grey, hatch-backed Pinto.

"I found a place!" She ran up the stairs to the studio. "I've got the cutest little apartment on Seminole Street—way out near the edge of town."

"When's the housewarming?" Patrick asked.

"Give me a day or two, for heaven's sakes. I haven't even moved in yet. But it will be great for a party. It has a little patio and high redwood fences and access to a pool. God, I'm in love with it, and I haven't spent a night there." She spun around. "Oh,

I love, love, love Grove Center!''

"That's a good address out there," Karen said. "You were lucky to get in an apartment in that area."

"I *was* lucky. It was the first place the agent took me, and I didn't want to go any farther.'' She gave a big, shoulder-raising sigh and looked from one to the other. "So—I'm now a resident of Grove Center."

"Before long, you'll be an inhabitant," Karen said.

"And never to leave. Oh, I'll have to wire my bank tomorrow, because it took almost all of my traveler's checks to make the down payment.'' She laughed, a good big laugh that filled the studio with its happiness. "But now, if you'll excuse me, I'm a little bushed and think I'll take a shower an lie down for a while. But call me for dinner. Jesus, a person can work up an appetite in this clean air.''

Around five o'clock the phone rang. Karen was preparing to take a shower, and Patrick had gone out to the shed to patch a canvas chair he was planning to take with him the next day. Jeff answered. In a moment, he called, "Mom, Mrs. Porter is on the phone."

Cynthia's telephone openings were usually direct and without preamble, and this one was no exception. "Karen, what are you and Patrick doing tonight?"

"Nothing. Why?"

"How about going on an old-fashioned double date?"

"Like where and doing what?"

"Drinking and dancing at the Golden Horn."

"Is there a special occasion?"

Cynthia laughed. "For a couple of stay-at-homes like Don and me, I guess you'd think there was something special, but there really isn't. We were just sitting here and decided we'd like to go out tonight. Want to have a fling at it?"

"I should say no, because I'm bushed and Patrick has to get up at down in the morning to go to Palm Beach. But maybe I have a death wish and want to keel over with exhaustion; so I'm going to say, yes. Can we bring Jeff over to your place? Jen's tired; she ought to have the house to herself."

"That was going to be my suggestion."

"Good. We've got a deal."

Karen was humming as she headed for the shower.

The Golden Horn was a hybrid. It had aspirations of being a cocktail lounge, with high-backed plastic booths, candles struggling for air in glass balls, and soft lighting fanning out across a star-speckled ceiling. The ceiling lighting caught the cigarette smoke drifting upwards so the ceiling appeared to be floating behind shifting clouds. But the place was in danger of actually being a road house. Somewhere there was a line of demarcation between a lounge built beside a highway and a road house—the clients, the tone of the music, the splits in the imitation leather on the barstools and in the booths. The lounge managed to retain a quiet mystery. The road house was blatant and open. The Golden Horn was a little of both.

The duo, an organ with synthensizer and electric piano keyboard and guitar, wasn't too certain whether it was an easy listening combination, a rock-and-roll twosome or a country-western duo. Like the club itself, the duo compromised and was a little bit of them all.

Both Cynthia and Don were surprised to learn that Jennifer had rented an apartment.

"Cynthia told me of her strangeness," Don said. "It's damn difficult for me to believe."

"Believe it." Patrick took a long swallow of his gin and tonic.

"Patrick! We are not going to discuss it. You hear?" Karen gave him a sharp stare. She did not want to continue on the subject. There was still something very personal about Jennifer's oddness—or lack of it—which she thought of as a family concern. Yet, these people were her family; no one was any closer than Patrick. And Cynthia, God knew, was more of a sister than Jennifer. So she said, "I think it's one of those things which happen now and then and even get written about in little esoteric quarterly magazines—but which never seem very real."

Cynthia said, "Oh, Kar, I hope you're right."

Don drew a long breath, hesitated, then asked, "Could she be a schizophrenic?"

"No!" Karen shook her head emphatically. "What we thought we saw in Jennifer was only our own imagination. Very odd things occurred around her, and we associated her with them. Guilt by association, if you will."

Patrick nodded. "What Kar says is true. We were hasty."

"Do you think she'll find her own circle of friends?" Cynthia asked.

Karen looked at Patrick who returned her stare for a moment, then looked away.

"I don't know," she said. "I've wondered."

"Let's just say she's going," Patrick frowned.

Cynthia looked from one to the other. "It seems like a loose end is dangling somewhere."

Karen shifted uncomfortably. "Come on, Cynthia. Let's talk about something else, shall we?"

The subject was dropped after that.

But what Cynthia had said was all too true, Karen knew. She sipped her drink. She had an uneasy feeling she and Patrick were hiding, hoping a problem would disappear instead of dealing with it. Something seemed to be wrong, out of balance. And she was ignoring the signals.

The evening wound itself through drinks and dances and laughs, but to Karen there were moments when all were heavy and dreamlike, and the four of them were traveling a predetermined path to something strangely menacing.

Eventually, however, the combo switched to vehement rock music. It got inside her mind and jumbled itself with the thoughts she was trying to keep organized. But she found the confusion helped. The fuzziness it created was like an insulation between her and the uncertainty life had become. Reality moved far back into the smoke-blurred club, receding far enough away that objectivity became a counterfeit point of view. She wanted to forget meaning, to forget everything which was definite and probable.

When the waitress came by their table, she ordered another strawberry daquiri.

"You don't need that, Kar," Patrick said sharply. "You've had enough. Those aren't strawberry milk shakes."

She said to the waitress, "Bring it, please."

"Are you sure you want it?" Cynthia asked.

"I'm certain."

Their concern for her was touching, but she didn't want them to be so conspicuous with it. There were things they just didn't understand, deep things which were shimmering slowly inside her, and which would forever be there burning at her insides and gnawing at her mind. So, what the hell. Let them be concerned. Let them watch her. That was all right. She was the one who had lost a sister. . . . So let 'em watch.

Debbie Margolis slumped in the La-Z-Boy chair watching a prime-time soap opera on Orlando's Channel Six. Actually she didn't care much for the program, but most of her friends, and a lot of adults, too, talked so much about it that she sometimes thought something was wrong with her tastes. Usually when she watched the unfolding drama, at the end of the hour she felt she'd wasted perfectly good time. She felt cheated.

Tonight was no different. Since the show was in its summer reruns, she had reasoned it would probably be even duller than it must have been the first time around. But Billy Porter wanted to see this particular episode because one of the many wives, who she found impossible to keep separated in her mind, was going to do some really wicked act.

Halfway through the show she grew bored, went to

the kitchen, and got a Pepsi from the refrigerator. She checked on the baby, who was sleeping peacefully. Billy was sitting on the floor watching the TV and Jeff on the sofa was leafing through a *National Geographic*. She went out through the front door.

There was no porch as such on the front of the Porter house, but a stoop between two full-grown croton plants offered three concrete steps to sit on. She sat on the top one sucking at the Pepsi and looking up and down the subdivision street. More darkness lay along the street then had been planned by the developers, because the town had cut back its power five years ago. Now only every other street light held back the night, and the darkness seemed thick and deep around them.

The door opened behind her, and Jeff came out. She moved over to one side to allow him to pass, thinking he was going to go down into the front yard; but instead of going down the steps, he sat beside her. "That show bores me."

"Me, too." She smiled. "Do you watch much TV?"

"Not too much. Mostly the Atlanta Braves."

"My boyfriend watches them."

Neither spoke for a moment. Far away a dog barked, but to Debbie it sounded more like a yelp. For some reason, the sound touched her wrong, and she shivered.

Jeff looked at her. "Are you cold?"

"No."

"You shivered."

"The bark of that dog . . . it sounded strange to me."

"I guess I wasn't listening." He stood up. "Did mom tell you when they were coming to get me?"

"Around twelve-thirty or one." She stood up, too. "Why don't we walk down to the corner and back? Billy's all taken up with the show and won't miss us. And the baby's okay."

"Okay."

They walked side by side down the short flagstone path to the sidewalk. Again, somewhere off to the north, the dog repeated its barking yelp.

Jeff looked in that direction and then at Debbie. "I heard it that time. It is kinda spooky, at that."

She nodded.

"How old are you?"

She looked at him in surprise, then smiled. "Don't you know you're not supposed to ask women their age?"

"Oh—yeah. I'm sorry. I just thought you looked maybe old enough to go to college, and I was going to ask if you did."

"Well, I'll tell you this time. I'm nineteen, and I'll be going to the University of Florida this fall."

"That's in Gainesville?"

"Yes."

"Patrick taught a class in watercolor there last fall for six weeks."

"He's a good artist, isn't he?"

"Yeah. So's my mother."

"That's what I've heard."

"What are you going to study?"

"Education. I want to be a teacher."

"Oh."

"It doesn't sound as if you approve."

He shrugged. "We need teachers, I guess."

She laughed an impulsively took his hand and squeezed it. She liked im. He didn't seem clumsy and inept like so many boys his age, and he wasn't afraid to make conversation.

They walked slowly, moving through a pocket of stickiness where falling dew seemed to be heavier than elsewhere along the road. The darkness seemed to curl around them like a being, gently stroking at their arms and legs and cheeks. Something not quite seen gave the impression of lurking ahead of them on the far side of the next wan pool of yellow light. Debbie stopped.

"I think we should go back to the house." Under the perspiration on her forehead and arms, her skin felt cold and clammy.

Jeff nodded. He looked at the pale street light, and squinted to see through its haze into the darkness on the other side. His heart beat faster.

She took his hand.

He gave a nervous little laugh.

"What's wrong?"

"I was just wondering what my mom would say if she saw us holding hands."

"Why? Is she against holding hands?"

"No. Not until Aunt Jennifer came, anyway."

"I don't understand."

"Well, she came to visit us several days ago from Cleveland. She was supposed to stay a couple of weeks, I think; but this morning she went out and rented an apartment for herself."

"She's going to live here?"

"Yeah."

"Why did your mother make you stop holding hands?"

"Oh, she didn't do that. I think mom thought Aunt Jennifer was too friendly with me."

"Too friendly? You mean. . . ."

"Sex, I guess."

"Oh." Debbie dropped his hand.

They turned back up the path to the stoop. From out of the corner of her eye she saw a shadow move among the tightly woven branches in the hedge beside the front lawn. She turned her head quickly and looked full at the place where the dark movement had occurred. She wasn't certain, she knew she never would be, but for one very short instant, she thought she was staring directly into two red glowing eyes. They were staring at her. She gave a cry.

"What is it?" Jeff asked.

She shook her head. "Let's get into the house."

"Did you see something, or hear something?"

"Jeff, let's just get into the house. Now, move along!"

"Okay." He sensed the sudden fear in her, and remembered the movement—or whatever it was—on the other side of the street light. He hurried for the door.

On the stoop, Debbie turned and looked back at the hedge. Whatever had been there was gone now. But as she turned to go in, she heard a low sibilant sound coming from the direction of the hedge.

The girl had seen her. The lamia narrowed her eyes and watched the door. It remained closed.

From far away the dog barked again.

She continued to watch the door. There was no hurry for her to leave. The woman body was safe. She coiled herself tighter under the hedge.

The girl who had been with the boy was healthy. When the hunger returned. . . . In a day or so. . . .

But the boy . . . he promised the great satisfaction. . . .

# CHAPTER 8

Thursday's dawn was still an hour away when Karen set a plate of eggs and bacon and instant grits in front of Patrick. Sitting hunched down within himself, he had already drunk a cup of black coffee while following her movements around the kitchen with eyes becoming brighter at each sip. His beard was curling with dampness from the shower he'd taken, and beads of moisture glinted like tiny gold pinpoints in his hair under the ceiling light.

She poured herself a cup of coffee and sat down.

"Aren't you going to have anything to eat?" he asked.

"No. You know I can't face food the first thing in the morning."

He grunted. Then, "Where's Jennifer? Still in bed?"

"Oh, God, no. She's gone to put her apartment in order."

"*Now?* In the middle of the night?"

There were things she wanted to say, but there was a great lassitude in her. So she merely said, "I guess she's excited."

He looked at the forkful of grits he held a little

above the plate. "It takes a lot of excitement to get up at this hour to clean an apartment."

"We know she's different."

He only grunted.

She studied him over the rim of her cup as she took the first sip of coffee. He looked so strong and satisfied and composed. The worry lines that had etched themselves into his skin the morning he had seen Jennifer at the mill ruins were smoothing out now. As the coffee burned its way down her throat and into her stomach, she felt tears fill her eyes. Then, as she blinked them away, she realize they weren't tears of pain. They were a part of her love for him, a love too great for her to control.

She set the cup down. "How long are you going to be gone?"

"Too long."

"No. Seriously."

"Well, three days at the art show. Then, I imagine, it will be another two days in Miami talking over the Bronze Hue posters with Lucas Sampson. Five days, maybe six counting traveling time."

She didn't try to make herself smile. It would have been a grimace if she had, and new tears would have come so easily. "That is too long, isn't it?"

He placed his elbows on the table and leaned towards her. "Why don't you and Jeff come with me, Kar? It would be a vacation for all of us—and I think you'll admit we all could use one. Jeff would have a ball. Come on! Throw a few things in a suitcase, and I'll phone the motel."

A sudden exultant mood struck her, the happy carefree mood of a young girl. "It sounds wonderful."

"You'll do it?" She heard some of the excitement she felt duplicated in his voice. He started to get up. "I'll phone the motel and tell them."

"No!" She shook her head slowly. "I can't. I have those damn frogs to finish."

"Oh—" He looked around the kitchen as if hoping to see a word or phrase floating above their heads. Nothing was there. "Oh, shit!"

"At least," she said, "you're not leaving us with the horror we had a few days ago."

"I wouldn't have done that."

"Oh, I know. That's not what I meant. What I mean is, everything here is fine and under control now. Jeff and I will get ourselves together, so when you get back we'll be ready to take a vacation—if you'll still be wanting to."

"That I will be, love." He looked at her, and she felt the blood in her cheeks warm into a flush. "I don't want to go," he said, deep in his throat.

They sat looking at one another. He reached across the table and took her hand. A heat passed from his fingers into hers. The silence around them in the kitchen became a web of protection against intrusions from the outer world.

He leaned across the table and kissed her.

"Can I come in?"

Jeff was standing in the door from the hallway. His hair was tousled, hanging down his forehead, and his eyes were heavy and puffy. A white T-shirt hung outside a pair of blue denim shorts. His feet were bare.

"You sure can, tiger." Patrick raised his left arm and beckoned. "Come here."

Jeff shuffled to his side, and Patrick encircled his

shoulders with the outstretched arm. Jeff looked at
Patrick. "Were you going to go without saying
goodbye to me?"

"No! You should know better than that." He gave
the shoulders a hug. "We just thought you ought to
get some more sleep."

"I'm okay."

Karen asked, "Do you want juice, or something?"

Jeff shook his head. "No, not yet."

"We were talking about taking a vacation when I
get back from the show and Miami. How does that
sound to you?"

For the first time, Jeff's face showed animation.
"That sounds terrific! Where would we go?"

"Well, that's for you and your mother to decide.
While I'm gone, you two talk it over, and we'll go
wherever you agree on. Okay?"

"Yeah."

After Patrick had gone, the back of his station
wagon crammed with framed and unframed
canvases, camp stools and knocked-down exhibit
stands, the remainder of the day became empty for
her. She felt herself relaxing both in mind and body,
as if all her brain had turned itself off and the
muscles all over her body had become flaccid. She
supposed she was like a machine which had been used
too long and too hard, waiting to be rejuvenated
under the hands of a master mechanic. She couldn't
help wondering how long it would take the delicate
mechanism of her mind to recover from the ugliness
and perversion through which she had passed. Scars
would remain. That she knew and accepted.

But all the hideous things which had become a part

of their lives for the past days were no longer making themselves felt. She knew it was only natural to have this sensation of fatigue. A dreadful phase of her life was ended, and she had ended a neutral period. A time untenanted. New events were waiting to be born and new life patterns to be formed.

After doing some shopping, Karen spent the afternoon in the studio. She found herself surprisingly interested in the illustrations and worked until dusk filled the room with shadow pools. When she had cleaned her brushes and dropped them in the coffee can, she sat staring out the window watching the twilight swallow the lawn. No fear came with it tonight. Even with careful scrutiny, there were no areas darker than the shrubbery moving stealthily across the lawn. The jasmine was sweet on the light air, and not the dead stench of dying funeral flowers.

Jennifer came in after supper, showered and sprawled on the sofa in the living room. "I think I'm on top of it. The place is ready to be seen."

Karen laid her book aside. "Tomorrow?"

Jennifer frowned. "Can we wait a couple of days, Kar? I have the place fixed up to be livable, but—well, before I go public with it, I want to fancy it up. And, I was thinking I'd like to wait until Patrick gets back and have one big blowout for you. Does that sound weird?"

It did, but Karen discovered she really did not care. If there was a why, she would forget it. If there was scar tissue in her mind where the terror had gouged it, she would let it heal slowly. And if the healing process called for accepting Jennifer, but not becoming too entangled with her, she would allow it to heal itself in its own way.

She said, "Not weird, but different. Let's do it that way. Where are you going to spend the night? Here or there?"

"Here, I guess. The place is ready to be seen, but not lived in. The water won't be turned on until tomorrow."

"What have you been doing about cleaning and mopping?"

"Imposing on the manager." She smiled. "He's an old dear."

After Jennifer left the following day, Karen's routine became what had once been normal. She phoned Joseph Waingard to tell him she'd have the illustrations completed within the week. Jeff went to a pickup baseball game and came home with a skinned knee from a slide into second base. A phone call came from Patrick in the evening. He had sold all but six paintings and accepted two commissions. Her memories of amber-hued eyes, sensuous stares at Jeff, vague movements through darkness, were fading. So quickly she thought, the mind can cleanse itself.

Sunday came. She didn't set her alarm; on Sundays when Patrick was not here she arose when she wanted to. It was the same with Jeff. Sometimes he was up and wandering the house and yard when she came down to prepare breakfast; on other Sundays it was she who waited.

Today it was Jeff who was up first. He was sitting at the table when she came into the kitchen, the comics spread around him and a half-full glass of orange juice at his elbow.

"Sorry to keep you waiting," she said.

"That's okay."

She filled the teakettle with water. When she set it on the stove and turned the burner to high, she asked, "What do you want to eat?"

"Oh, I don't know. Do you have any of those frozen waffles?"

"About a half a package. That sounds good. We can each have a couple. Do you want anything with them—an egg, bacon?"

"No. Just butter and syrup."

She got the waffles from the freezer, took two from the package and dropped them into the slots in the top of the toaster. Jeff gathered the paper together and stacked it neatly on one corner of the table.

When butter and syrup were out, and hot waffles on their plates Karen sat down and reached for the paper. She glanced at a couple of headlines, but refused to allow herself to read the articles. Too many times she'd scolded Jeff for reading during meals, telling him it was boorish, that meal times were for the exchange of ideas and news. As she took a sip of coffee, she thought how damn difficult it was to practice what you preached.

"You do anything interesting while your mother was sleeping the morning away?"

He shook his head and swallowed a mouthful of waffle. "Not much."

"Well, what?"

"Oh . . . I went down to the river and walked along it."

"Down to the river? Why in the world?"

"I don't know." He looked down at his plate, frowning. "I really don't know. I just . . . wanted to walk along the river."

Suddenly she had a dry metallic taste in her mouth. She forced herself to take a slow sip of coffee. "What did you do down there?"

"Nothing, mom!" His face stiffened and, for a fleeting instant, he looked angry. "Why are you asking me all these questions?"

"Because I'm interested in what you do."

"I'm fifteen, mom. I can handle myself."

"I'm not saying you can't. But it seems you're being secretive."

"Oh, mom!" He gave an exaggerated sigh. "I've told you what I was doing. Nothing."

She sat back in her chair and suppressed the impulse to yell at him. "Do you think I'm being nosey?"

It was a moment before he answered. "No. I guess not."

"You're not certain?"

"Yes, I *am* certain. Geez! I wouldn't have told you if I knew it was going to cause all this."

She looked away from him, suddenly feeling guilty. She was, she knew, being illogical. "I'm sorry, Jeff. You know I trust you. It seems I'm feeling overprotective this morning."

He said nothing while he took a bite of waffle and chewed it slowly. Then he finished his orange juice. When he set the empty glass on the table, he said, "I'm sorry, too, mom. But can I ask you a question?"

"Certainly."

"You've been very uptight lately. What's wrong?"

She couldn't answer him, because she didn't know. Something was ebbing and flowing in her, threatening to shred her nerves at one instant and making her feel foolish the next.

He looked at her while licking syrup from his lower lip. Suddenly Karen thought of Jennifer running her tongue around her lips.

"That's okay," he said, grudgingly. Then, like a person obliged to make a statement against his will, he added, "I'm really telling you the truth."

"Of course you are. I know that! Let's forget it, what do you say?"

He nodded as if in agreement, then said, "I kinda wish Aunt Jennifer hadn't moved out."

"Jeff, when she decided to stay in Grove Center, she needed her own house. She's going to make new friends and live her own life, and we'd be in her way; and, believe it or not, she'd be in our way if she stayed here. It's just as simple as that."

Jeff's face was closed; expressionless.

"Maybe." He stood up. "Can I be excused?"

"It looks as if you've already excused yourself."

"Can I *leave*?"

"Yes. Go ahead."

He left the kitchen with a slowness that seemed insolent. The coffee tasted cold and bitter. The remains of the waffles were sodden, stuck to the plate by the sticky goo which had been syrup. She had lost control of something vital, and there was a chance, a terrible chance, she would never regain it. Some of her motherhood was gone. In the final moments of their conversation, Jeff had warned her.

She heard the outside door slam and looked out of the window. Jeff had gotten on his bicycle and was riding down the driveway. Watching him disappear, she felt he was riding away from her in more ways than one. . . .

She stacked the dishes, scanned words in the newspaper which did not relate to one another in stories making no sense, and walked out into the garden, noting that the grass was still unmowed and some of the shrubbery needed trimming within a few days. Up in the studio she stood staring at the illustration taped to the drawing table, hating it, wondering if it was a waste of time and talent to spend her life involved in such garbage.

The day seemed to be taking on a life of its own. In spite of the sunshine and warmth, it had developed a secret personality, a bleakness like the inside fear a person suffers when the face shows no emotions. It was having its effect on her, turning her more inward on herself. Once, when she was walking down the upstairs hallway, she looked through the open door into the room in which Jennifer had slept. She wondered why her sister hadn't phoned, but gave it no prolonged thought. Even though they were now living near each other, they were again living their separate lives. And she was pleased. The delicious days of their childhood were long past.

Outside in the driveway a horn honked, blaring through the silence of the house and the emptiness of her emotions. At first she thought of ignoring it, of letting whoever was out there go away, but it blared again, and this time it found the hidden places where her nerves were not yet healed and strummed them like overtautened wires.

She went to the window.

Cynthia was leaning out of the driver's window of her old Datsun. "Hey! They're having a big sale at Penny's. Come on, let's rummage!"

She did not want to go shopping; yet the activity might provide a counterbalance to the grim mood descending on her. At least she could hope it would. So she called down, "Hold on just a minute, Cyn. Let me throw on a face."

Cynthia was a dangerous driver. Rules and reguations held no meaning to her. She did not ignore them intentionally. They just didn't exist when she was behind the wheel, not compared to her much more important conversations. She got them to the Grove Center Plaza after running only one stop sign, a feat which Karen considered remarkable.

"If you're not going to shop, Kar, what are you going to do?" she asked as they got out of the car.

"Browse. I really don't need anything. What I needed was to get away from the house."

"Well, I'm glad I came along when I did."

"You always come when I need someone, Cyn. Thanks."

Cynthia looked at her, then away, trying to hide the embarrassment she felt. "I'm a friend, Kar."

While Cynthia went to Penny's to pick up the jeans she wanted for both Don and Billy, Karen wandered aimlessly through the shops, drifting with the casual herd of shoppers. She kept her mind blank, not allowing it to think of anything but the merchandise her eyes wandered over, transforming all the glitter and sparkle into a cushion on which the workings of her mind could rest. That way everything would remain in proper alignment.

Once a bouncing mass of golden hair made her think she saw Jennifer, but it disappeared into a store, and when she arrived at the entrance she had no desire to enter.

Ten minutes before she was to meet Cynthia, she went into the appointed coffee shop and took a booth far to the back of the narrow room. Cynthia would find her. A pert little girl with a blank face took her order for iced tea, and she settled back to wait.

Sipping the tea, she felt herself moving away from what had become comfortable confidence. The familiar apprehension was closing in on her, enveloping her in its coccoon of isolation.

"Hey, come back, come back from wherever you are!"

Cynthia was sliding into the opposite side of the booth.

Karen set her glass down. "Back so soon?"

"So soon? Gawd, gal, I'm ten minutes late." The girl took her order for hot tea. "Where were you when I sat down? One million, two million miles away? You certainly had a faraway look in your eyes."

"No, I was here." She looked at the bundles beside Cynthia. "You outdid yourself."

"I've no control. I'm compulsive and impulsive."

Karen smiled. With Cynthia in the booth across from her, the apprehension moved away, withdrawing ever so slightly so that the world of light seeped through her isolation.

Cynthia's tea came and she took a sip, made a face and poured a teaspoon of sugar into it. "I saw Jennifer."

"Yes. I thought I did, too."

"She wasn't friendly. She didn't ignore me, but I wish she had, because the way she looked at me sent chills up and down my back." She looked down into her teacup. "Kar, her eyes were venonmous. I guess they frightened me a little."

"Oh God! She's come back."

"What do you mean? She never left."

"The other one. The other Jennifer."

"Oh Christ, it wasn't imagination then?" Karen nodded slowly. "It wasn't hasty decisions. She's everything you told me about at lunch the other day, isn't she?"

"I . . . I think so."

"What are you going to do?"

"I don't know. Take me home, please. I want to make sure about Jeff."

He wasn't there when they arrived. Cynthia stayed for a few minutes, but Karen finally insisted that she leave.

Suddenly she felt terribly tired. There was no pattern to it, not a muscle ache here or flesh pain there. It was a complete exhaustion, draining her of energy until it felt as though she might crumble in on herself.

Around her the walls of the old house loomed in eerie silence. It was the oppressive silence behind which secrets hide, a heavy stillness which squeezed in on her, pressing against her like something

physical. Now and then a dry timber groaned somewhere in the old structure, sounding like a moan
coming from a distant place. It touched her nerves,
tingling them so her flesh crawled. As much as she
tried to convince herself it was a product of her
imagination, she could not help feeling evil had
moved through the house—and some still lingered.

Forty-five minutes later, as she was sitting on the
veranda, Jeff came riding back up the driveway. He
looked at her but kept slowly pedaling his bicycle
towards the garage. Then he stopped, as if with
second thoughts, got off, and walked over to the foot
of the steps.

"I'm sorry," he said. "I shouldn't have done
that."

"No, you shouldn't have done that, Jeff." There
was so much more she knew she should say, but she
also knew that perhaps it would be better left unsaid
for the present. "Put your bike away and go wash
up."

For a moment he stood looking at her question-
ingly, then turned and walked away. Another
mistake had just been made, she knew. A little of his
respect for her had just vanished.

Patrick didn't phone that evening. She wanted him
to. Oh God, she wanted him to! She hadn't been this
lonely since the days immediately after Jason's
death. She would have called him, but he had been
planning to go on down to Miami that afternoon, to
spend the night there before meeting with his client
tomorrow. She didn't know where he was staying.

The evening meal was skimpy, both in food and
conversation. She had hoped it would be different, a

time when they approached each other on common ground. Right now, she knew, a pit was being dug between them which, if permitted to become too wide and too deep, would never be crossed. If that occurred, destruction awaited them.

"How's the batting coming? You raising your average any?" she asked.

"It's okay."

"Is it being raised?"

"Yeah. I'm one hundred and eighty."

"Well, now. That's not too bad. Is it?"

"It could be better."

"Most everything can be better."

"I guess."

She felt a tiny touch of fear. She wasn't reaching him. It disgusted her, because she knew she should have solutions, should have some kind of a positive action planned.

She tried again. "Is the big game going to be with Apopka this year?"

"I suppose so. It usually is."

"When? Patrick and I will want to go and watch you play."

"I don't know. They haven't set a date yet."

There was nother silence. She cut one of the hot dogs lying on her plate into eight tiny segments. It was something to do. Jeff folded one of his in a slice of bread and smeared mustard on it. She noticed he didn't take a big bite as he usually did, but only a nibble.

Once more she sought to find an opening. "You haven't been doing much work recently on your boat model. How come? Need more material?"

"No. I've been busy."

"You have that."

"It's worth it, isn't it? The clinic's helping me with my ball game."

"Yes, it is."

"Like, you know, if I can get good enough, I'll make the school team and maybe win a scholarship."

"We could use that."

He grunted.

"By the way," she tried to keep her voice jocular, "do you think you could find time to mow the lawn? It's getting hip-high to a six-foot Indian."

He nodded. "Is there gas in the mower?"

"I think so. I think Patrick put some in."

"Okay."

It ended there. The meal finished in silence. And she blamed herself. Too much room had been left for worry over a future which might or might not materialize. God, there were so many conflicting elements within her now.

When they went to bed, their good-night kiss was short, but she thought she noted an easing of the tension in him. Today was behind them. Tomorrow it would simply be a bit of history. Normalcy would be waiting for them at the breakfast table.

At first she wasn't certain what had awakened her. Then there was a great splash of light sizzling through the air outside the house and bathing the room in an orange-green fire as it reached in through the open window. Sound crashed into the earth just beyond the row of pepper trees and rolled along the ground with a booming roar. Faraway there were other flashes of light ripping at the black bowels of the night sky and more rumblings of things falling and tumbling across the heavens. A summer thunderstorm was roaming across the land.

She sat up in bed, her breath short, her skin prickly. Outside the window rain hissed in a wet monotone of sound.

She slipped off the bed and went to the open window. A spray of rain was coming in, dampening the sill. The curtains were blowing into the room like ghostly forms trying to escape from the storm. She closed the window and shivered, the rain mist cold on her warm flesh.

Another explosion of lightning: the trees and shrubs and the shed stood out in brilliant bas-relief, their details lost in flat white light and opaque shadows. She blinked and stepped back, quivering. A vast domain of sound, building upon itself with monstrous vehemency, shook the earth and rattled the house.

"Mom!"

She quickly took her housecoat from the chair by the bed and slipped into it.

Out in the hallway she saw the door to his room was open.

"Mom! Come here!"

The call came from downstairs. Now, for the first time, she was aware there was no alarm or anxiety in his voice, so the first pangs of fear lessened and the tightness pressing against her chest eased. Still she descended the stairs too fast and stubbed her big toe.

Jeff was coming from the living room, dressed in white undershorts. He saw her and looked sheepish.

"What's wrong?" she asked.

"Nothing." He looked around the foyer and then

down at his feet. "I came down to close the windows, and I guess I got a little excited. I didn't think I'd get them all shut by myself."

"But you did?"

"Yes. I—I'm sorry to have gotten you down here."

"Don't be." Her whole body suddenly felt light and free and rested, and she straightened a little. "I'm happy you did."

He continued looking down at his feet, embarrassed. She knew he wanted to say something.

To help him, she said, "You did a good job. The storm came up fast."

He gave a little shrug. "I—I shouldn't have gotten you up."

"You didn't. I was already up when you called."

"Oh—"

She pressed her arms tight against her sides to keep from reaching out and pulling him to her. If she did that, it would disconcert him even more; what drawing together was taking place between them would be snapped.

"How about some ice cream?" she asked lightly.

He looked up at her in surprise. "At one thirty in the morning?"

"Why not?"

He grinned. "Geez, that would be neat, mom."

She laughed. "I think so, too. Come on. I'll get it out of the freezer while you put the dishes and spoons on the table."

A couple of times the kitchen light flickered as thunder crashed through the outside darkness. One peal was so close and so loud, they both jumped in their chairs. Then laughed at each other's startled expressions.

"You know," he said, "it might just be too wet for me to mow the lawn tomorrow."

She smiled. "It might just be."

He frowned. "It might be too wet for the clinic to be held, too."

"You can phone the Jay-Cee office in the morning and ask them."

"Yeah." He looked down at his dish of chocolate ice cream. "You know, I'd kinda forgotten about the boat model until you mentioned it at dinner. Maybe if it's too wet to mow the lawn and go to the clinic, I'll work on it."

"That sounds good to me. Maybe I'll get some work done on my illustrations, too."

The center of the storm had moved off over the western rim of the world when they went back up to their bedrooms. A steady rain still fell, though, blown by an eastern wind, so the windows had to remain shut. The inside of the house had begun to feel steamy and close.

At the door to his room, Jeff stopped. Slowly, still uncertain of himself, he reached out and took her hand. "Thanks, mom. I—I love you."

She squeezed his hand. "And I you, Jeff."

Sh lay on her hot bed with the perspiration running from her; her mind was refusing to accept sleep. Her stomach was squeamish, her lungs didn't seem to hold enough air, and her skin was so tender the damp sheet chafed her back and shoulders. The day had been filled with stupidity and impatience. And then there was the spawning of the new fear. Once more, it seemed, it was sending its tentacles out, slithering them through every portion of her body.

She lay staring at the ceiling, fighting to sleep; and, as usual in that circumstance, becoming wider and wider awake. In a little while her head began to ache, and she knew she would have to take a couple of aspirin. She looked at the table clock. It was ten after three. If her mind still refused to relax after the aspirin, she'd work on the illustrations, she decided. Fighting them would at least keep her thoughts in some order, and maybe prevent them from running back to grasp the bad times when Jennifer was still there.

On the way back from the bathroom, she looked in on Jeff and saw him sleeping the deep relaxing sleep it was impossible for her to find. How near to animals the young were, she thought, how able to clear the mind and let it spread its soothing anaesthetic throughout the body. In the morning, he would get up without the least fatigue, the young muscles taut and strong.

She went into the studio. She wanted to sit down at the drawing table, turn on the light and work. To do that would be the sensible thing. But she couldn't. She sat limply, feeling undone in spirit and determination. A murmuring in the back of her consciousness was telling her she had become only half a woman, that there wasn't enough left left of her for any sort of work . . . for her to bring back any sense into this incomprehensible tangle their lives had become.

Outside the rain still fell steadily, a grey membrane between her and the darkness of the shrubbery and sky. On the northern horizon lightning still flared, its reflection touching the hanging bellies of the clouds with swift traceries of green and purple. Her skin crawled and the goose flesh rose as she watched. Out there, where that faraway light was, something terrible was being born.

She moved on the stool, trying to see past her own reflection in the dark windowpane. She made a slight twist to the right—and vanished from the black glass.

But she saw something else. Something down there on the lawn in the rain next to the jasmine bushes. It shone dully, coldly, a misty thing very much like the rain itself.

She leaned closer to the window, hunching across the drawing table no more than three or four inches from the glass. Her stomach knotted, and, for a brief moment, she thought she was going to bring up the ice cream and the aspirin. The rain running down the pane in squiggly rivulets distorted her vision, but she could see whatever it was move off toward the left, following the line of the pepper trees and the jasmine bushes. Her heart began to pound, and the blood it sent through her carried the coldness of fear.

The thing hesitated. Then it moved again, slowly, with a rippling movement between an indulation and a glide. It was heading for the side door, the one leading to the kitchen.

"No!" Karen cried. "No!" She pushed herself back from the table.

A wayward finger of lightning skipped across the sky. It blinded her. She shrieked and pushed her face down against the table top. Around her the smashing roar of thunder hammered the earth and shook the house until the old timbers moaned.

As suddenly as the noise had struck, it was gone, leaving a vacuum of silence and a darkness as deep as the universe. Karen drew a long breath, a sighing whimper. Around her the house seemed to be sighing, too, though it was a passing wind caught in the eaves and fretwork of the gothic sculpturing.

She looked out the window again.

The thing was where it had been, halfway to the veranda from the hedge. But now she had the vivid impression it was looking up at her. She could discern no outline change in the vague silhouette, but she had the feeling that if it had a head it was turned up towards the lighted window. She could feel eyes staring at her.

She clenched her teeth and returned the unseen stare. A moment passed, then another. A terrible strength was down there. She felt it like a shock wave engulfing her. Then she became aware of an almost physical power boring through her eyes into her skull, then into her brain where it tried to find her terror and increase it.

"No, damn it! No!" She ground her clenched teeth. "No more fear. Do you hear me? No more fear!"

The rain splashed hard against the window for an instant; the water cascaded down, obliterating what was on the outside. Then the window cleared.

The creature was gone.

She had no idea how long she stood looking out the window at the empty lawn and the unfathomable and disturbing darkness. The thing had been coming to the house when the lightning and thunder struck and stopped it.

Was it coming for her?

Or for Jeff?

She stood looking down into the rain-swept darkness. Drawing deep breaths, she got her breathing to return to normal and the trembling of her hands to go away. But there was no interest in the illustrations. She turned away and walked slowly down the hallway to her bedroom.

Sleep came faster than she would have thought possible, probably because she refused to lie in the darkness trying to evaluate and dissect what had occurred. But it was not a peaceful sleep. She was aware of thin grey light and dark shadows through which an undefined creature of terrible evil slithered.

When she got up, her body ached and her mind struggled with a fuzziness that made it difficult to perform even elemental functions.

It was mid-afternoon when the new fear, or the rekindled old one, returned. Her vow at the window the night before had dissolved.

She was in the studio. The window was open, allowing the rain-washed air to come in. The scents borne on the air were sweet and vibrant and provocative. Big white cloud mountains puffed their peaks high into the blue sky. It was one of those rare days of a Florida summer—slanting sunlight, yellow and lavenders and whites hidden among the shrubbery bushes, drowsy insect sounds and dancing butterflies.

She paid the beauty no heed. There was a darkness in her mind left over from the darkness of the night. Even her brush strokes were done by rote, lines crisscrossing lines to form a design, which, in turn, formed a picture. Experience gave weight and emphasis where they belonged. What should have been moments of unreality in the rain had been reality, the reality of terror returned, and all joy was forfeited.

"Mom! Hey, Mom!"

She looked out the window. Jeff was pumping his bicycle furiously up the driveway, making heavy work of it in the loose stone and shell.

She stood up and leaned a little way out of the window. "What is it?"

"Mom, I just talked with Aunt Jennifer!"

He dropped the bike and ran up the veranda steps. The screen door opened and then slammed shut. Then his feet were running up the stairs, coming closer, the sound of approaching ugliness, the sound confirming the return of terror. She sat waiting, head bowed, hands clasped together on the table. Everything was out of balance again.

He burst through the door and all but skidded to a stop next to her.

"She invited me to visit her."

She suddenly felt very small and very weak. "Where was she?" She stared at the illustration.

"Out on the road. She was driving real slow, right by the end of the drive, in that Pinto she rented."

Her eyes blurred, perhaps because tears were trying to form. She blinked, and the drawing came into focus.

"I was going to call to her, but she saw me and stopped. She said she wanted me to come to the place where she lives."

"Her apartment?" she asked.

"I guess. She just said the place where she lived. Can I go?"

"No."

"Why? I'm fifteen, mom. I can choose my friends."

"I can't say, Jeff." She sucked her lower lip in between her teeth and looked away.

He stepped back and looked at her. She looked back, reluctantly. The withdrawing into himself was occurring again, the moving back into that very secret, very private part of his mind. His look became a bitter stare.

"You don't like her, do you? Even if she is your sister. Isn't that right, mother?"

She dropped her eyes to avoid his accusing stare, trying to tell herself she wasn't as alone as she felt at this moment.

"Jeff, please try to understand. Your Aunt Jennifer is a sick woman—maybe very sick. Not sick like a cold or the flu or a stomach ache, but ill in a way that makes her sometimes not know for sure who she really is. She's like a person who has played make-believe too long, and now can't remember if she's the real person or the make believe person. Do you have any idea of what I'm trying to say?"

"Yes. You mean she's not all together in her head."

"That's a harsh way of putting it."

He shrugged. "I don't believe it, mother. I think you're just telling me that, so I won't like her. The way you don't like her."

"She's dangerous, Jeff. Damn it, she's dangerous

for you to be around! That I want you to understand.''

For the space of a breath, he stood silently; then he turned and went to the door. Just before he crossed the threshold, he stopped and smiled at her. ''She's nice, mother. Real nice. . . .''

He went to his room and closed the door. She heard the lock click.

''Damn you, Jennifer Logan! Damn you to eternal burning hell!''

She laid her head on the table and sobbed.

At first she ignored the ringing of the telephone, allowing its sound to fill the silent house as though it was taking place in another realm of time.

On the ninth ring, she picked up the extension. She held it away from her ear, staring at it, not wanting to hear any words that might come through it. She shook her head, and felt an instant of disgust, because she knew she was behaving like a child scaring itself with shadows. Holding her voice steady, she said, ''Hello?''

If a voice can have a sweaty, fleshy sound, this one did. It mingled gruffiness, boredom and indifference. ''This is Sergeant Simmons,'' it said, ''of the county sheriff's department.''

For some reason, the words had an odd cadence to them. Rather mechanical. A litany repeated until it had no meaning.

''Yes, sergeant?''

''I'd like to speak with a Mr. Patrick O'Shawn.''

''I'm sorry. Mr. O'Shawn's not here.''

''When will he be back?''

''I can't say. He's out of town on business. Maybe

I can help you.''

"Are you his wife?''

"No. But I am a very close friend. I'm sure I can help you, sergeant, if you'll tell what it is you want."

During the short pause, he sucked his breath in through his lips; she visualized them as plump and wet.

"One of our deputies was out to his place the other day and picked up some clothes he'd found buried at the old Ludlow Mill. I need to ask him some more questions, and then have him come in and talk with us.''

"Yes, I remember that, sergeant. I was here when the deputy came. So I think I could help you. I'm Mrs. Sommers. It's my place the deputy came to.''

"Oh. Well. Were you with Mr. O'Shawn when he found the clothes?''

"No, I wasn't at the mill with him, but he told me everything, I think.''

"No, we'd have to talk with him. What our people want to know is what the ground looked like around the place he found them. If there were signs of a struggle. That kind of information, you know. It would have to be him, since he's the one who saw the site.''

"Yes, I understand. Well, it will be several days before he returns. He's in Miami."

"Have him phone me when he comes back. Will you?'' He gave her two numbers. "Thank you, Mrs. Sommers.''

"Thank you." She hung up.

Dusk was sending its creeping shadows across the lawn and filling the rooms with squares and oblongs of

dark. Twilight. She hated it. She had always hated it.
Since she had been a little girl, shadowed nooks and
vagrant gloom had made her want to cry, for reasons
she could never explain.

She knocked on Jeff's bedroom door. "Are you
going to come down for dinner?"

"No. I'm not hungry."

"All right." There was no argument within her. He
could go without dinner. She didn't care.

She ate alone at the kitchen table. Once she thought
of phoning Patrick, but dismissed the impulse. He
would be back in two or three days; surely she was
perfectly capable of handling whatever happened
without interrupting his pursuit of a livelihood. From
childhood she could remember her mother refusing to
phone her father at his office, saying the house was her
responsibility and she would run it to the best of her
ability without disturbing him. She had never phoned
Jason at work; she would not start now with Patrick.

But she did call Cynthia. Don answered.

"Don, this is Kar. Is Cyn there?"

"No, she isn't, Kar. This is the night she goes to
macramé class at the Hanging Fern Garden Shop."

"Oh, that's right. I forgot."

"Anything I can do for you?"

"No, not really. I just wanted to chit-chat."

He gave a chuckle. "Well, she's better at that than I
am. But if there's anything you want, or need, I'm here
to help."

"No, no. I guess I'm just a little antsy tonight."

"Kar, I'll have her phone you just as soon as she gets
home."

"No, don't do that, Don. It wasn't anything important—honestly. I think I might just go to bed and read. I'll talk to her tomorrow.''

"Okay. But if there's anything I can do—''

"Thanks, Don.''

There was no use trying to read, and watching TV would knot her nerves even tighter. She went to the studio. She turned on the table lamp and studied the three small tearstains on the illustration taped to the board. What she wanted to do was rip the illustration off and throw it out the window. Dear God, how she hated this assignment! Instead she dampened a corner of her paint rag and began dabbing carefully at the area around the blotches. Slowly the harsh edges melted and the area blended. She dabbed at the other two smears. Tomorrow, when they were dry, she'd apply new paint and reblend them into the overall area.

When she first heard the sound, she thought Jeff had turned on the portable radio in his room. But listening closer, she could tell that it was a voice, coming from the darkness of the yard.

She turned out the light and listened.

It was a woman's voice calling, piquant and wistful. There was a misty quality about it which set it apart from reality; it was the sound heard in imagination or a dream.

"Jeff . . . Jeff, come out and visit with me.'' Was there a movement near the jasmine? "Jeff, come out. Come out and visit with me, Jeff.''

She stepped back into the darkness of the studio and stood very still.

Again the dream voice called. "Come out, Jeff.''

She turned and almost ran down the hallway to Jeff's room, pushed open the door and looked in. He was lying on his side, legs pulled up and hands clasped under his head on the pillow. Little purring sounds were coming from his mouth.

The calling voice wasn't reaching him.

She closed the door and went back to the studio, where she stood in the doorway watching his room.

The earth along the river bank was cool. Dew clung to the weeds, sharp pinpoints of light. She narrowed her eyes against them.

The hunger was on her again. It gnawed at her stomach. Was it too soon? Was the return of the cold emptiness in so short a time a warning of too much activity within the woman body? In a time far back she had seen one of her kind waste away when she had driven her host into exhaustion.

She slithered through the damp weeds until she reached the nest. At its entrance she stopped and raised her head. She flicked her tongue out to catch vibrations on the air. There were none. She moved into the hollow beneath the overhanging foliage.

The woman body was as she had left it, sprawled on its back. She struck it viciously on its side. The relaxed flesh quivered. She hissed in satisfaction.

Very carefully, feeling the tiredness within her, she stretched full length on the soft body—and entered it.

The hunger. . . .

# CHAPTER 9

Karen wanted to plead with Jeff, to beg him to cross the rift which had opened between them while it was still shallow. She wanted to take him aside and lecture him, maybe even take a yardstick to his rear. Somewhere between these two extremes there was a middle ground, she knew, a rational adult approach, but it eluded her. Try as she might, her mind was swamped by the deadly, violent intrusion which had once more entered their lives. Rationality was beyond her reach.

Early Tuesday afternoon the Grove Center police phoned. A young-sounding man introduced himself as Detective Sam Cooper. The pleasant, intelligent voice pumped confidence into her.

"Mrs. Sommers, the sheriff has asked our department for assistance in the investigation of the possible murder of Sue Ann Miller."

"Murder, Officer Cooper? You think Sue Ann has been murdered?"

"We're working under that assumption, Mrs. Sommers. As the detective in charge, I'd like very much to come out and talk with you."

"Are you assuming Sue Ann has been murdered

because of the Simpson girl's death?''

"I'd rather not talk about that on the telephone, Mrs. Sommers.'' His voice was crisper. "If you'll permit me to come out, I'd be happy to discuss with you as much as I can concerning the case.''

"May I ask one more question, Officer?''

"Of course.''

"How do you think I can help?''

"I'd like to go over with you Mr. O'Shawn's finding of Sue Ann's clothing.''

Her heart took an extra beat. "Mr. Cooper, I have to come into town on an errand. I'll be happy to stop by the station and talk with you.'' She was lying; but she was obeying an instinct which told her to keep the whole affair away from the house—away from Jeff.

"That would be kind of you, Mrs. Sommers.'' He gave a deep chuckle. "I'll buy the coffee—straight from the urn in the detectives' room.''

"I'll be there in about an hour.''

"Ask for me, Mrs. Sommers. Sam Cooper.''

She changed from her blue jeans to a summer dress and dabbed make-up on her cheeks and lips. She was surprised, when she noticed it, at the effort she was making to control herself. Looking at her reflection in the mirror, she knew what she wanted to do: she wanted to leave all this and go away somewhere and hide. To scurry away to a place where time was forever kind.

She found Jeff in the tool shed rummaging through a pile of cartons. Looking at Jeff in the interior gloom, and seeing the remoteness on his face, gave her the feeling that he was unrelated to her, a stranger, actually.

"I'm going to go into town for an hour or so. While I'm away, I want you to stay right here at the house. Do you understand?"

He nodded.

"Jeff, I want to hear you tell me you understand."

"I understand."

Anger struggled with apprehension as she left the shed.

As usual the Dodge pick-up didn't start on the first try. Jeff was standing back in the darkness of the shed's interior watching her, and it made her nervous; she pumped the accelerator too hard on the second attempt, and the engine flooded.

"Damn it! Why now? Why in front of him?"

Dear God! She *was* thinking of Jeff as a stranger, a hostile one at that. She looked back at the shed doorway. He had moved farther back into the darkness, and all she could make out was the white blob of the T shirt he was wearing. Why? Why did she suddenly feel that he, too, was an adversary?

A car came up the driveway. In the rearview mirror, she watched Cynthia stop her Datsun too close to the pick-up's rear bumper.

"Going somewhere?" Cynthia was leaning out of the driver's window.

Karen leaned out of hers. "Into town."

Cynthia got out and walked to the truck. The hem of her brown skirt canted to the left several inches below her knees; her hat was floppy. Karen wondered how a hat could appear wrinkled.

"Don says you phoned last night. I'm sorry I wasn't there, then this morning I couldn't seem to get the day going in the right direction, so I decided to run out here." She ran her tongue around her lips as if tasting her lipstick; her vivid eyes behind their huge lenses roamed around the area. "Do you still believe as you did the other night about Jennifer?"

"Yes." Her hands tightened on the steering wheel. "No. I don't know. I'm going to the Grove Center police station now."

"Good lord, what's wrong?"

"Nothing, really. A detective phoned and asked if I'd give them as much information as I could about Patrick finding Sue Ann's clothing. They're starting to think she was murdered. The sheriff has asked them to help. About Jennifer . . . Patrick and I met her at the ruins the morning Sue Ann was murdered."

"Holy God! You never mentioned that."

"No."

Cynthia looked off across the lawn, and Karen thought she saw a shadow move across her friend's face. "What are you going to do, Kar?"

"Go to the police station now and tell them what I know about the clothes, which isn't much."

"Have you phoned Patrick?"

Karen shook her head.

"Don't you think you should?"

"Not right now. I'll tell them what I can, and if they still want more information, then I'll call him."

"I'm going to go with you."

"What?"

"To the police station."

"No, that's not necessary."

"Kar, I want to help."

"You can—by staying here at the house."

"What do you mean?"

She took a deep breath, and wondered briefly why she felt cold. But she knew.

Very slowly, trying hard to pick the correct words, she said, "Cyn, this has been a hell of a twenty-four hours here."

"Jennifer?"

"Not in person. But I'm sure she's the root of it. Jeff and I have all but lost contact with one another. I can't get through to him, and I'm sure he doesn't want me to."

"Oh, you mean he's in some kind of a sulk? Billy gets that way frequently, and I find it's better to ignore him. I think it's got to do with the chemistry in a fifteen-year-old boy's mind. No one's supposed to understand but them . . . and they seem to be rather vague about it."

"It's more than that. Those I'm used to, and I can shrug them off. No, this is different. He won't even speak with me like a person. He uses only two-syllable words and grunts when I ask him things. He's accused me of trying to turn him against Jennifer. When I tried to explain to him she was a sick person, a person he should stay away from, he told me I was lying."

"Oh, Kar. What is happening?"

She shook her head. "I don't know, but I had to talk with you. Only another mother would have the special ability to understand."

"I'm trying, Kar. But this is all so beyond anything I've experienced or studied, I'm having a hard time grasping it."

"And don't you think I am, Cyn? There are

moments when I'm alone that I know I've slipped over the edge into hysteria. There's too much happening for me to cope with.''

"Don't say that, Kar! Don't even think it. Do you hear me?''

Karen nodded. Then she looked at her friend and, as calmly as she could, told Cynthia about the voice calling to Jeff from the lawn the previous night.

"Oh dear God!'' Cynthia quickly looked at the row of jasmine bushes and then towards the upstairs window. "Oh God, Kar.''

"So, would you stay here with him, Cyn, while I go into the police station? Don't let him turn on you, but if you can, somehow, ask a question or two about Jennifer. There has to be a . . . a relationship of some kind between them.''

"I'll do my best, Kar.''


Detective Sam Cooper wasn't what Karen expected. His tall lean frame, topped by a bush of black unruly hair, was more like the police officers she saw on TV, members of big-city narc squads. A busy mustache grew like a shrub on his upper lip and drooped like black icicles on either side of his mouth. His black eyes, she quickly noticed, danced with pinpoints of blue. He wore suntan slacks and a floral-patterned sport shirt, opened at the neck. Curls of black chest hair grew up to his collar bone.

He took her into a small office; two desks were jammed into the tiny space. One stingy window, high up on the back wall, allowed a thin shaft of sunlight to slant into the room. Fluorescent tubes cast their cold light. It was a depressing space. Karen wondered if it had once been a cell.

Cooper pulled a straight chair up to one of the desks and nodded to her. "Please sit down, Mrs. Sommers." He gave a little shrug. "I'm sorry I can't offer you better surroundings. It's dreary, isn't it?"

She smiled, put at ease by his open friendly manner. "At least it shows the Grove Center Police Department doesn't spend the taxpayers' money frivolously."

He laughed. "That it certainly doesn't. No, it's a very tight-to-the-belt operation."

He opened the center drawer of his battered metal desk and withdrew several sheets of paper. Spreading them on the desk top, he said, "We're just beginning to draw all the facts together from which we'll make the basic picture of the jigsaw. As you can see, we're damn skimpy on these murders. But we'll get there."

"Mr. Cooper, you are saying the murders. That does mean you believe Sue Ann is dead, doesn't it? That she has been killed like Shirley Simpson?"

"We're working on that assumption, Mrs. Sommers. We know she was a carefree spirit who sometimes just took off with friends, but according to her mother she'd return after only a day or so. This time, of course, she hasn't. And there are the clothes Mr. O'Shawn found buried at Ludlow's Mill." He shook his head. "A person, even a free spirit, doesn't undress, bury her clothing, and disappear."

The wooden chair was unyielding. She felt its back pushing against her spine. "It doesn't seem logical, does it?"

"It isn't. That's why the finding of the clothing

interests me.''

Karen looked around the tiny room. Blood on a piece of fallen masonry. Dirt and dirt stains on elbows and knees.

"Now," Cooper was saying, "if you can tell me as much as you can about how Mr. O'Shawn found Sue Ann's clothing."

"I'm beginning to think I don't have enough details, Mr. Cooper; and I'm wondering if Patrick— Mr. O'Shawn—has enough to help."

"Anything will help, Mrs. Sommers. Anything at all. Did he say anything to you he didn't tell the deputy? Anything he might have remembered after the deputy left?"

"No." Blood and dirtstains. "I'm sorry. I thought I'd be of help, but I guess there are different degrees of observation and Patrick's wasn't very high on the scale that morning."

Sam Cooper leaned back in his chair. "I had my hopes built up. I was hoping you could tell me what he said about the area around the burial spot, or even a few yards a way. Signs of a struggle. Anything. Any damn, dumb, insignificant thing."

She shook her head.

"How did he find them? Why did he go to a place hidden from the ruins by a heavy overgrowth? Something must have called his attention to the spot."

"I believe he mentioned hearing a sort of rooting noise, as though an animal was digging. And he went to see." She made in a little gesture of uncertainty. Blood and dirtstains. "I'm not being any help at all."

"No, don't feel that way. But I had hoped for

more, I admit."

"I'm sorry."

Without changing his casual expression, he asked, "Are you sure you're telling me everything?"

She controlled her expression, but fear tightened within her. "Yes. Everything about Patrick's finding Sue Ann's clothing."

"And there's nothing else? Nothing related to it?"

"Blood—"

"What?" He leaned forward in his chair, putting his forearms on the desk top. "What?"

She sat rigid, her eyes fixed on his empty desk top.

"Mrs. Sommers, what did you say?"

"There's a big piece of masonry out there, which at some time fell from one of the walls. It's coquina. There was blood in one of the crevices that morning. Patrick and I saw it when we went out to sketch."

"That morning?"

"Yes."

"Why didn't you or Mr. O'Shawn tell the deputy?"

"I don't know."

"Damn it, you do! You're an intelligent woman. You would have associated it." He wiped his forehead, leaving white streaks on the tan. "Tell me, please."

She bit lightly on her lower lip as she tried to put her thoughts into a logical sequence. Cooper was holding his pencil over the spread out papers.

"I hadn't seen Jennifer for three years before she came on this visit, and a lot can happen in three years, I guess. Something has happened to Jennifer. It's as though she drifts in and out of contact with people; one moment she's full of life and frivolity, and the next she has moved into a remote corner of her mind and stares at people. She seems to be examining them; but for what purpose, I don't know. She has always had some kind of a long-range plan for her life, following it by the milestones of accomplishment. Never anything hasty—always well thought out. But she'd been here only two days when she decided to go out and get an apartment and make her home here in Grove Center."

Cooper looked up. "Just like that? On the spur of the moment?"

"Yes."

"Any reasons?"

"Only that she's fallen in love with the town and wants to escape the big-city life." She hesitated. "She's not even going back up to pack her personal belongings or quit her job. She's going to have her things packed and phone in her resignation."

Cooper's dark eyes glanced at her, then moved off and stared over her shoulder. "It sounds like an escape action."

"From what?"

He shrugged. "I don't know. Just an observation."

"A rather harsh one."

He looked at her and nodded. "I'm sorry. Now, tell me exactly where that blood was, where the stone is in relation to the walls of the mill."

She did, and when she finished asked, "Why?"

"I'm going to have the blood analyzed if I can find it—if it's still there. It might match that of the Miller girl."

"And if your scrapings of the dried blood match hers, that will put Jennifer in a bad light because she was lying on the stone."

Cooper didn't look at her. "Probably no more than she is now, Mrs. Sommers. Now, is there anything else for you to tell me?"

"I don't think so."

"Are you sure? You forgot about the blood, and that's a critical item. The most critical. If we can get scrapings it will be the only hint we have of what might have happened to the Miller girl."

"There's nothing else."

"Okay." He ran his pencil through his fingers in a tiny windmilling motion. "I'm going to have a watch put on her, Mrs. Sommers."

"She has her own apartment, Mr. Cooper, and I don't have the address."

"We'll find it."

"Officer Cooper, you're—you're making her sound like a criminal. She isn't that. She's a sick person."

He nodded and got up. "I'm sorry."

He walked her to her pickup. She drove straight home, feeling like a traitor.


Cynthia and Jeff were sitting on the side veranda when she stopped at the foot of the steps. Jeff was drinking a Pepsi from its bottle; Cynthia was merely sitting, looking off into space.

Karen turned the pick-up's engine off, and sat in the cab for a moment pulling her thoughts into a cohesive, workable pattern. The very first thing she had to do was plan her approach to Jeff. And she found she could not. She had absolutely no idea how to walk up and speak to her son. None at all. She sat with the afternoon sun glinting on the hood of the truck, ricocheting through the windshield into her eyes, and fought to keep from crying.

Cynthia got up and came down to the truck.

"Everything's okay," she said. "He's feeling pretty embarrassed and contrite."

"I suppose I should, too; but I can't, Cyn. I just can't help but think it's not all my doing."

"It's not yours at all, and in some ways, it's not his, Kar. It's Jennifer's."

"Were you able to bring her name up?"

"Some, yes. And I found out a few things I'll tell you about when we're alone." She opened the truck's door. "Come on. Let's go up so you and your son can make up and get back on the beam."

As she walked toward the steps, where Jeff now stood, she wasn't at all certain either one of them could overcome the resistance of the other.

But then he jumped down and ran to her.

"Mom. Mom." He threw his arms around her waist and buried his face between her breasts.

She hugged him, drawing him close, trying, it seemed, to pull him into her, back into the safety of her body, back into the time when no harm to him was possible.

She looked over his head at Cynthia and watched her smiling friend blur into a fuzzy image. The tears hung briefly on her lashes, then spilled and ran down her cheeks.

When the phone rang that night, she knew who it

was and answered it on the third ring.

"Kar?" It was Patrick. His voice boomed along the wire.

"Yes, darling, it's me. Where are you?"

",I'm in Miami. At the Holiday Inn on 163rd Street. Room 404. Got that?"

She scribbled on the phone-side pad. "Got it. How are things going?"

"Just fine, love. The show was a sell-out, and the negotiations with the suntan oil people are going great." He chuckled. "If finances are a consideration in our marriage, Kar, I'm coming back with a wallet full of cash and two fat signed contracts."

"You're the biggest consideration. You know that."

"How are things up there, Kar?"

She hesitated and a strange chill went through her. It was as if some latent sense was telling her to keep quiet. But if it was a warning, she refused to grasp it. "I've talked to the police."

"About Jennifer?"

"Yes."

"Has she done something else to upset you?"

"No, I haven't seen her. But . . . but I believe we were wrong, Patrick, and I felt we might need help in the not too distant future. They were asking about your finding of Sue Ann's clothing, and while I was with the detective, it just suddenly seemed so logical to tell him. About her. About the blood."

"Damn it, Kar, tell me! What's going on up there?"

"It's just as I said it was. The detective wanted to know if you'd seen signs of a struggle near where you found the clothes, and . . . well, one thing led to another. . . and I suddenly wanted to have them aware of Jennifer. I felt like hell after I told them— very irrational and disloyal. But, darling, I think it was for the best. She hasn't invited me over to her apartment, she hasn't been here. I think that's unnatural.''

For a moment he said nothing. She could hear him draw in his breath. ''Okay. I'm hightailing it back up there.''

''Don't you do one thing to jeopardize your position down there!'' Then she put a smile into her voice, and said with a quiet humor, ''We're going to need all the work you can bring in, Patrick O'Shawn. It takes a lot of money to feed a three-member family.''

''By God, you're still going through with it! You're still agreeing to marry me.''

''You don't have a chance of wriggling out of this marriage, Patrick O'Shawn.''

''You're a magnificent woman, Karen Sommers, and I love you. Keep remembering that. Make it the one thing on your mind. Have you talked yet with Jeff?''

''Not yet.'' She prayed her voice didn't sound too downbeat. ''Things have been in their usual hectic state around here, but I'll do it within the next day or so.''

She wasn't sure, but there might have been a slight hesitation in his voice, before he said, ''Well, just keep on thinking about that love. I'm on my way to Grove Center to make you prove it.''

After Jeff was in bed she sat on the veranda. She

just sat looking up at the meadowland of stars twinkling and gleaming from horizon to horizon. This was a good night. A good time of the night. For the first time in the last two days, she felt calm, assured. She slid lower in the wicker chair, thrusting her long legs out before her, feeling drowsiness claim her.

Debbie Margolis looked at her wrist watch. It was ten minutes after nine. A little twinge of apprehension touched her. She had stayed far too late at the library. Now it would be full dark long before she arrived home, and she had no light on her bicycle. She wished she had driven her mother's car, but she hadn't planned to stay anywhere near nine o'clock. Besides, bike riding was supposedly healthy. The last thought didn't make her a bit happier.

She put the two books, each with a divergent view of America's ills, back on the reference shelf and tucked the two she would check out under her arm. She shoved her blouse down into her jeans, pushed her dark hair back from her forehead, and hurried to the desk.

"Oh, Debbie. You still here?" Miss Ahearn squinted up at her through thick, blue-tinted glasses.

"Yes. I guess I lost track of time." She handed the two books to the gnome-like librarian.

"Did you drive, or are you on your bicycle?"

"My bike."

"Oh, child, that's dangerous. It's almost dark out there now, and it will be pitch black by the time you get out to Crestwood. You be very very careful."

"I will, Miss Ahearn. I didn't mean to stay this late, or I would have driven my mother's car. She wanted me to."

The little woman cackled as she pushed the books across the counter. "I guess mothers still know best."

"I guess."

"Outside, Debbie put the books in the basket on the handle bars, then unlocked the chain and wound it around the seat post, out of the way.

As she swung out onto Sloan Avenue, the realization of how dark it had become surprised her and laid another touch of worry on her, like a cold hand on her shoulder. For an instant, she considered going back to the library and calling home to ask her mother or father to come pick her up. But she dismissed that as pure selfishness. It was her fault that she was caught this way by the nightfall, and it wouldn't be fair at all to ask either of her parents to inconvenience themselves to put right what she had done wrong.

She pedaled slowly at first then faster as gaining courage, she saw that motorists were swinging out as far as they could to avoid her. At least, even without lights, she was visible. When she got out past the town traffic she'd feel better. The road to Crestwood Homes was wide with a good solid shoulder on which she could ride when headlights approached.

She swept past the Quick Stop store and shifted into third gear, wondering if the girl who worked there had ever been found. She shivered. That made one girl, about her age, who had been murdered and another who had disappeared. Debbie had begun to think she had been murdered, too. She pedaled faster, feeling perspiration on her forehead and back.

She passed the driveway of the Sommers' place. There was a car pulled off the road, facing toward her, its lights out. As she went by she thought she saw a blonde head in the darkness of the vehicle. She couldn't be certain, it was more sensing a movement than seeing a person, but she thought the head turned in her direction, as if eyes were following her. It was a creepy feeling, like something cold, but at the same time hot, reaching out for her. She began to pump faster.

The road was straight and smooth; it was the only one serving the orange groves another six miles to the north, so the county kept it free of potholes. She knew she was making good time—possibly twenty miles an hour. About half a mile past the car, she threw a glance over her left shoulder.

The car's headlights were on, and it was moving. She looked back again. It was making a U turn and coming after her. A dagger of fear stabbed her between the shoulder blades, and for an instant she lost control of the bicycle. It swayed left, then back to the right as she fought it back under control. Frantically she tried to pump faster, but couldn't do it. She gave a little cry.

The car gained on her.

Her heart gave a violent slam in her rib cage. She knew the car, or whoever was in it, was after her. She could almost feel danger moving down the headlight beams after her, drawing nearer and nearer. A vile bitter taste filled her mouth. It was becoming impossible to draw a breath. She began to feel dizzy. The sweat was running down into her eyes now, blinding her, and making the plastic handle grips slippery.

She was whimpering.

The car drifted in closer. The light from its headlights touched her, now.

Down the road . . . down the road . . . just a little bit farther was the lane to the Ludlow ruins. She could turn in there. Yes. . . . The car could follow her, but she could ditch the bike and take off on foot through the woods. She felt better. There was hope. She managed to pump a little faster.

Then it was there, the narrow lane slanting off into the wall of dark foliage. She made a quick left turn and gave the pedals an extra hard push. The bicycle leaped across the asphalt and into the rutted dirt. It wavered, bucked, and started to topple. She steadied it.

Behind her, out on the road, the car passed the entrance to the lane. Then it stopped, idled for a moment, and slowly backed up. She traveled another fifty yards along the lane. When the car turned into the lane, its lights cutting a brilliant swathe through the trees and bushes, she had rounded a bend. To the right was a clump of cabbage palms. She skidded the bike to a stop and jumped off. Panting, whimpering, she dragged it behind the palms and dropped it at their base. She wanted to cover it with weeds and fallen branches, but the headlights were approaching and she could hear the car's motor straining in low gear. She turned and ran.

The moon was a crescent lying on its back, a dry moon according to farmers and those who studied almanacs. Its pallid, slender weakness gave little light.

Debbie picked her way slowly through the tangled underbrush, unable to see obstacles until she ran into them. Now, with scratches on her arms and cheeks, her blouse torn, and her mind beginning to function normally again since the immediate danger was behind her, she stopped for a moment, to draw several deep breaths and allow her heart to slow.

It was too dark to see her watch, but she judged she must have been in the woods almost twenty minutes. Instinct told her not to hurry, that caution would help her more than speed. She would creep a few yards through the foliage, then stop and listen for any alien sound out in the darkness. Only once did she hear a disconcerting noise, one unlike any she had heard before. It was a loud hissing like that of a serpent filled with fury, but undertoned with what could have been the deep indrawing of a human breath. It had startled her, and she had held her breath for a long time waiting for it to come again, but it never did.

She wasn't exactly lost, but there was some confusion in her mind. She kept going on what she thought was a northerly course. It would take her fifty to a hundred yards east of the ruins, she thought; from there she could turn to her right and get back out on the road.

But somewhere in the darkness, weaving and twisting through the matted branches and clinging vines, she had lost direction. Suddenly she was in the clearing, the ragged ruins huge, dark, and threatening forms over her. She stopped and looked around, trying to orient herself. And while she stood there, her nerves suddenly began to tingle. Something was behind her. She whirled around.

In frantic desperation, her mind slammed itself shut against the vision her eyes were conveying to it. Her nerves shrilled again.

On a huge jagged piece of masonry, balancing itself on the flat top of the rock, was a creature escaped from a nightmare. From what might have been a face, red eyes glared malevolence through a pulsing nimbus with such a terrible force they were like knives slicing into her brain. A long tongue flicked out from between two fangs, stretching and curling towards her.

She stumbled back a step, her mouth opening and closing as she gulped for air and tried to scream all at the same time. Then the muscles in her long sturdy legs collapsed and she fell to her knees.

Inside her something was swelling bigger and bigger getting ready to burst. She opened her mouth, but only a croak came from her straining throat.

The creature moved to the edge of the stone, swaying, weaving, stretching to an undulating slenderness, faintly glowing in the moonlight.

For a long moment while the world revolved and the stars swam in the depthless sky, the two stared at one another across the void of hate and fear. Then the thing gave a long hiss and sprang.

Debbie rolled back on her shoulders and thrust her legs upwards with her feet braced. The creature attempted to twist in mid-air to avoid them, but failed. Debbie's feet drove into it. It hissed in pain and fury and rolled to the left, the end of its body falling over Debbie's right thigh, tearing the denim of her jeans as though it was cheesecloth. Debbie squealed with pain and rolled away to her left. As she did, her right hand brushed against a stick. She closed her fingers around it, and rolled onto her back to see where the creature was.

It was stretched to its full height, advancing slowly, hissing, its tongue darting in and out, its eyes burning like coals. It lunged; Debbie swung the stick in a wide sweeping arc between them. She continued swinging the stick back and forth, lashing the air with such force the wood made a swishing sound between them. The thing circled her, around and around, seeking an opening. Debbie got to her knees, wincing from the pain in her lacerated thigh, and began to alternate the swinging motion with thrusting jabs of the stick. The thing hissed.

Very deliberately, feeling the ground behind her with her feet, Debbie started moving towards the ruins. She didn't know what she would do when she got to them, but at least she could place her back to one of the walls. Then the thing could only come at her from one direction.

She moved slowly, one step at a time. The muscles in her legs began to quiver with the strain, and her arms were growing tired. She'd have to move faster; she'd never make it at this pace. She turned her head to see how much farther she had to go.

The thing sprang.

She landed on Debbie's back full force, her weight driving the girl to the ground. Her hisses became wild with hatred and vengeance, piercing the night with such vehemence the night creatures around the clearing scurried in terror for their burrows.

Debbie dragged herself towards the ruins even as

the entwining body tore the flesh from her back, ripping her open with a pain she could not bear. She screamed. It echoed through the night like the death cry of a mutilated animal, filling the darkness with its agony.

The thing turned the writhing girl over on her back and coiled its coldness around her, contracting, breaking the pliant flesh against vibrating ribs and spine. Debbie's heels beat a week tattoo against the earth, and her fingers clawed into the dirt at her sides. Her eyes bulged out of their sockets as the pain in her head began to expand.

The coils pulled upwards, forcing Debbie into an arch, lifting her torso off the ground so her head fell back and her throat was bent in a long arch. From out of the vapor something cold and glutinous ran along her throat. Debbie whimpered. The coils tightened, quivered and strained at the crushed waist, lifting Debbie's torso higher off the ground, at the same time jabbing with its tail at the underside of Debbie's upraised chin.

Debbie stared at the black nothingness of masonry, the pain gnawing her like a thousand fires. Vaguely she understood that the creature wanted her to tilt her head back farther than it already was. Anything to stop the pain. She laboriously pulled her arms to her sides, dug her elbows into the ground, and arched herself upwards. Her head tilted back until all she could see through the mist in her eyes were the frail stocks of weeds.

The thing uncoiled and raised itself. Debbie made no move. A coil nudged her in the side. Debbie whimpered, but struggled and arched herself even more. Her throat tautened to the bursting point; the pulse beating in it was heavy.

A night animal rustled on the fringe of the forest, and a bird, awake for some reason, called several times then became silent again. Up in the sky an airplane droned, and on the distant highway a lonely automobile blew its horn.

Debbie was grunting now. Her muscles were shaking; she would be unable to hold the position too much longer.

The thing moved toward her shoulders and bent down. It lowered its mouth, and, swiftly, drove fangs into the proffered throat.

It was twenty after seven when Jennifer turned the Pinto into the parking lot of the Quick Stop store. The juices were flowing heavy in her now, and her loins were swelling with desire. They would be unable to use the ruins this morning; the finding of Sue Ann's clothing had made the place a destination for sightseers and law enforcement personnel. All privacy was gone. Danger was there. But she would take the young clerk, Terry, down to the river nest. After she turned off the ignition, she sat thinking of the ancient witcheries she would perform on him under the coolness of the trees.

She walked across the dew-dampened asphalt with eager steps. Her hand was outstretched to the misted door of the store, ready to pull it open, when he heard a girl giggle. Her hand dropped to her side.

"Terry, you behave yourself until we leave here. You hear me?" Another giggle. "You know, I think maybe it was worth getting up this early."

Terry laughed. "Just wait until I get you out to Ludlow's Mill, baby doll."

"No, Terry, not there. That's where they found Sue Ann's things. I don't want to go there."

"Okay. There're other places. You're not going to let where we do it stand in our way, are you?"

A giggle. "Nooo."

Jennifer turned and went back to her car. This time, as she crossed the parking lot, she saw a Datsun parked beside Terry's VW.

In the car she allowed the anger within her to grow. Her eyes narrowed and she sat without seeing as she stared through the floodlighted area into the darkness beyond. She must do what she planned to do faster now, setting forward her time schedule.

She hissed.

# CHAPTER 10

Karen was in the wide bed with its sweat-dampened sheet and soggy pillow, wandering through a dream which led her down dark passageways, twisting and turning and opening here and there into tiny ante-rooms in which human-seeming forms moved, watching her go by. She tried to run, to get past those ill-defined creatures, because she knew they were evil, filled with abominable intent. But her feet were too heavy to lift; she was forced to slide them along the uneven flooring. Then ahead was a pale light, no more than a grey blotch in the overall blackness, but a signal that the end of the passage was near.

But from behind her there was a sudden thumping noise. A voice called out to her. She tried to hurry. The sound rolled down the passage after her and the voice became louder. She moaned.

"Mom! Mom, wake up!"

Unexpectedly the voice became familiar. The thumping was a recognizable noise—a knocking on her bedroom door.

"Mom, wake up! Mrs. Porter is on the phone."

The dream vanished; morning sunlight slanting through the open windows. She blinked and uncurled herself.

"Yes?"

"Mrs. Porter is on the phone and says she must talk with you right now. She told me to wake you up."

"I'll get it on the extension in the studio."

"Okay. I'll tell her you'll be right there."

She rolled out of bed, feeling stiff and unrested, full of lumps and indiscriminate little aches, and struggled into her housecoat, her fingers fumbling with the zipper up the front. She didn't bother with slippers; the hardwood floor felt cool under her feet and helped to get her moving.

The Baby Ben on the bedside table told her it was eight twenty-five. Good God, why had she slept so late? And why was she so tired? It was a chore walking to the bedroom door. As she opened it, she realized there was no joy in facing this day. And she realized, too, that it had been a long time since she had felt excitement in the morning. Where, in this strange world, had the fun all gone? Replaced with plastic, she thought, like everything else.

She picked up the handpiece of the telephone. "Cynthia, I'm sorry to keep you waiting. I haven't slept this late for I don't know how long."

Cynthia ignored the apology. "Kar, have you heard the radio?"

"No."

"Debbie Margolis was found murdered this morning out at Ludlow's mill. Kar, the radio says she was mutilated, torn, as if attacked by a big animal."

"Oh, dear God!" Her empty stomach churned and she had the sensation of wanting to vomit. "My

God.''

"You knew her. She was—''

"Yes, of course, I knew her. She sat with Susy last week when we went to the Golden Slipper.''

"Something terrible is happening here in Grove Center.''

"Yes. When did it happen?''

"Last night. She left the library a little after nine, according to the reports, and was riding her bicycle home. They've found the bike out in the mill area.''

"That means she would have ridden by here.'' What was it in the far back of her mind, trying to force its way up to consciousness?

"Yes. She lived out in Crestwood Homes.'' There was a silence. Then: "Oh, Kar, I feel so terrible. She was such a fine girl with such big ambitions and such a compassionate way of thinking. She wasn't so offbeat like some of the younger people, but she was popular with them just the same; I think they secretly admired her.''

Cynthia was taking the death hard. Karen said, "I'm not much in the mood for work this morning. Why don't I come over for a late cup of coffee?''

"That would be splendid.'' There was a new energy in her voice. "I've got some of those frozen Danish and will stick them in the oven. Bring Jeff, Kar. Billy is really upset. He liked Debbie immensely.''

"Give me an hour, Cyn.''

She went into the shower. At first the water stung, as though ants were crawling over her; but then it soothed her, and she felt her strength flow back until her body felt sleek and glossy. She rather wished she had one of those massage heads on the nozzle.

She put on a pale blue sleeveless dress and accentuated with a white belt. It came as close to being conservative as anything in her wardrobe; however, as she turned in front of the full-length mirror, she decided it wasn't exactly prim, because it fit snugly across her breasts and drew attention to their thrust, even though in a quiet manner. She put on the only pair of white shoes she owned and felt, suddenly, overdressed. They were high heels; it wasn't exactly a cocktail party she was preparing to attend. Nevertheless, she kept them on and left the bedroom.

Downstairs, Jeff was at the side of the house working on his bicycle, doing something with its chain. He looked up and saw her standing in the door. "Are you going out?"

"We're going over to the Porters. We'll eat breakfast there."

"Right away?"

"Right now."

"Okay." He wheeled the bike into the garage.

The pickup started on the first try. It was an enormous relief to her, because the day was closing in upon her after Cynthia's call, shutting off her mind. She felt as if the world was growing fuzzy, indistinct.

"Are we going to get back by eleven?" Jeff asked, as they turned out of the driveway.

"I don't know. Why?"

"Oh, mom! You know I told you there's a clinic meeting this morning."

"I don't remember you telling me that."

"Well . . . maybe I forgot. But I've got to be there. They're having a half hour on showing us how to slide into base. That's important."

"Well, so is what we're doing. Mrs. Porter and Billy need us. And I'm not sure you'll make it today."

"Aw, geez, mom. That's not fair. What's so important with Billy and Mrs. Porter?"

"Jeff, they're friends, and they need us. That's about as good a reason as there is. Now, look. I'll phone Mr. Pritchard and explain to him why you couldn't be there this morning. Okay?"

He sighed. "I guess it will have to be. But you still haven't told me what's so important about us going to the Porters—other than them being friends."

She pretended to concentrate on her driving while she fought to gain control of the cold, ugly shudder of revulsion and fear slithering through her. Too many things were tugging at her for her to choose the words to tell him about Debbie's death. She had to be careful and gentle; the words simply wouldn't come.

Finally she asked, "You remember Debbie Margolis, don't you?"

"Sure. She's a nice person. We had a long talk and took a walk the other night when she stayed with the baby at the Porters'."

"Well, Jeff, she's dead."

"*Dead?*"

"She died last night."

He sat staring straight ahead through the windshield. "Was she sick?"

"No, Jeff. She was murdered. Out at Ludlow's Mill."

"Murdered? You mean like Shirley Simpson?"

"Yes, and maybe Sue Ann who worked at the

Quick Stop store.''

He looked at her, seemed about to say something, then turned his head and looked out the side window, watching the lawns slip past the truck. "That's three," he said, as if to himself.

"That's why we're going over to the Porters. That phone call from Cynthia this morning was the first I knew of Debbie's. . . . Cynthia is very upset, and Billy is taking Debbie's death very hard. Debbie babysat the baby a lot, and Billy came to like her a whole lot. She asked me to bring you to try to help cheer him up.''

He was silent for a long, long time. She wondered how he would respond.

The sun was higher now; she could feel it drying up the coolness, and forcing its way into the asphalt to leach out during the day, making the roads even hotter. She reached up behind the sun visor for her sunglasses, put them on, and found there was a fingerprint in the middle of the right lens. She took them off and handed them to Jeff.

"Will you clean these for me, please? There's Kleenex in the glove compartment.''

He rummaged through the maps and notebooks until he found a squashed pocket-sized packet of tissues and pulled two free. He seemed to concentrate on the glasses to the exclusion of everything else.

He handed them back to her. "Try that.''

"Great. Thanks.''

He nodded and looked away again. "I don't know if I'll be able to cheer Billy, mom. I liked Debbie. I liked her a whole lot, and I think we could have become friends.''

She was dismayed. "Try," she said, softly. "Just try, Jeff."

Cynthia let them in, dressed in a halter and shorts, and that made Karen feel even more uncomfortably overdressed. The house smelled of the baking rolls. Coffee perked cheerily in its pot.

"Thanks for coming, Jeff," she said, and laid a hand on his shoulder. "Billy's upstairs in his room. Would you go up and talk with him, please? He's very depressed."

Jeff looked at his mother. Karen nodded. "You can do it, son. Go ahead."

He went slowly toward the stairs.

When they were alone, Cynthia shook her head. "I'm embarrassed about letting you come over, Kar, but I needed help with Billy. He's not having any spells of wild crying; he's just withdrawn very deeply into himself and I've been unable to draw him out. It's disconcerting."

"Don't be silly, Cyn. What are friends for, huh? And Jeff's certainly a friend of Billy's."

Cynthia went to look at the oven timer. Her slenderness, which looked like thinness when she wore dresses, in the shorts and halter became a tight-knit body well proportioned to her height.

"I guess they're ready," she said, and began piling the rolls on a plate. "Would you pour the coffee, Kar? I'll go up and see if the boys want anything."

"I can save you a trip. I know Jeff's hungry. He asked about eating before we came over."

Cynthia poured out milk and orange juice and placed six rolls on a plate. She put it all on a tray. "I'll be back down in a minute, I hope."

Karen poured two cups of coffee and took them into the dining room.

Cynthia came in smiling. "I think Jeff's a budding psychologist. Billy was actually grinning when I left them. They'll be down later."

They ate slowly, neither having any desire to bring this interlude of tranquility to an end. Neither spoke much. There was no need. What they possessed, they knew, was a very special relationship many people never have the opportunity to enjoy. It was friendship.

"Want any more coffee?" Cynthia asked.

Karen shook her head. "I'm about all coffeed out."

"Me, too."

There was another long silence, and Karen became aware that each, within the other, was finding strength and confidence and peace.

"When does Patrick get back?"

"In a couple of days. He phoned and said the show was a sell-out and that he's doing all right with the suntan oil people." She looked down at her coffee cup. "We're going to get married, Cyn, when he gets back."

"Kar! That's wonderful! Oh, I'm glad to hear that. You two are such a perfect couple. Oh, Kar, that is wonderful!"

"I haven't told Jeff yet."

"He'll take it okay. He loves Patrick. In fact, Don and I've always said Jeff took to Patrick before you did."

"I hope so."

"Hey, he's pretty adult. He's handling Billy like a

pro."

Karen laughed. "This is one of his better times."

At that moment, the telephone rang. Cynthia went to the kitchen to answer it. Karen watched an oblong of sunlight creep across the living room floor and start to crawl up a hassock.

Cynthia returned. "That was Lois Rutherford."

"About Debbie's murder?"

"Yes. There's a meeting tonight at the Lincoln Heights school auditorium. I guess it was on the radio, but I turned it off right after phoning you. The police and sheriff will be there; it's open to the public. She asked that I attend, being a teacher; though I don't know why that has anything to do with it."

"Are you going?"

Cynthia nodded. "Yes. I don't want to harrass the law enforcement people, but I am interested in learning what they have in mind to combat this— this terror which has descended on us. Why don't you come with me, Kar? Bring Jeff over, and Don can keep tabs on him and Billy while he babysits Susy."

Such a few days ago, Karen would have laughed and declined. But back then she had no reason to become involved with the interlacings of society. She had sat back smugly, giving damage appraisals on the rents and tears in the fabric called civilization.

But that was before the tide of life had swept over her, smashing her isolation and throwing the debris in all directions. Like it or not, she had been sucked into the undertow, and now she must fight it alongside those whom she had not considered. She must stand with them now.

She nodded. "I'll go with you, Cyn. What time is it?"

"Seven-thirty. Why not come by about six and we'll have something to eat here? Bring Jeff back, if you can."

"If you promise not to go to too much trouble."

"Hamburgers, trouble?"

Perhaps ninety people were knotted in the seats near the stage when Karen and Cynthia arrived. Sam Cooper, in a suit and tie, was sitting on the small stage with a man in a neat deputy sheriff's uniform. Squeezed into one of the narrow front-row seats, Lois Rutherford was holding a miniscule court with several followers. Dressed in a pseudo-western outfit, she looked like a middle-aged follower of the Urban Cowboy fad.

A man who introduced himself as Mr. Alan Clark, principal of the Lincoln Heights elementary school, called the meeting to order.

Sam Cooper stood up and walked to the lectern. He looked over the assemblage and smiled. "Let's keep this informal," he said, "but let's not get carried away. Okay?"

There were a few assenting murmurs.

"Okay. I'm Sam Cooper, and I'm a detective with the city police. I'm here to tell you what we are doing and what we are planning to do about the two, and possibly three, murders of teenaged girls. Now, I'm going to be very frank and very truthful with you. So far we haven't done much."

There were one or two angry mutters from the

audience.

Cooper held up a hand. "Now I know you don't think we've turned our backs on them, that we've slipped their files into a bottom drawer where they can be ignored. What I mean is, until the two young people found Debbie Margolis' body this morning out at Ludlow's Mill we have treated each one as a separate case. Last night's murder has changed all that. They have become one case.

"As you know, the two bodies which have been found were very badly mutilated and the blood drained from them. Now, I've been authorized by my superiors, including Chief Wilson and Mayor Stockton, to tell you facts which would normally be confidential police information."

He paused and looked around the faces below him. Karen realized it was for dramatic affect, and she began to wonder a little bit about Sam Cooper's background.

"We are not at all certain what we are dealing with. Human or animal."

Breath was sucked into startled mouths.

"Okay, here's why. Both bodies have had the blood drained from them, almost down to the last ounce, and it has been drained from the throats . . . and in the throats are puncture holes. They look like the marks of two big . . . fangs."

Lois Rutherford called out, "Then it has to be a wild animal of some kind, young man."

There were mutters of agreement from those sitting around her.

Cooper nodded. "Also, both bodies were squeezed under great pressure, as though they had been

encircled by heavy constricting coils. And the flesh
was covered with abrasions. Something had wound
itself around those girls. Perhaps—''

He paused again and swept them with his eyes.

''Perhaps a reptile-like creature. But the only
reptiles capable of exerting that kind of pressure on
human bodies are pythons and boa constrictors—and
they do not drink the blood of their victims.''

''What the hell are you trying to tell us, Cooper?''

''Yeah, man! Don't try to be mysterious. I got a
daughter who's sixteen, and I damn well want to
know what's going on!''

''For heaven's sake,'' a woman said, ''will you let
him talk?''

Cooper nodded and smiled at her. ''There's really
not much more to tell you. That's it. But we are
starting our counteractions. Deputy Giles is going to
talk with you about that.''

The deputy was a man in his mid-thirties, alert and
serious, with a hint of military background showing.

He spoke slowly with a slight drawl. ''Everything
Detective Cooper has told you is true. The findings
around the bodies are baffling. We don't pretend to
understand them; however, we have requested aid
from the Criminal Investigation Department in
Tallahassee, and there is a team of three officers on
their way down here now, including a forensic
specialist who can give authoritative analysis of the
wounds. When we have his report, we will have a
definite direction to follow and will be able to
pinpoint our endeavors much more precisely.

''There is one other thing I'd like to tell you. The
sheriff's department is recommending to Mayor

Stockton and the Grove Center police that a dusk-to-dawn curfew be ordered for all teenaged girls.''

This brought exclamations from the audience, most of them negative.

''We know,'' Giles said, when some quiet had been returned, ''that is an unfair, unpopular, and archaic way to handle the problem. But, on the other hand, where would a girl out after dark obtain protection? None of the law enforcement agencies have the man-power. Can you parents travel with them? Can we form a band of volunteers to accompany each and every girl? We don't think so. That's the reason we are recommending the curfew.''

Lois Rutherford was on her feet. ''I'll tell you the kind of volunteer group you need: vigilantes! Women vigilantes who'll stand up and protect all womanhood in this town!''

Again there was a chorus of agreement from those sitting around her.

Calmer voices rose, fought to be heard, then faded away. Karen sat and watched the audience drawing into two hostile groups, forgetting facts, glaring at one another balefully. The meeting was falling apart, degenerating into shouts and twisted faces.

She looked at Cynthia, who was slouched low in her chair, a disgusted look on her face, and asked, ''Do you think they're going to accomplish anything?''

Cynthia shook her head. ''My God, Kar, this is absolutely appalling. Watching them makes me think we shouldn't have to look too far for the creature murdering the girls. This is senseless.''

''Let's go.''

They were almost at the exit when Karen felt a light touch on her arm. "Mrs. Sommers."

Sam Cooper was smiling at her. "I saw you in the audience and wanted to have a word with you before you got away."

She smiled, once more feeling the man's warmth. "Do all your meetings end in donnybrooks, Mr. Cooper?"

He laughed, a good laugh all the way up from his chest. "Only the ones where I'm supposedly speaking to rational adults."

Karen introduced Cynthia, then said, "I suppose you wanted to speak to me about Jennifer."

"I think you have a phantom for a sister, Mrs. Sommers—the blonde-haired lady who wasn't there. We've seen no activity around her apartment, and she gave your address when she rented the car. Twice one of our patrol units have spotted the Pinto, but it's always disappeared before the men could investigate."

"Did you phone Mr. Holscomb at Neutronics?"

"Yes, and he told me the same thing he told you. She was a real belle of the ball around the office."

She wanted to get away from the turmoil behind her and go home. The tightness in her chest was becoming acute; soon she would have to scream to relieve the pressure. "Thank you, Mr. Cooper."

"I'll keep you informed, Mrs. Sommers."

"Please. I'd appreciate that."

As they were pulling out of the school parking lot, Cynthia asked, "Let's stop somewhere for a drink. You look as though you could use one."

Karen shook her head. "I'll wait until we get to

your place and have a good stiff one."

"And I, I think, will have two."


Don Porter reclined in his La-Z-Boy chair, ignoring the characters moving across the television screen. He was struggling with himself, trying to understand the uneasiness attempting to overwhelm him.

He swung his feet down to the floor. Something very alien was playing a cat-and-mouse game with his well-being. It disturbed him. Everything just seemed so damn uncoordinated all of a sudden, like when the lights went out in a house you'd lived in for years and on the way to the kitchen for the candles you bumped into a dozen pieces of furniture.

The baby was upstairs asleep; the boys were out in the Florida room doing something or other with a plastic model of the space shuttle. He could hear their low drone of conversation, punctuated now and then with a laugh. Whatever was giving him the quivers wasn't coming from out there. And then, as he sat there, his uneasiness turned into something he could put a name to, and that name was colder than the air conditioned coolness of the room. Premonition.

Along with the realization, as though the one had called the other forth, there was a low scraping sound outside the house. A slithering, like a soft body pulling itself through the ornamental bushes outside the window. It was a vague noise, barely audible over the television and the hum of the air conditioner.

All interest in the TV show was gone. He hoisted himself out of the chair and turned off the set. A startling silence wedged itself into the room. At first he didn't like it. It seemed heavy, almost physical, a substance as out of place here as a tombstone.

"Jesus!" he said, half aloud, "you've got the willies tonight."

He went to the sliding glass doors opening on to the Florida room. The boys and their model were lying on the woven grass rug. Billy looked up, saw him and grinned. Then Jeff did the same.

There was such innocence there. How long would it last, he wondered. Soon life would begin to chafe the boys' trust; the years would not be as kind as these in the protection of family and home. Shit, it was a goddamn shame that kids had to grow up.

He looked at his watch. It was eight-forty. He wondered when Cynthia and Karen would get back. Personally, he considered the meeting a waste of time, because nothing was ever settled at those affairs. A speech; talk; disagreement; argument; chaos. A town meeting was, he thought, incapable of a frontal assault on any problem.

Restlessly, still carrying the weight of premonition on his shoulders, he wandered out into the kitchen and rummaged through the refrigerator, not finding anything which enticed him to break his vow not to snack.

Then he heard it again. Along the back of the house, now; perhaps whatever was making it was circling the building. What was it doing? Trying to find a way in?

"Now that damn well does it!" What the hell was getting into him? Things crawling around the house seeking a way in? "God Almighty!"

He went back into the living room, determined to turn the TV back on, sit down and enjoy whatever was being broadcast. His damned mind was all out of kilter.

But halfway to the set, he stopped. As asinine as it possibly was, something might be out there, and he knew he would be more at ease if he did go out and look.

On his way to the front door, he glanced over his shoulder through the glass door into the Florida room. And through the screening around it, into the darkness of the backyard.

It was there, like the first image on a double-exposed negative. Through the veil of reflection on the sliding doors and the scrimming effect of the screen, from what might have been deep sockets, two slitted eyes glowed with a violent redness.

"God!"

He started for the glass doors, then remembered the Florida room had no door leading outside. He turned and dove for the front door.

He rounded the corner of the house, running faster than he had for years.

The yard was empty. He stood still in the spill of light coming from the Florida room, close to the wall of the house, straining his eyes and ears, his flesh tingling. There was nothing alien in the darkness.

He wanted to walk back the hundred and fifty feet to the rear fence and look deep into the shadows beneath the punk tree growing there, but he could not make himself move. He stayed where he was chilled with fear, disgusted with himself. Several minutes slipped by. It was lying out there watching

him with its slitted eyes, while he standing here, was
somehow preventing its escape. He had the definite
sensation he was in battle of wills with the creature.

But finally he knew he had lost. Whatever it was
out there in the dark had entered the battle of wills
with him—and it had won. He had the feeling it
could stay out there until morning patiently watching
him, but, at the same time, alert to protect itself
should he advance towards it. Damn, if he'd only
brought a flashlight with him! But there hadn't been
time to search for it in the kitchen drawer. Now, if he
went back in to get it, the thing would escape. But it
was going to escape, anyway, because he didn't have
the courage to walk back to the punk tree. He was so
goddamn ineffectual. He ran a hand over his wet
forehead, took one last glance at the cave of shadow
beneath the tree, and retraced his steps to the front
door. He was weak and shaky. And he wanted to
vomit.


"Isn't that Don going into the house?" Karen
asked as they drove up the street.

"I wonder what pulled him away from the TV."

They passed through the weak pool of a street
light; Cynthia slowed and turned into the driveway,
the headlights sweeping in a great arc across the street
and yard.

In the middle of the driveway, something waited.
At first the headlights sprayed around it as if
reluctant to isolate it in the darkness. Then, glowing
like two windows into the fires of hell, red eyes
burned with fury. A snarling mouth pulled open.
Between two long glinting fangs a tongue darted in

and out, in and out. A slender amber-hued body swayed, light splashing from it like reflections from tight-woven scales.

Cynthia jammed the brakes on and screamed. The Datsun swerved to the right, its engine coughing, ran onto the lawn, and it stalled.

Karen heard herself screaming, felt the terror bursting in her throat, as she brought her hands up to cover her face. Behind her closed eyelids she saw the creature advancing, crouching toward them.

Cynthia's cries had changed to an animal whimpering. "No . . . no . . . no. . . ."

Karen dropped her hands. She could feel the veins and muscles standing out in her throat and neck as she fought to hold in the scream exploding in her. She opened her eyes and stared past Cynthia to the window on the driver's side. Framed in it was the creature's head.

It glared its malevolence at her, its breath harsh and raspy in its flared nostrils, and its tongue darted out as if trying to reach across Cynthia and spike itself into her throat.

For a time that outlived eternity, they stared at one another, the thing, Karen felt, looking deeper and deeper into her until it saw into her soul, and she unable to see past the depthless eyes of fire.

Then the creature gave a violent hiss and moved back from the window. An instant later it was a portion of the night.

Cynthia had regained partial control of herself, and her mewlings were heavy pantings. She sat staring straight ahead.

The car door clicked open. "What was it? What in

the name of God is going on?''

It was Don, reaching in and gently helping Cynthia from under the wheel. Behind him Jeff and Billy watched, their faces blending curiosity and fear.

"Some—something . . . terrible,''          Cynthia moaned. "Oh my God, Don, you should have seen it . . . those horrible red eyes, the fangs. . . .''

He held her close to him, patting her shoulders. "I did, love. I did see it.''


She lay snuggled in the river nest, beside the mortal body, thinking of the boy Jeff, of the deep desire in her.

She pressed closer to the woman body, absorbing some of its warmth through her scales.

Fear was on her side. They did not know how to combat her.

Not long, she thought. Not long.

Soon the boy would be hers.

# CHAPTER 11

Sam Cooper leaned back in his desk chair and windmilled his pencil through his fingers. Karen now recognized it as a nervous habit.

He looked at her, and then at Cynthia. A little grin formed under his mustache. "I know you two hadn't been drinking, because there wasn't enough time between when I saw you at the citizens' meeting and the time you reported the incident. So I grant you did see something."

"Thanks," Cynthia said. A hint of exasperation sounded in her voice.

Karen said nothing. She looked around the little cell of Cooper's office and tried to understand why she and Cynthia were being considered unstable by so many people. What they, and Don, and the boys had seen in the driveway, was a creature no mind could devise—not even one soggy with alcoholic fumes. She was wishing they had not reported it.

"Look, you've got to admit the timing was . . . well, not in your favor. You had just left a meeting in which I, myself, hinted we were dealing with an unknown kind of creature. Almost everyone in this town is uptight—so when two people leave a meeting

in which a ghost-like creature is blamed for the
murders and report seeing such a thing . . . well.
. . ." He shrugged his shoulders. "People on the
verge of panic have to have something against which
to turn their emotions."

Karen looked at him. "You mean Cyn and I are
being made into scapegoats?"

"Something like that, yes."

"That's absurd," Cynthia said.

"The human mind can be an absurd thing when
not controlled, Mrs. Porter."

Cynthia gave a dry chuckle. "That's undeniable.
But it doesn't solve our problem, Officer Cooper."

"She's right," Karen said. "Because we reported
an encounter with a . . . a thing, the likes of which
has never been seen, we're being branded as two
hysterical women contributing to a growing mass
hysteria. We've been questioned by the Grove Center
police, by the sheriff's department, and by that man
with the Criminal Investigation Department from
Tallahassee. And we've told each and every one of
you exactly what we saw. Together and separately. I
admit, very frankly, it's hard to believe—but what
we reported happening happened."

Sam Cooper stopped windmilling his pencil,
leaned forward and rested his forearms on his desk.
"I believe you. I'm more than certain that what you
say occurred really did take place—and for one very
big reason . . ."

"What's that?" Cynthia asked.

"You both have described this thing as serpent-
like. That is, what you could make out looked like a
big serpent. Now, that fits in with what I said at the

meeting, but you both said it raised itself up and accomplished movements in a vertical position. Now that's what makes me believe. Both those girls were very strong. Neither one of them would have been unable to hold her own against an ordinary serpent; in fact, both of them could well have bested any snake, no matter what its size. But a creature which is partially invisible and which has abnormal movements . . . well, it could have killed them."

"Are you alone in that theory, Mr. Cooper?" Karen asked.

"For now, yes." He smiled. "But I am persuasive."

"I'll take that as encouraging," Cynthia said.

"I want you to." He looked at Karen. "As for your sister, Mrs. Sommers, I've nothing to report. I'm sorry."

"I suppose this has pushed it aside for a while."

He nodded. "For a little while. But the file is still open, and we're trying to find the apartment you say she rented. Frankly, that's become more difficult than I imagined. I'm starting to think she used an assumed name and probably changed her appearance. But we'll home in on it, believe me."

"I'm sure you will. Thank you for telling me."

Cooper stood up. "I guess there's not much more we can cover now. Thanks again for your cooperation. I hope we can get you both off the hot seat before too long."

Lost in their own thoughts, neither said much on the drive to Karen's.

The next three days crept by with an agonizing

slowness. As usually occurs after such incidents, Karen and Cynthia's notoriety lessened when the first accusations of self-seeking fame were past. Sam Cooper did phone, however, telling her it was possible Jennifer's apartment on Seminole was discovered. But it was not being used. And where the car was kept, they had no idea. He sounded sincere, and Karen thought he was sincere; but she also had more than a vague suspicion the case wasn't being given high priority, because he admitted there were persistent reports of sightings of a blonde woman driving a grey Pinto. Yet, in all truth, even in a town as small as Grove Center it would not be difficult to become a phantom if a person used care and imagination.

Karen forced herself not to think of serpents and of a disappearing sister. But she was only partially successful. Nothing would fall into proper perspective as long as those two affairs went unsettled. But she was determined. She had bastions to rebuild, behind which she would gather her strength and return to the life which had become obsolete. Now, before Patrick returned, she was going to eliminate her own personal terrors moving through the murky gloom of her subconscious. And she was going to stop her ears against the wails of her own personal banshees.

The storm had made the lawn too wet to mow and left the Jay-Cee Field too wet to conduct the baseball clinic; Jeff had been busy in the shed constructing his ship model. He had become as intent on it as he usually was on his baseball, hardly taking any time for meals during the three-day period. Occasionally, sitting at her drawing table, Karen wondered if his concentrated endeavor was not an attempt to hold away from himself the many inexplicable things he had had forced on him in recent days. No matter how adult he tried to act, or think of himself as, he was only fifteen and still so very vulnerable.

After lunch, on the fourth day, he came into the house carrying the model sloop.

It was beautiful; the most delicate whittling, joints perfectly glued, sails and rigging which looked just right. She said, "They don't do any better in the shipyards along the coast."

"I'm taking it down to the river to try it."

Intuition screamed at her to object, to make up some gentle, but firm, story which would keep him here, make him feel that staying at the house was what he should do. But the eagerness and the pride on his face stopped her. And it was broad daylight; what, after all, could happen to him?

"Don't stay too long."

He grinned. "Yes'm."

"Have a good sail."

There wasn't any breeze on the river, so he couldn't really tell how well the sails worked; but the hull was almost watertight, with only a trickle of water seeping in where he'd missed gluing a joint. It floated upright, too.

Using a stick, he pushed it over the dark water, keeping it about three feet out from the bank. He'd give it a shove and stand back and watch it glide its way over the mirror-smooth surface. It really did look wonderful.

"Jeff."

He looked around.

"Jeff. Over here!"

She was standing under a willow tree, its drooping slender branches like a feathery green curtain around her. She was wearing blue shorts and a skimpy blue halter, standing with one hip outthrust, one arm holding back the willow strands and the other hanging at her side. Thin shadows played over her tawny hair and honey-colored skin, giving the impression of tiny tremors running through her. There were little glints of amber in her eyes, and her lips glistened a deep red.

"Aunt Jennifer!" He walked toward her. The boat drifted into a clump of water hyacinths, where it stuck between two purple blossoms. "Where have you been? Geez, everybody's looking for you."

She smiled and chuckled, low in her throat and husky. "I imagine they are."

"Why didn't you come back to the house?"

"I think you know why, don't you?" Her voice was lazy.

He nodded and looked down at his feet. "Mom made you go away."

"You don't have to be embarrassed about it. I wanted to go."

"I missed you, Aunt Jennifer," he blurted out.

"And I missed you, Jeff." Her voice became even lower, almost purring. "Remember that night in your bedroom? I do. I couldn't forget it."

He sucked his lower lip between his teeth and his eyes furtively crept over her body. What he could see of it between her shorts and halter was so strong looking, and yet so soft. He could feel her warmth, too. And there was a subtle spicy scent about her. For the first time, he became aware of the true sensuousness of a woman. Down in his stomach a tight feeling tied his mucles into knots.

Jennifer gave a murmuring laugh. "I invited you to my apartment, but since you didn't come, this place will have to do. Why don't you come in, Jeff—and we can . . . talk?"

"In there? Under the tree?"

"Yes."

He looked around. "Let me get my boat, first."

"Oh, leave it, Jeff. It will be all right there." She stretched a hand out to him. "Come on in under the tree and visit with me."

He reached out and took her hand. Very gently she pulled him into the green-hued twilight beneath the tree. It was like being under clear water. There were clothes hanging from some of the branches and a heavy blanket spread like a carpet, covering the ground.

"Do you live here, Aunt Jennifer?"

"Mmm, most of the time. I have a small apartment where I go to take showers."

"It's kind of camping out, isn't it?"

"Just about." She squeezed his hand. "Do you like it in here?"

"Yeah, it's real nice."

She dropped to her knees and pulled him downward. "Let's sit down and talk."

He was looking at her again, watching the sleek way the muscles worked under her skin. When she bent forward to brush a twig from her knee, they rippled along her back. He thought he had never seen anything so delicate.

Then he pulled his eyes away and looked at the clothes hanging from the branches. "It looks like you really do live here."

"I do."

"Why, when you have an apartment?" He thought the idea was dumb, but didn't want to say it.

"Oh, I have my own commune here. I was so tired of people when I came down here, I just had to get away from them. Do you understand what I'm trying to say?"

"Yeah, I guess. But I think I'd rather live in an apartment and keep the doors closed."

"I'll be moving back into a house before too long, Jeff. I've had just about enough of camping here."

He started to say he thought that was a good idea, but she smiled and arched her back, pushing her breasts against their halter.

"Do you like me, Jeff?" she asked.

"Sure. You're a neat person."

"I mean as a woman, not as your aunt."

He started to say he did, but he couldn't find his voice, so he just nodded.

She made a low sound in her throat like a big cat purring and once more pulled down on his hand. This time he dropped to his knees beside her. Then, before he completely realized what she was doing, she dropped his hand and pulled his T shirt up his torso. Automatically he raised his arms, and she removed it from him with one swift and easy motion.

"There," she smiled. "You'll be more comfortable."

He nodded, not knowing whether to stay on his knees or hunker back on his rear, and not knowing what to say. But he wished she would take off her halter. The memory of her breasts was occupying a big portion of his mind.

She was starting to breath a little harder and a little faster. Under her long lashes, her eyes stared at him intently. It was as though she was examining him to see if he would fit into some plan she had. For the first time in her company, he felt embarrassed and awkward.

He was going to ask her what she was thinking, when she suddenly leaned forward and kissed him. At first she put the softness of her lips gently on his, then pressed them harder, forcing his apart. When his lips were forced into an oval, she darted her tongue into his mouth and probed it against his until he felt his own stiffen and push back. She moaned and attacked his tongue with her own in a renewed frenzy, keeping her mouth tight to his. In a little while he began to run out of breath and tried to pull away. For a moment longer, she held the kiss, then straightened.

"You have never been kissed like that before?"

He shook his head.

Her lips, now with a faintly bruised appearance, quivered in a tiny smile. "That's only one of the things I can teach you, Jeff, if you want to learn. There're many more, too. And you should learn, because someday you'll need to know all the ecstasy of love so you'll find pleasure yourself and give pleasure to the woman who you love. It's a secret most men don't know, but I'll give it to you. Do you want to learn?''

This was weird talk. Right now he couldn't think of any girls he wanted to excite, but someday knowing how might be useful.

He nodded.

''Good. And we'll have fun while I teach you. Don't you think so?''

He nodded again. Damn, it was all he could do. His throat was too dry and his heart was beating too fast for him to try to speak. Something, he knew, very important was happening to him, something which was about to change his life; and, though it excited and mystified him, it frightened him a little, too.

''In the act of love, Jeff, remember all women are the same: be she a high-society member or one who walks the street selling herself. A woman's body is the same no matter what the brain that guides it or the clothes which adorn it. All have their secret points of passion. Learn these, Jeff, and all women will be yours. One by one, I'll show them to you and, in time, among women you'll be as masterful as a king.''

If possible, his heart beat faster and he ground his teeth together to hold back his heavy breathing. He had never felt like this before. He had never been this close to delirium. He struggled for control of his voice and obtained it long enough to ask, ''Are you going to start teaching me today?''

She shook her head. ''No. Today will be a time when you discover what a woman's body is, its frailties and its strengths—which are many.'' She raised a brow. ''You have never slept with a woman or taken her in the act of love?''

He shook his head.

She laughed. It was a trilling, bird-like sound. ''Then this afternoon will be the most wondrous you have ever spent.''

''Maybe we should wait, Aunt Jennifer.'' In spite of himself, he found he was a little frightened. This was his aunt!

Her eyes narrowed. ''Waiting accomplishes nothing, Jeff. And I am Jennifer, not Aunt Jennifer.''

''I just don't think it's right.''

''You will, Jeff. You will.''

She reached behind her and undid the ties to her halter. In a very slow, erotic movement she removed it and dropped it at her side. Her heavy breasts swung free before him.

''Take them,'' she whispered. ''Take them in your hands as you did the night in your bedroom.''

He reached out and laid his hands flat on them. The tightness in his stomach slipped even lower into his loins and became a true pain.

Jennifer leaned forward, pressing into his hands. ''Do you think it is all right now?''

His brain was clogged. Nothing existed but the softly firm flesh in his hands.

His aunt pressed harder against his palms, moaning low in her throat. Her lips found his and mashed against them.

Karen looked at the paint-spattered clock on the taboret. The time was nearing four o'clock. Where was Jeff? He had been gone nearly three hours, and allowing for a time slippage caused by the novelty of a new toy, he still should have returned by now.

She got up and looked out the studio window towards the shed, hoping he might have returned and been too thoughtless to call up to her. But the door was closed and it had that special look only empty buildings have. She knew he was still down at the river.

She cleaned her brushes hurriedly, driven by a uneasiness which she knew was going to become stronger until it turned into fear.

She almost ran down the stairs and across the veranda. When she was on the lawn, she did run until she reached the path winding through the fields to the river.

"Damn it, Jeff!" she said out loud, and heard it coming from her mouth in as much a sob as an exclamation. "This is the last time I'll trust you to go out alone. Damn it, why did I let you? Why?"

She came to the river bank before she expected. He wasn't there. She stopped, baffled as to which direction to take, then remembered he usually made his way north.

And then she remembered something else!

Jennifer!

It was north of here where Jennifer had taken him not too long after her arrival to talk with him and start to weave her spell.

"No! Oh my God, no!"

She started to run as best she could on the uneven, root-covered, ground. Once she fell, skinning her knee, not feeling the sharp pain of the abrasion. She sprang back to her feet and half stumbled, half ran, on.

She spotted the little boat, lying on its side among the hyacinths, trapped and helpless, almost as though the long-stemmed plants entwining it were preparing to devour it.

She stopped, full of a new fear. Should she dive in? Or turn back to the house and phone for aid?

She heard a moan. It was coming from her right. There was nothing there, only a willow tree weeping among its coarser neighbors.

Once again a moan came to her. This time it had substance and direction. It was the whimpering sigh of a woman; it came from behind the veil of the willow's branches.

Anger and terror took her swiftly to the tree. She thrust aside the thin branches and stared into a watery green world, at confusion of naked flesh her mind refused to untangle.

Then understanding came. Jennifer was on her forearms and knees, her body almost concealing Jeff, who lay on his back beneath her, his hands wandering over her nakedness.

"Goddamn you, Jennifer! Goddamn you!"

She sprang into the green light and kicked her sister with all her might. Jennifer, surprised and hurt, squealed and rolled the ground, grasping left side. Jeff lay on his back staring up at his mother, disbelief and shock on his face.

"What kind of bitch are you?" she screamed. "Damn you!"

"Mom," Jeff cried. "Don't—"

"Shut up!"

Jennifer was on her feet, now, facing Karen. If

there had been any shock and surprise on her face, it was gone, replaced by rage.

"Stay clear, sister," she rasped, a hiss curling around the words. "Jeff is mine now."

"Are you out of your mind, you crazy bitch?" Karen's fingers were clawing, the muscles in her thighs and calves bunching for the leap upon the naked, sneering woman.

Jeff scrambled to his feet and stood looking from one woman to the other.

"Mother, Aunt Jennifer—"

"I told you to be quiet. You and I will have this out when we get home."

"He's not going home with you, Karen." Her eyes slitted. "Jeff is coming away with me. For a day or two."

She laid a hand, as if protectively, on his shoulder.

"You're mad!"

The eyes slitted more, taking on an amber hue. Very deliberately she pulled Jeff tightly to her side, so he leaned against her sturdy nakedness. "You'd like to come away with me, wouldn't you, Jeff?"

He looked up at her, then at his mother. His face was a mask of indecision, but underlaid, Karen saw with a terrible wrench of her heart, by wanton sexual desire.

"I'd like to, Aunt Jennifer." Then to his mother, "I'm a man now, mother. I'm fifteen, remember?"

"Jeff . . ."

"Just for a little while, mother. Just for a day or two."

Jennifer laughed. "Now, sister. Back off and let us go."

She made no move, but stood dumb and empty and disbelieving. Around her the world had slipped away.

"I control you, sister. With Jeff in my company, I control you. Do you hear, you stupid cow?" Jeff stirred slightly; she ignored him.

Karen nodded.

"Then stand aside and let us pass."

She put one foot behind the other and stepped aside.

As they came even with her, Jennifer's hand tightened slightly on Jeff's shoulder. She said, "Go outside and wait."

With a final look at his mother, a little more uncertain than he would have liked it to be, he pushed his way through the willow curtain.

The amber tint in Jennifer's eyes was glaring, now; the breath hissed through her flared nostrils.

"Get down on your knees."

Karen hesitated.

"Remember I have your son."

Karen fell to her knees. She felt no loss of dignity. She had lost so much more.

With a grunt, Jennifer drove her foot in a vicious kick into Karen's hip, knocking her sprawling halfway across the area.

She lay there. Her mind fled to some nonexistent place seeking peace and rest.

Very vaguely, she heard Jeff ask, "Did you kick mother?"

"Yes."

"Why, Aunt Jennifer?"

"She kicked me, Jeff. She deserved it, don't you

think?''

Silence.

"Come on, Jeff. Let's get dressed and leave here."

She listened to them dressing, and, after a moment, she heard them move away. She drifted off into a grey kind of consciousness where nothing existed. The last sound she heard was her own hacking sob.

She had been in the mortal body for so long, lugging it through its cumbersome movements, that her own muscles were becoming weak, responding to her demands more slowly.

But the boy was there, sitting in the archway of the ruins. She watched him take a handkerchief from the pocket of his jeans and dab at a thorn scratch on his forearm. Even covered, he was a beautiful thing. There would be many delicious moments with him. The woman body provided its delight as well.

Soon . . . soon this hiding would be over.

# CHAPTER 12

A portable quartz movie light snapped on, filling the living room with the uncompromising glare of a hundred white suns. Somewhere behind it, a camera began to whir. Then a perfectly modulated voice started talking.

Karen looked up from her chair, trying to see the face of the correspondent, but he was silhouetted against the light. All she could hear were his words.

"This first day of summer, Monday, June twenty-first, has not been a day for Mrs. Karen Sommers to celebrate. This afternoon her fifteen-year-old son, Jeffrey, was kidnapped while at play along the river by her own sister, Miss Jennifer Logan. We at WTAW have learned there are many bizarre twists to this incident, not the least of which is that the authorities have been looking for Miss Logan for a number of days—asked to do so by Mrs. Sommers."

Another camera began to whir, taking advantage of the first one's lighting.

"From what we have been able to gather," the voice continued, "Mrs. Sommers and Mrs. Logan fought over the boy." The silhouette turned towards her. "Is that correct, Mrs. Sommers?"

She blinked, trying to focus her eyes as well as her thoughts. "Yes."

"You actually did battle, so to speak, on the river bank—you to save your son, and she to take him away?"

"Yes . . . we fought."

"And she overpowered you, and took your son?"

"Yes, yes . . . She knocked me unconscious and, when I came to, they were gone." She looked around. Her face, she knew, was starting to twist with the desperation she felt. "Please. . . ."

The correspondent quickly said, "Thank you, Mrs. Sommers. This is Lyle Jenkins reporting from the home of Mrs. Karen Sommers for Eyewitness News in Grove Center."

The lights went blank.

"Mrs. Sommers!" A pointed-faced woman, glasses pushed up on her severe hairdo, pointed a pencil at her. "Aren't you one of the ladies who reported seeing a monster several days ago?"

"I saw a creature, yes."

"You have a vivid imagination, don't you?"

"What does that mean? What does that have to do with my son's kidnapping?"

"It seems you're good at telling stories. Could this be another one?"

Karen felt her muscles knot. She wanted to reach out and rake her nails down the smirking face. "Let's say I'm good at seeing monsters."

"What does that mean?"

"I saw one the other night, and I saw another one today."

"It was your sister, you say, who kidnapped your

son."

"Yes . . . and she's a monster!"

A chorus of voices shouted at her. One, a man's, rose above the others. "Mrs. Sommers, if your son is fifteen he must be of fairly good size. Why didn't he help you fight off his aunt?"

Instinctively she recoiled, her mind closing in on itself until it blanked out all remembrances. Around her the jumble of faces leered at her, while the jumble of sound they created hammered at her eardrums. A tremor of panic ran through her.

"I—I don't know," she stammered. "I was knocked unconscious."

"Before that," a voice shouted. "Why didn't he come to your assistance before that?"

"I think he tried," she lied. "After I was unconscious, Jennifer might have used a gun to make him leave with her. I—I just can't say."

"That doesn't sound very good, Mrs. Sommers."

"No, are you telling us the truth?"

"Mrs. Sommers, did you and your son get along together?"

"How long have you been a widow, Mrs. Sommers?"

"Why did you have the police looking for your sister, Mrs. Sommers?"

"Is Jeffrey a victim of a family feud?"

All the voices asking, demanding, but none of them offering sympathy, none of them telling her where Jeff was.

Then from nowhere, amid the contorted faces, came one set in determination, cutting through the wolfpack, backing them from the room, using slender shoulders when necessary; pushing them from the house. Cynthia.

Eventually only two strangers remained, a deputy sheriff and the man from the Criminal Investigation Department, but they were unobtrusive, sitting at the kitchen table where a command center for the investigation had been set up. They sat huddled over area maps and CB radios.

"You need rest," Cynthia said as she sat Karen down in the living room. "You need lots and lots of rest."

Karen's entire body, every muscle and tendon and fiber, ached with exhaustion. But she said, "I need it, yes. But you know I'm not going to get it, Cyn. I'm blowing up inside. Voices are screeching in my head."

"Try, Kar. For God's sake, try. What good will you be if you collapse? Answer me that. What will a body in intensive care do to help?"

"Oh, Cynthia. You're exaggerating again."

"Well, I've got to get your attention, and I don't have a two-by-four to whomp you with."

"All right, you win. But first I've got to talk with you. I've got to, or I really will blow up. I've got to tell someone the truth, and you're the only one, other than Patrick, I have."

The concern deepened behind Cynthia's oval glasses. She hunched forward in her chair. "What is it?"

Karen felt awkward; words didn't want to come. She closed her eyes and let her hands hang from the arms of her chair. "Cynthia . . . Jeff chose Jennifer over me. It was his decision to go with her.''

"Oh dear God! I'm not believing you're saying that, Karen.''

"I'm saying it, Cyn. It's the truth." She was talking into the darkness behind her closed eyes. It took the embarrassment away, and words began to come to her.

"Jennifer didn't take him away from me in a fight, they way I told all those people out there. She took him, and that's truth enough for them.''

"What happened out there, Kar? What, in God's name, really happened?''

She squeezed her eyes shut tight and drew a long breath. She wondered if the pain she felt was contorting her face, if when she did try to tell Cyn her voice would be more than a formless sound. In the darkness behind her closed eyelids, she saw it all played over again, each detail a graphic image.

"Are you all right?" Cynthia's voice sounded close to fright.

She nodded. "Yes. I didn't tell those people the truth, Cyn. I lied to them, because I don't want to face the truth of what happened out there.''

"You don't have to tell me, Kar. You really don't.''

"I want to."

"Then do it slow, Kar. There's no hurry. We have as much time as you need.''

"As you know, Jeff went down to the river to test the boat model he'd been working on, and when he didn't come home by four, I went looking for him. All that's true, Cyn. That's how it began. I was frightened, oh God, I was frightened. I knew

Jennifer was playing a role in it. As I ran down the path to the river, something told me she was the reason Jeff hadn't returned. Oh God, Cyn, it was terrible!"

"Easy, Kar. Just take it easy."

She opened her eyes and looked at Cynthia. "You can imagine the terror, can't you, Cyn, if it was Billy who had not returned?"

"I know what you felt."

"And then I found them—under a willow tree. She had piled branches around it to form a cozy hideaway with blankets spread on the ground and her clothes hanging from the branches. I heard them before I saw them. I found the entrance to the nest and went in. And they were there. They were. . . ."

"Kar?"

Suddenly her memory stopped, then began again, flickering like a cheap movie. "They—they were having sex, Cyn."

"Oh, my God!"

"She was on top of him, working herself into sexual gratification. I could smell her, musky and woodsy. For a moment, they didn't see or hear me, and, as I watched them, I had the most terrible feeling that it was me straddling my son, enticing him with my dangling breasts and naked loins."

"Karen . . . Karen! What, in the name of God, can I say to help you erase that from your mind?"

"Nothing, Cyn." She looked at her friend. "That picture, and that feeling, will always be in the back of my mind."

"That bitch! That incestuous bitch!"

"I kicked her off of him, screaming at them both.

But it did no good, Cyn. Jennifer asked him if he'd want to go away with her . . . and . . . and he said yes." She felt a sob forming in her throat and swallowed. "He told me he was a man now, that he could make decisions like that."

"And he went with her? You're telling me, he turned his back on his mother and went away with that—that slut? Oh, Kar, something had been done to him. Jeff isn't that type."

"Sex," she said. "It was his first time. He wasn't thinking straight."

"You couldn't stop him . . . talk to him . . . even beg him?"

She shook her head. "She laughed at me, telling me she controlled him absolutely. And she did, Cyn. He looked confused, but he was determined to go with her. I was helpless. I was at her mercy, knowing I had to do what she demanded if I wanted to see Jeff safe again." She clasped her hands in her lap and stared over Cynthia's shoulder. "She made me get down on my knees before her then kicked me on my hip like I'd kicked her. That's how my hip got bruised, not in a fight with her."

When she was finished, Cynthia did not speak. The voices of the men in the kitchen came to them, muffled; they were talking low. Out on the road they could hear cars passing slowly in low gear, so the occupants could gawk at this latest house where tragedy had struck. But there were none of the sounds of normal summer, no rustling leaves, no high-pitched insect songs exploring the open windows. Nature seemed hushed and pulled in upon itself.

The phone rang.

Cynthia answered and came hurrying back into the living room. "It's Patrick. The operator has finally located him."

Karen went to the phone.

"Kar, what's wrong? The operator said it was an emergency. What's happened?"

"It's Jennifer, Patrick. She's come back and she's taken Jeff away."

"No! No!"

She knew the disbelief on his face was turning to rage.

"When, darling? When in hell did it happen?"

"Just a few hours ago. Late this afternoon. He was down at the river with a model boat he'd made, and when he didn't come back in time I went down to find him. She was there, and she . . . she took him away from me."

"How? How did she do that?"

"I'll tell you when you get here."

"That, by God, won't be long. I'll leave here as soon as I hang up."

"Be careful, Patrick. Please be careful, darling. I need you so very much."

"I will, love. I promise you, I will."

He hung up. She listened to the hollow sound of the telephone wires. Desperation hovered near, like a tremendous blow about to strike her.

The night slipped towards its darkest hour. Don Porter came, bringing Cynthia her night things and a change of clothing. He didn't stay long. After a few words of condolence and a quick kiss on Karen's cheek, he went back out to the car where Billy and the baby waited and drove home.

Cynthia made coffee for them and the men in the kitchen, who were commencing to show signs of strain and frustration.

When sleep came, it struck Karen without warning. One instant, it seemed, she was awake and staring blindly through the window, and the next she was gone into a huge nothingness. Several times she felt Cynthia fussing over her, placing a pillow behind her head and raising her feet to a stool. It was a depthless sleep in which no hideous forms wandered, no eyes bored into hers. It was the sleep of total exhaustion.

The day was brilliant when she awoke with a start. She had overslept. She pushed herself up and winced as cramped muscles protested the sudden stretching. A pain dug into her hip, too, where Jennifer had kicked her, and she suspected the entire side of her buttock would be black and blue.

Before she'd taken the first step, Cynthia was at her side offering support.

Karen forced herself to smile. "I'm no cripple, you know." But even as she spoke, a twinge of pain from her hip jerked her erect.

"The hip?" Cynthia asked.

She nodded.

"The bitch!"

"Is there any news?"

"Good and bad."

"Oh God, a game. Not so early, Cyn."

Cynthia shook her head. "It's no game."

"Well, okay. Give me the good first."

"They found Jennifer's rented car. It was parked

off the lane about two miles up the road from the ruins. The sheriff's man said it appears she's parked it there several times and covered it with brush.''

"The bad news?" Before she asked, because he wasn't there, she knew concerned Patrick.

"His fuel pump broke along the road, and he had to have the car towed into Hanes City. Naturally there isn't the right one in the whole town, so they're ordering it from Miami. He's trying to get a bus out, but there's nothing coming in this direction until close to noon."

Suddenly, from nowhere, Karen was overwhelmed by a vivid sense of catastrophe. She saw the end approaching for them all. She gasped and swayed.

"What's wrong?" Cynthia grabbed her arm.

"Nothing. Just a dip from the hip."

"No, Karen, it's more than that. Give."

Karen shook herself. There was no point making the day darker by telling Cynthia. "Honestly, it's just my hip. What I need is a good hot shower."

"Are you sure?"

"Yup. Help me over to the stairs, will you? I'll make it from there."

As she climbed the stairs, Cynthia stood below, watching anxiously, a vaguely puzzled expression on her face.

The shower drained most of the soreness from her. She had been right about the bruise on her hip. A ragged purple stain covered the skin; it looked as though a big plum had been squashed and smeared against the flesh.

Cynthia had a bowl of cereal and a cup of coffee waiting for her when she came down. No one else was in the kitchen. "It's not much, but I don't think you should put too much on your stomach yet."

"Where are the policemen?"

"Oh, they left early this morning, right after Jennifer's car was found. They moved to the police department in town."

"Then there's just you and me."

"Don't let your thoughts turn in the direction I think they're going to. Don't you dare!"

"It is lonely here, Cyn."

"It won't be for long. Now eat your breakfast."

She was only halfway through when a car pulled into the driveway and stopped at the veranda steps. It was a dusty blue Plymouth; if the dents and waves in its fenders were any indication, it had traveled many hard miles.

The door opened. It was Sam Cooper.

Cynthia went to the screen door and called for him to come ito the kitchen for a cup of coffee.

When he was seated on a chair at the table, he looked from one to the other and smiled. "You two are close, aren't you?"

"Closer than sisters, and I'm not referring to what's happened," Cynthia said.

"Too close," Karen said, pouring him his coffee. "I want her to go home and get some rest and spend some time with her family."

"I don't need rest, and Don and Billy insist I stay here. A neighbor lady is helping with Susy and will phone if there's any emergency."

"You both are very lucky. Maybe sometime I'll be fortunate enough to find a friendship like yours."

"Did you come with news of the investigation?"

Karen asked.

"This is all very unofficial," he said, "because I'm about four miles out of my jurisdiction. But I wanted to see you, Mrs. Sommers, to tell you how sorry I am we couldn't find your sister before she did this. It's one of the things that makes police work so damn frustrating."

"You did everything you could, Mr. Cooper."

"I wonder. Oh, we did everything we could think of, but there's always that nagging thought that we overlooked something very obvious."

"It happens. It happens."

"But not with such disastrous affects."

She didn't know what else to say. Maybe, if it hadn't been her sister, and her son, she could mouth more platitudes.

"One very odd thing has been unearthed, though." He looked away, hesitating, turning words over in his mind. Then: "Your sister must have been living mostly under that willow tree, because the apartment manager has stated she used the apartment only occasionally—possibly only for showers and the like."

"God, that's sick, sick, sick," Cynthia said.

"Very sick, Mrs. Porter."

Karen looked through the window. A grey cloud was resting on the northern horizon and spreading itself like a cloak along the tree tops. Was Jeff under that cloud some place with his aunt? With his sick, sick, sick aunt?

She brought her eyes back from the window and saw they were both watching her.

"Don't allow your mind to wander too much,

Mrs. Sommers," Cooper said. "Keep it occupied with trivialities.

"How? I don't even know what's trivial anymore."

"Most of our conversations fall in that category," Cynthia smiled. "Just keep talking to me."

Cooper laughed. "That sounds like good advice. You know, you're lucky to have a friend like Cynthia."

Cynthia reached across the table and laid her hand on top of Karen's. "I'm the one that's lucky, Mr. Cooper. I have Karen for a friend."

He got up. "Whatever. I'm sorry, but I must go."

They walked out to the veranda with him, and as he was getting into his car, Karen said, "Come back any time. You're always welcome."

"Thanks." He started the engine. "I'll keep you informed the best I can."

They went back in. The stillness of the house was oppressive. Is this, Karen wondered, what the stillness of a tomb is like? Cynthia turned the radio in the kitchen; hard rock smashed from the speaker. She quickly fiddled with the dial and flipped the switch to FM. Easy listening music filtered into the silence, pushing it back, making it retreat into the rooms away from the kitchen and foyer.

Even with the silence gone, Karen felt as if the old house was squeezing in on her, blaming her for the loss of Jeff's feet running up and down the stairs and his voice calling from one room to another. And it was right in its assessment. Oh, it was so right. So many things she could have done to save him instead of groveling on her knees. But what? God, tell me

what I could have done! Nothing. You did right.
Jennifer had Jeff. You had to protect him as best you
could under the circumstances. Yes. Keep telling
yourself that, Karen Sommers. Keep telling yourself
that cowardice and degradation were discretion.

She went out on the veranda. The cloud had spread
its darkness over more of the sky and was beginning
to take on the shape of a thunderhead.

Once upon a time—how many eons ago?—when a
restlessness settled on her, she'd hike to Ludlow's
Mill. There all the undercurrents of trouble ceased
tugging at her, and her well-disciplined beliefs
returned. But all the magic was gone from the
crumbling stone. Hate, and maybe death, were the
only visitors now.

Maybe they weren't. Maybe there was another—

She turned and, in spite of the pain in her hip,
almost ran into the house.

"Cyn!" She called. "Cyn, the mill!"

Cynthia came from the living room, the morning
paper in her hand. "What?"

"The mill, Cyn. Ludlow's Mill is where she is."

"Oh, Karen, remember what Mr. Cooper told
you. Keep your mind on trivialities."

"Cynthia, listen to me, please. There was something about the mill which attracted Jennifer. They
were like a magnet drawing her to them time and
again while she was here. It was almost a mystical
attraction, like a force she couldn't have resisted even
had she wanted to. That's where she has Jeff. That's
where she is! I know it!"

"Then let's call the sheriff and have him send some
men out there."

"No, there's no time. I'm going there, Cyn, and you phone the sheriff to tell him."

"Karen, for the love of God, use your head. That woman's dangerous. If she's there, she's got Jeff—and she'll make you give in again."

Strength gushed into Karen from a fountain of confidence. Inside her things were drawing together, shaping her into the creature of vengeance that could vanquish the monstrous ugliness that was Jennifer Logan.

"No, not again, Cyn. I've learned my lesson, and I know what to do to save my son."

"You're crazy, Karen. But I can see there's no shaking you. If you insist on going out there, then I'm going with you. I don't care what you know, or what you think you know. You're going to need help."

Karen didn't want Cynthia to accompany her, but she felt strongly that there was no time to argue. "All right."

It took three tries before the pickup started. It sputtered and coughed all the way down the driveway, finally giving itself a metallic shake when Karen turned onto the asphalt and gave it full power.

"You really should get that engine worked on," Cynthia said.

"It's the carburetor. Patrick's going to fix it." She turned into the lane leading back to the mill.

"How far along this are we going to go?" Cynthia asked.

"As far as we can."

"Maybe we'd better not go too far. If she's there, she'll be able to hear this truck a quarter mile away."

"You're right."

The old Dodge bucked and swayed and rattled, but it kept on going. When they came to the last bend in the lane, still out of sight of the ruins, Karen braked to a stop and turned off the ignition. The engine continued to run for a few seconds, then sighed and settled into silence.

They climbed down, and Karen said, "Cyn, you should have worn shoes rather than those sandals. This place is covered with sandspurs and nettles."

"I know I should have, but you wouldn't have given me time to change, and if I'd tried to, you'd have gone off without me."

"You're right. I'm sorry."

Cynthia shrugged. "If she's here, where would she be?"

Karen looked towards the mill. The tumbled walls were squat and black, seeming to crouch at the eastern end of the clearing brooding over a time long past. She saw only ugliness where once she had seen beauty. The cracks between the coquina stones swallowed the sunlight, making the walls shadowless from this distance, turning them into a dark malignancy against the green trees. Though she knew it was her imagination, she sensed a chill coming from them, reaching for her across the sun-warmed clearing.

"Most any place, I guess." She pointed at the large flat-topped piece of masonry. "Let's go over there first. That's where she was lying the day Patrick and I found the blood. We can use it as a starting place, anyway."

Cynthia nodded.

About three-quarters of the way across the clearing, Karen stopped. "Do you hear anything?"

"No." Cynthia cocked her head. "I don't hear anything at all."

"Then somebody's here. Somebody has frightened all the woods creatures into silence." She turned and faced Cynthia directly. "Cyn, go back to the truck and wait for me. Please."

"No, Karen. Now don't try to scare me."

"I wish I could." She turned and walked along the narrow path towards the stone.

Cynthia pushed her glasses up on her nose and followed.

She lay almost flat on the ground behind one of the old boiling vats, watching. As the women came closer, tiny tremors shook her body, causing the cold flesh to ripple on the sandy soil. The tightly woven scales covering her rattled thinly, sounding like dead twigs in a breeze. Instinct told her the venerable ones were smiling a blessing on her from their hallowed places. Surely, now, she must be one of the Chosen Ones.

She had warmed herself on the stone; the sun had leached the exhaustion from her body. For too long she had been in the woman body; its weight and cumbersomeness had weakened her muscles and tired her to her very bones.

After the mortals had trampled and torn up the old one, she had made a new nest along the river. There the woman body lay in its coma, the boy in a deep slumber.

The two women were at the stone, leaning against

it, talking in low tones.

She inched forward. How stupidly unaware mortals were. She narrowed her eyes as the scene became tinted with amber. The women continued to talk. She slithered forward another half a body's length, her head now under a thorn bush.

Then the mother of the boy walked slowly towards the far side of the clearing.

The one named Cynthia stayed near the stone, looking at the ruins through the round ovals of her glasses.

She inched forward again, coiling now under the bush.

She hissed her warning.

The woman looked, but saw nothing, the sunlight making blank circles of her glasses.

She moved out from under the bush, raised her head above the weed tops and looked for the mother of the boy. She was standing at the far edge of the clearing.

She hissed again.

This time the woman turned, her mouth opened as though to speak.

The lamia sprang.

# CHAPTER 13

Cynthia's scream struck the coquina walls and bounded and rebounded from angle to angle, frantically seeking a way out into the forest. It started low and trilled higher and higher until it became a raw, hysterial shriek throwing abysmal terror over the clearing.

At the edge of the trees, Karen spun around, her heart skipping a beat, her flesh crawling.

Cynthia was writhing, bent over, struggling with something; she seemed to have a great hump swelling from between her shoulders. It was almost impossible to see in the sunlight, a twisting gossamer mass of amber with an undefinable form writhing within it. Part of the mass wrapped around Cynthia's hips, part around her breasts, part around her throat, pulling her head back at a grotesque angle.

Cynthia was stumbling in blind circles pulling at the thing with one hand, gouging at its side with the other.

"Cyn, my God, Cyn!"

Karen ran towards her friend. At her cry, the creature gave a powerful yank at Cynthia's neck.

Desperately she struggled for balance, but the weight of the horror riding on her back unbalanced her, and with a cry of dismay she fell. The creature landed separately and whirled to meet Karen, red eyes blazing.

With a vicious hissing, it sprang to meet her face on, but she threw herself to her left and the hell-thing rushed past, lashing out, as it did, at her face.

It raised up for a moment; what must have been its head swung from side to side. Its eyes moved from one to the other, quicky, quickly. It did not lunge again.

Karen backed slowly towards Cynthia. Her friend was getting to her feet, blood running from her breast down her side and stomach, whimpering to herself.

"Get hold of my shoulder, Cyn. I'll lead you." She put her arm around Cynthia's waist. "We'll start down the path."

Cynthia clutched her shoulder. Slowly, too slowly, Karen lead her a half a dozen steps down the path.

Then the thing was at them again. It lashed at Cynthia's back. She screamed and staggered; Karen lost her grip around her waist. Cynthia stumbled and fell.

Karen spun to face it. It was raised up like a glimmering serpent standing on its tail, weaving, watching, the hot sun glancing from it and through it, so it became almost unseeable. Hissing louder, it moved nearer.

Karen fell back a step.

The creature came on, its eyes glowing fiercely now, with a deep, coruscating red. It stretched itself tall, then suddenly whirled towards Cynthia, its head poised like a hatchet to smash down on her skull.

"Cyn, look out!"

Karen drove herself forward, shoulders hunched, and slammed into the creature, driving it off balance to the ground. Her momentum would have carried her over and past the hissing, writhing creature, but with lightning speed it clamped a coil around her left ankle. She fell on her stomach, half on and half off the creature, her fingers digging into the sandy ground and her right cheek scraping across a sand spur. Under her the thing squirmed. She had a split-second blurred glimpse of gleaming eyes in a dart-like head coming down on her skull.

Then there was nothing.

Some time later a high piercing sound knifed its way into Karen. She stirred. Then pain throbbed in her head, not much yet, but enough to hint at what was to come later. She stirred again, and this time dug her fingers into the soil. Then the shriek came again. It drove deeper into her brain.

She opened her eyes and saw the light brown sand of the ground. She turned her head a little to her left. The pain that enmeshed her head tightened its grip. Blood from her forehead began running into her left eye, and trickled on her right cheek where the sand spur had scraped the flesh.

She blinked her eyes to bring distance into focus. It moved in and out, blurred and sharpened. Now, trying to ignore the pain, she drew a long breath and forced herself to concentrate. Everything became clearer. Sand. Dockweed. Nettles. A lizard sitting desperately still.

Another one of the horrible cries echoed around the ruins. Desperation and despair underlay the pain and fear in it. It was the sound of all the horror in the world.

Karen pushed herself to her knees, shook her head and wiped the blood from her eye with the back of her hand—then looked in the direction of the screams.

The creature had bent Cynthia back over the flat stone, pinning her shoulders on the rough surface by lumping itself on her chest. And very methodically, with strokes of slow deliberation, it was tearing her arched belly to bloody shreds with what appeared to be the tail of its slender body. Cynthia was writhing and flailing at the pointed head swaying over her, clawing with her fingernails at the translucent coils squirming on her chest. Her long legs were thrashing as her tortured muscles spasmed.

Her head turned, and she saw Karen swaying on her knees. "Help me, Kar. Oh, God, help me! Help me—"

Crying herself, now, although not aware of it, Karen managed to climb to her feet. She took a wobbling step, and then another. The creature turned its head and glared at her. It hissed.

She stumbled forward another step, her head whirling on a pivot of pain, bringing waves of dizziness. The throbbing mass hissed again, this time vehemently, as if telling her to come no closer. She gulped a mouthful of air and shuffled forward. Once more the thing hissed, now holding its tail poised over the bloodied flesh of Cynthia's belly.

"Help me . . . Kar. . . ."

Karen forced her clumsy, heavy legs to move again. She advanced another awkward step.

The creature, watching her with flaming eyes, lashed down and tore Cynthia's belly wide from her breasts to her loins.

A pure animal sound of horrible agony erupted from Cynthia.

Karen stopped. Its head suddenly distinct, the creature watched her balefully, its eyes wild and filled with seething flame, its tongue darting out and in, out and in.

They stared at one another.

Then the creature slipped its tail from Cynthia's belly to her throat.

Cynthia's pain-twisted mouth opened wide and she whimpered. Karen moaned.

With a wild hiss, it tightened itself around Cynthia's throat, hesitated as the woman whimpered and turned her frightened pleading eyes toward Karen. Then, with a powerful yanking motion, it tore Cynthia's throat out.

Cynthia's scream turned to a choking gurgle; blood fountained from her throat. Before the echoes of her final cry lost themselves among the fallen walls surrounding them, Cynthia's flaccid body rolled off the stone to the sand and curled there, a bloody piece of meat.

Karen whimpered.

Perhaps a half a minute went by while the creature crouched staring at her. Then it began to move. It undulated slowly towards her, seeming to swim in and out of the sheets of sunlight, until it was no more than six feet from her. She dropped her eyes, unable to look at it; now she could smell its aroma of woods and earth and blood. It hissed. Then it turned away and glided across the clearing, towards the trees on the west.

Unable to hold back the tears of misery squeezing from her eyes, she went to what was once Cynthia and knelt by the contorted dead flesh. Already flies were buzzing over the body, and ants were running across the cooling skin.

Something should be said, but what did one say to a dead friend who was beyond hearing? Cynthia Porter was gone. This bloody ruined flesh by the stone was not her friend.

She looked across the clearing. The creature had almost reached the trees; it was passing a small bush struggling for life amid the weeds. And while she watched it, all the terror which had writhed within her began to fade away, as if leached away by Cynthia's death. In its place, as she knelt by the remains of what had been her friend, she felt the change settle on her, a warm cloak covering her emotional nakedness. Determination. Confidence. Weak, but there, building her will.

The creature disappeared into the trees.

She looked down at the poor mutilated body. "I'll be back, Cyn, I'll be back. But I'll never be far away."

Pulling together all the strength she could find in her body, she half-stumbled, half-walked across the clearing. The blood was still flowing from her forehead. She found a sizable gash there. She kept wiping the blood to keep it from her eye and dabbed with her fingertips at the blood on her cheek.

At the place where it had disappeared, she hesitated, looked back towards the ruins where the body lay, then entered the tangled underbrush. There was no trail of broken weeds or twisted tree foliage; but an instinct, an almost audible whisper, told her to go ahead, to go to the river.

Dizziness came on her in spells, forcing her to stop and lean against the closest tree. Gnats and stinging insects swarmed at the blood on her face. In the breathless twilight world under the interwoven trees, the air was stagnant, and full of the smell of decay. Sharp thorny things scratched at her blue jeans and tore rents in her blouse. Perspiration oozed out of her skin and mixed with the blood on her face, and dripped from her chin.

And then there was the river, dark snaking body of water with no current and the rotting smell of water plants. She stood on the low bank, swatting at the insects buzzing around her head, and looked up and down the bank. South, she decided, south towards where Jennifer had hidden before.

She went more cautiously along the treacherous bank than she had through the forest. Instinct was whispering to her that it was this way the creature had traveled.

She almost didn't hear the sound of swishing water. When she did, she stopped. Not too far ahead, just beyond that clump of cabbage palms, something or someone was washing in the river. She stood very still, hardly daring to breathe, forcing herself to refrain from swatting at the insects clouding before her face. There was no other noise, only that of washing.

Then it ceased. Silence.

She remained still. Her mind, which had traveled down so many long corridors of darkness and fear, was working furiously. Then it found an answer.

She inched forward a half step at a time. She knew, now, she would discover one of two things beyond the cabbage palms. The creature—or Jennifer. This time with Jeff.

She pushed aside the fan-like fronds of the palm.

An oak tree stood some feet back from the river; its bottom limbs were dipping low on the water side. Brush had been placed against them to make a lean-to. On the bank, cat-o'-nine tails had been thrust into the water in quite a naturalistic way.

She crept closer.

A noise came down inside the lean-to. Feet, walking on dried leaves and moss. Holding her breath, choosing the ground for each step carefully, she went slowly around the corner of the lean-to. On its south side she found the doorway, a triangular opening in the piled brush. She was about to peep into it when she saw a small fault in the wall. Two of the interwoven branches had pulled apart. Leaning to it, shading her eyes with her cupped hands, she looked within.

At first she could see nothing in the interior gloom. And when she could, everything in her that was human wanted to scream and scream and scream.

The creature was an undulating mist hovering between the bodies of Jeff and Jennifer. Jennifer was on her back, stretched out with her arms at her sides and her feet together, all tidy-looking, like a body in

a morgue. Jeff was on his left side, his legs pulled up
a little. It was the way he slept at home. Both of them
were nude.

Then she backed shaking, but no longer on the
verge of screaming, she went back to the peep hole.

The thing had gotten down to the ground beside
Jennifer. It wove back and forth over her as if
drawing warmth from the living flesh; its slitted
amber eyes roamed up and down the still form. A
sibillant whisper came from it. Then slowly, drifting
like a grey shadow, it moved onto Jennifer's body
and stretched itself full length on top of her.

Almost immediately, wraith-like coils intertwin-
ing, it began to disappear into the long voluptuous
contours. Not with any speed, not slowly, either, but
with a steady downward sinking, until it vanished
completely within her and was no more. Only
Jennifer lay, still and rigid, on the mossy floor.

Karen backed away one step, then another, and
then another, and found the rough trunk of a tree
and leaned against it. She closed her eyes to shut out
the whirling world, but all she saw was Cynthia's
blood spurting in sunlight. She leaned her head back
against the bark and drew in a long breath.

Finally the surrounding trees quit spinning and
spilling their green in a blur before her, but her heart
still hammered in her chest and her breathing came in
short ragged gulps.

But after a little while gradually the strength she
had lost began to find its way back into her, and she
gingerly pushed herself away from the tree. She
found she was capable of standing alone.

From inside the lean-to there came rustlings, the

sounds of bodies changing position, a throaty laugh
and a sleepy murmur.

Dear God, she knew what was about to happen.
Hatred ripped through her at that abomination
which, she knew, had destroyed Jennifer and held
Jeff in its spell, a spell a great deal deeper than that
of the flesh.

She stood immobile. Rushing in there helter-
skelter would be folly, a folly very dangerous to Jeff.
She knew beyond any doubt that that thing was the
killer of the girls. . . .

God, you didn't save Cyn, but now help me! Show
me the way to avenge her!

She would have to attack the creature, even though
it was in Jennifer. But was Jennifer Jennifer anymore, even when the thing was not within her? Had
she been destroyed, eliminated, as a person? Turned
into a witless host? Too many questions, too many
horrors. Her mind was only functioning on three-
quarter power.

Through her unbloodied eye she stared up at the
sky. Are you going to help me, God? Are you going
to help my son?

A weapon. She neeed a weapon. Its strength was
probably increased by Jennifer's when it was in
possession, and Jennifer herself was a strong woman.

There was only one kind of weapon available to
her, a good heavy tree branch she could swing as a
cudgel. She looked around and saw nothing, and
knew she'd have to search for one back in the forest.
This area must have been picked clean during the
construction of the lean-to.

Dreading what she would witness, but knowing she

must take one more look into the hut, she went back to the peep hole.

Jennifer was lying on her left side. Jeff was on his right, snuggling against her, stroking her right breast, while Jennifer's right hand stroked his back in slow, gentle strokes.

Jennifer's voice, low, almost furry, asked, "Are you ready for a lesson, my Jeff?"

He nodded.

Sickened, Karen turned away. But she had gone no more than a dozen steps into the forest when the nausea turned to cold fury. Ten yards or so from the lean-to, and she had no trouble finding the piece of wood she wanted. It was covered with a deep-veined bark which would give her a good grip, and one end was forked. Just right, she thought, for gouging at eyes. Time had rolled back from her, stripping the veneer of civilization from her. She swung the wood several times, learning its weight for the hold she'd use. Then she turned back toward the lean-to.

Not too far from the entrance she stopped, careful to stay out of sight, and began to gather in all her strength. She ran her tongue over her lips, taking the dryness from them. It would return as soon as she sucked air.

A hiss.

She whirled her head to the right, torn between hope and fear of what she would see under the trees, watching her.

Nothing was there, only rippling shadows. Again the hiss. Down . . . down by her foot.

A rattler was coiled not a yard away, its head raised and its slitted eyes watching her. She made no move. There was no great fear in her. She had feared too much in recent days; she had no more capacity for it. She turned away. Then realization struck her. There, by God! There was the certain weapon—watching her with amber eyes, like Jennifer.

Very slowly, trying to hide the movement, she shifted the stick in her hands until the forked end was pointed at the snake. The sweat ran heavier down her back.

From inside the lean-to flesh slapped flesh. Jennifer's voice moaned; Jeff said something she couldn't understand. Time had almost run out.

She looked back at the rattler. It returned her stare.

Without allowing herself to think about the consequences, she lunged, driving the forked end of the stick toward the back of the rattler's head.

Too late, the rattler tried to strike. The fork caught it; its head was jammed into the ground. Its body twisted and coiled. She was amazed at its strength.

Thrusting down hard on the stick, she reached down and replaced its forked end with her fingers. The skin was warm and dry; the muscles beneath it like steel springs. She grasped the neck with all her strength. Her arms trembled with tension; ribbons of veins and muscle stood out on the back of her hand.

Holding the struggling serpent at arm's length, she darted for the opening in the lean-to. Jennifer, kneeling, turned her face toward the blocked light.

"Jeff! Get out of here! Get out!" Karen yelled.

The yell startled him. Without thinking, he obeyed—rolling away from the kneeling Jennifer, coming to his feet and diving for the outside.

Jennifer was scrambling to her feet, her blue eyes wide, staring not at Karen but at the writhing, hissing snake. Karen lunged, thrusting the snake at her sister's body.

Jennifer threw an arm in front of her and swung with the other at the hand grasping the snake. Karen kicked, driving her foot deep into her sister's belly. Jennifer grunted and struggled to hold her balance, at the same time grabbing for the snake's head. Its fangs glinted, and its tongue darted out. Quickly she withdrew, leaving her throat unprotected for an instant. With a cry, Karen jammed the snake at it. But Jennifer brought her hand down sharply. It smashed on Karen's wrist, diverting her thrust.

Karen felt a convulsive leap in her hand. At the same time Jennifer screamed.

The snake had sunk its fangs into the heavy mound of Jennifer's breast and hung there lashing back and forth, whipping her stomach with its tail.

Jennifer cried out again and wrapped both hands around the squirming body, frantically trying to pull it loose. Just as she fell to the floor the rattler released its bite, turned its head up at her and hissed. She dropped it, whimpering. It slithered across the hut. Just before it disappeared under the brush wall, the snake stopped, looked back at Jennifer, and hissed again. And the sound of the hiss was gentle, like a condolence.

Jennifer lay quiet, looking up at her sister. Some of the blue seemed to have faded from her eyes.

"Mom?" Jeff called from outside.

"You stay out there, Jeff. I'll be out in a minute."

She looked down at her sister, or what her sister had been. She felt nothing—no sorrow, no regret, not even hate. It wasn't her sister she had killed, but a creature out of place in time, something unspeakably unholy. And yet, looking at the woman lying quietly at her feet, she felt sorrow creep over her. She had grown up with that dying body, shared loved Jennifer as one loves those who share their blood. Somewhere, some place, they had passed into a shadow world.

"Jennifer," she said slowly. The words were hard to find. "It wasn't you I killed. It was that thing inside you, the creature who owns you. That's what I killed, sis. Not you. If you can, please have compassion for me. I had to save my son. I loved you, sis. I will always love you."

Perhaps there was a slight twitching in the blue eyes—she wasn't certain, things had gone blurry. Her sister didn't move.

She turned and went to the doorway. There she stopped and looked back. All decency said she should stay with her sister and comfort her during her last moments of life. But that wasn't her sister, her Jennifer.

In the sunlight, Jeff was dressed in his T shirt and shorts. Whether it was the way the sun touched his auburn hair or the solid stance he had taken by the river bank, she wasn't certain; but the boy looking at her was not entirely familiar. He was no stranger, but neither was he the Jeff who had been attending the baseball clinic, or the Jeff who had come down to the river with his boat two days before. He returned her stare with a steady gaze. And then she knew. Jeff had taken the first step into adulthood. She didn't know whether to be happy or sad.

"Where did you get your clothes?"

"They were hanging on a branch drying." He looked down embarrassedly. "I fell in the river."

"Oh."

"Where's Aunt Jennifer?"

"She'll be following us in a little while."

He turned his head and looked across the river. Sunlight limned his features, accenting the bone structure. God, she thought, how he resembles Jason.

"Mom, I'm sorry I went away with her. I guess, like they say at school, I got the hots for her and wasn't thinking straight."

"I think I understand. I'm trying, anyway."

"I hope you do. I'd had enough and wanted to come home."

"Why didn't you?"

"She kept putting me to sleep."

She looked hard at him. He might have taken that first step into adulthood, but the innocence and vulnerability of a boy remained.

"Jeff, I'm going to be busy around here for a while helping Jennifer pack her things and then going to the mill. Would you go home and stand watch over the telephone? Patrick should be arriving, too."

"I'd be glad to help."

"No. I'd rather you go home and clean up and watch the house."

"Well, okay. I'll see you at dinner. I wonder if Patrick is back."

"He should be. If he is, tell him where I went."

"Okay."

He took off along the river. He walked with the easy grace of a young athlete. His shoulders were broad and his hips narrow, his long legs developing thigh muscles hinting at a future strength. He moved with an unconscious use of power. As he moved farther away from her, she became aware of the way he blended with his surroundings, not as an inconspicuous nonenity, but as a person so at ease with them he gave them no thought. Pride filled her. She watched until he rounded the clump of cabbage palms and disappeared.

Then she turned towards the mill.

At the edge of the clearing she stopped. At the far end the ruins lifted their darkness into the slanting afternoon sun, irregular, rigid shapes against the background of shaggy trees. A shadowy monument to a shadowy past. How had she ever found escape among them? The dreams she had enjoyed among them had turned to nightmares. Forever more, Ludlow's Mill was a thing of the past. She would never return.

Reluctantly, she moved out into the clearing.

Behind her something rustled in the underbrush. She turned. There was nothing. An animal, she thought, and slowly, unwillingly, began to cross the clearing.

She knew there was safety in the future once more, but its price had been so monstrously high it was tarnished. How would she live a life bought by the deaths of a sister and a friend? Moments would come out of nowhere full of loneliness and sorrow.

A tiny breeze, coming from nowhere, going nowhere, drifted past her. She thought she detected a faint tang of wood and earth and blood on it. She drew a deeper breath; the smell was gone.

The old ways would return, but they would be different. All the goodness would have evil mixed within it; there would be no dividing line between them as there once had been.

She was twenty yards from the stone now. Ahead was the buzzing of many flies, feasting on the lifeless thing lying in the dirt.

Two families destroyed. Survivors who could never find peace; there was no comfort for them to find. Hurting was such a terrible business.

Off to her left, light twinkled dully among the ruins. Sun on a discarded beer can?

If only it were possible to turn away from today and tomorrow and all the days following. If only she could retrace the steps back to the days before the horror had come.

But what was—was. Reality was reality. To try to change it was self-deception. She would find a way to live. She *would*.

Around her the afternoon sunlight turned to amber, warming the weeds and tinting the ruins. The future was not all black oblivion. She had Jeff. She had Patrick. And she had herself.


From the ruins she watched the woman named Karen approaching with slow steps across the clearing. While she waited, she began the incantation of possession. It had been many months since she had spoken it over the one named Jennifer.

By lying still in the nest, she had delayed the venom racing toward her heart. Yet the time had been closer than she wished, and she had shed the body only at its dying.

She slithered out of the archway and moved through shadow toward the stone beside the dead one. No harm could come to her now. Now this mill was hers.

And this new body approaching across the clearing. It was hers. Hers. The lamia's. The thirsty one's.

Her eyes narrowed. Her tongue darted out. This body was a good body. She coiled tighter on the warm sand. A ray of sunlight struck her scales and glanced off. The woman looked, hesitated, then came on.

The lamia continued the incantation.